ABOUT TH

Ross Merrin is a professional musician with a science education, a background in both charity and corporate sectors and a fascination with the nature of the world, both external and internal.

He is never happier than when he is creating music, writing, when fortunate enough to be diving in the world's tropical seas or simply watching as the world goes by.

He loves to facilitate the output of other musicians and creatives and is the Director of Deaf Fret, a production, recording and development company.

www.deaf-fret.com

Moments of Tiny Violence

How Beats the Original Heart

Ross Merrin

Copyright © 2024 Ross Merrin

The moral right of the author has been asserted.

Apart from any fair dealing for the purposes of research or private study, or criticism or review, as permitted under the Copyright, Designs and Patents Act 1988, this publication may only be reproduced, stored or transmitted, in any form or by any means, with the prior permission in writing of the publishers, or in the case of reprographic reproduction in accordance with the terms of licences issued by the Copyright Licensing Agency. Enquiries concerning reproduction outside those terms should be sent to the publishers.

This is a work of fiction. Names, characters, businesses, places, events and incidents are either the products of the author's imagination or used in a fictitious manner. Any resemblance to actual persons, living or dead, or actual events is purely coincidental.

Troubador Publishing Ltd
Unit E2 Airfield Business Park,
Harrison Road, Market Harborough,
Leicestershire LE16 7UL
Tel: 0116 279 2299
Email: books@troubador.co.uk
Web: www.troubador.co.uk

ISBN 978-1-83628-019-4

British Library Cataloguing in Publication Data.
A catalogue record for this book is available from the British Library.

Printed and bound in Great Britain by 4edge Limited
Typeset in 11pt Minion Pro by Troubador Publishing Ltd, Leicester, UK

Author photo by Vessi at www.vessives.com

To those going, those still going and those already gone.

Characters

The Fifth Season

Kick Vivid	Singer
Bat Fantastic	Bass
Zip Furious	Guitar
Riot Malign	Drums
Powdermouth	Manager
Iodine	Security
Entenne	Security
Yo-Yo	Public Relations
Crunch	Front of House Sound
Slopehound	Onstage Sound
Mangler	Head Roadie

Universal Services

Dessel	Senior Outreach Representative
Tapper	Assistant to Dessel
Drumbeat	Assistant to Dessel
Hammer Flower	Enforcer, Retired
Frankie Finesse	Enforcer
Bubon	City Leader, The Mean City
Mister Five	Bubon's Aide

Single Malt	City Leader, The Indulgence Junkies
Myelle	City Leader, Destination Beautiful

Other

Tempra Kay	Kick's Mysterious Friend and Confidante
Eventually Kelly	The Young Girl Who Asks For Kick's Help
Ben Tempo	The Missing Boy Kick Promises to Find
Honeytongue	Kick's Love
Llo Spuntinoh	Senior Citizen, The Out-Of-Towners

Before

Without sentiment he noted that, whilst killing someone on purpose was often extremely difficult, killing someone by accident, it would seem, was surprisingly easy.

With his lean figure pinning a long shadow to the ground, he surveyed the flames from the car below, a fiery intrusion amongst the shattered trees.

One moment was all it had taken.

One moment of distraction for his car to kiss the other, a brief, chaste union, a touch so delicate that he wondered whether the other driver – who he had clearly heard singing along to his stereo – had even noticed. Yet it was enough to nudge the other car off the road and into the valley below.

He had spent years perfecting his work but taking this life had been the easiest and, standing alone high on this elevated route, he knew it might go entirely unobserved until later when someone might react to distant smoke.

He stared down with glassy resentment at the other driver, thrown free from the rolling car – he wasn't singing now. He would be dead before he could get to him. No need to make sure.

That this killing was a surprise, a bonus if you will, made no difference; as he returned to his car, he still felt cheated – the dying man below would give him no pleasure and no insight.

You come into this world alone and then you die alone – or so they say – but what thoughts keep you company, what visits you in that last moment of your own end?

THE END

The Light that Came from Beside the Sea

deaf fret

presents

Chapter One

Drifting back into awareness from thoughts already tumbling away beyond his reach, it struck Kick Vivid that this was a long way to come for a meeting.

Vehicles could get only so close to the restaurant, hanging from the side of the cliff such as it did, its transparent floor suspended over the water as though defying the waves below to make good on their ceaseless crashing menace.

Yet, at this height above the sea, the Standard Candle remained as untroubled as the menu of the occasional diner touched by vertigo.

Even those stepping out from its dining area into the capricious weathers featuring in rolling guest-spots on the outside balcony were mostly only vulnerable to being left wordless at the beauty of the venue.

Appetites already sharpened by the walk over the headland feasted first on coastal views, the visceral impact of which were resolutely breath-taking in all seasons; on this occasion, the defiant jags of the cliffs stood drenched in a sunset bleeding over a sea made pink courtesy of Universal Services.

Gradually becoming more aware of the room from his position at the busiest table, he took in only what he had to

– something he had learned to do by necessity over many years.

Tonight it was business and, more than usual, he wanted no interference.

Of the twenty tables in the dining area only half were occupied and Kick thought it odd that so many tables were free, their 'Reserved' signs patient waiting testaments to unknown future guests.

The flavour of the room was typical – some tragedy, some joy but mostly it was the usual mix of tolerance, acceptance, disappointment and hope.

Powdermouth had reserved the long table next to the window for them – far too long for their small party of five but it meant that, with the sea on one side and no occupied tables directly around them, they were as undisturbed as they could be.

'What will it be?'

Kick jumped slightly as the waitress broke into his reverie bringing him more fully into his circumstances – something that did not go unnoticed by his fellow band members.

Powdermouth, composed and slightly removed – his most natural orbit – betrayed his amusement, allowing the faintest of smiles to alight on his face before moving it on almost instantly.

The others were less inclined to such restraint.

Bat Fantastic spoke first, his tone tempered, though probably only for the benefit of the patiently-waiting waitress, very much the outsider here, the audience for another band performance.

'Hey Vivid, you need a count-in before you can open your mouth perhaps?' he inquired casually, prompting

Riot Malign, the band's giant of a drummer to tap two knives together and count a slow four in the deeply reassuring yet playfully provocative way he could use both his words and his presence.

Zip Furious, the band's fizzing tight-wire guitarist, who mostly had to tire himself out to shut himself up, looked at Kick seriously before contributing:

'You know we're all laughing now but it seems to me you might want a little more than a count in, seems to me you might need a little extra coffee in your coffee, keep you focussed, keep you a little bit more on the straight,' he carved the air directly in front of him with a chop of his right hand, 'and narrow. Just want to be sure you've got your motivation for the task ahead because it's not the skills but the cause you bring to the battle that matters, not that I doubt it, just need to be sure and sure again is all I'm saying but in a more immediate sense, you being all filter-out-the-world is not conducive to the healthy fulfilment of my nutritional needs and with that in mind I'll have black coffee and the all-day breakfast, eggs with legs please.'

He snapped the menu shut and it was the waitress's turn to jump, having been hypnotised to distraction by Zip and totally unaware that he had, in his own way, been placing an order.

Powdermouth hosted a smile a while longer this time while Kick smothered one of his own, amused not that Zip could ignite like this but that he could ever maintain silence for any length of time.

Kick valued Zip's energy, his enthusiasm and that he said just exactly what was on his mind, often a little inappropriately but never with malice and never with the lazy irresponsibility of those who thought speaking their mind excused any offence caused, presenting honesty as a trump card over thoughtlessness.

He was a law unto himself, no doubt, but Zip knew what rude was. Zip was rarely rude. And if he was, he knew to apologise.

The waitress, not yet fully aware that she was really only dealing with a wide-eyed child, a fussy bundle of curiosity in a lean adult body, enquired carefully, 'Eggs… with legs?'

Zip looked at her, 'Runny,' and then as though acknowledging that it might not be obvious to everyone else how his mind worked, 'please.'

Kick knew that any discomfort she felt had evaporated with Zip's almost apologetic last word; Zip could be unnerving and he often noticed a little too late but Kick needed him to be this person.

Like that of Kick, like that of the other band members, Zip's disciplined zest was a large part of why, despite this initial excitability of old friends who hadn't seen each other for a while, they would soon settle into what the waitress would notice but not name as the quiet charisma of hard-earned success.

'Eggs with legs? Where do you get this stuff?' teased Riot, all smiles and Kick knew when his luck was in and stayed quiet.

Bat was too alert for that.

'You think you're off the hook sleepy-head?' and in a moment of further mischief asked, straight-faced, 'Would you like me to order for you Kick?'

Kick smiled, raised an eyebrow, knew full well the strawberry-jam-in-soup-lettuce-on-the-side combination Bat was already gleefully designing in his mind.

Addressing the waitress, he said simply, 'I'll have what he's having,' and pointed to Bat.

'You're a very dull man so you are Vivid,' mourned Bat, turning to the waitress and – seizing another opportunity – began walking his fingers slowly up Zip's arm.

'I think I'll also be having the breakfast, extra coffee in my coffee…and eggs with leeeeegs!' he finished, his fingers scurrying up into Zip's ear.

Zip giggled, Riot and Powdermouth placed their orders and as the sea crunched a steady beat against the rocks hundreds of feet below, for a moment, just a moment, Kick felt The Maze.

♪

On the balcony outside stood Dessel, motionlessly occupying the only spot that could not be seen by Kick's party, focussed so totally on the conversation inside that his eyes sparked with life only from the reflected sea he stared out towards but didn't see.

He appeared to be asleep, perhaps meditating but, in reality, he was operating at an intense level – he allowed himself no thoughts, other than those he was listening to, playing shadow, camouflaging his presence by limiting his cognitive activity to almost nothing and letting their thoughts be his own.

He knew he would get nothing from Powdermouth and he knew Vivid would be too alert as usual but he could get what he wanted by proxy, reading the thoughts of the other three as they listened to the details of the preparations that an audience would never be aware of, now being laid out by Powdermouth.

What was it with that guy anyway? How did he manage to be so lucid and controlled when his thoughts were such a shambolic mess?

And in that instant, the moment that he had the thought, realising his concentration had been broken, he worked to resume his passive reconnaissance.

Looking steadily into Kick's eyes as though needing to be sure he had his full attention before starting, Powdermouth said:

'Let me take you through this.'

With an intellect that could either make the world seem bigger or the room seem smaller he, naturally, had Kick's attention but broke off from speaking, momentarily distracted, a quizzical look on his face as he sat back and casually looked around the restaurant.

Moments like this drove Zip crazy, even short ones like this – silence, inactivity – but he, like all of the other band members, had too much respect for Powdermouth to do anything other than wait for him to take one more glance around before continuing with the details, the travel, the accommodation, the contingencies.

Kick listened with the others, still surprised at having felt The Maze. It meant there was another superimposer in the room, or nearby, but it had been so brief as to have possibly come from one who was unaware of who they were, perhaps a moment of understanding or insight for someone in the room, significant enough to unlock something for them.

Carefully he allowed everyone in the room in as he sometimes did, time permitting, and found nothing of note beyond his initial impression; a possessive boyfriend, tense that his date was being glanced at too often being the only stark mood in an otherwise unruffled room.

So, no, Kick felt fine; he was with his people and they were about to go on tour again, a feeling almost alien to him after a break – yet still reassuringly familiar.

The food arrived and the table, despite a cold sea rain announcing its arrival with percussive insistence on the windows, relaxed in the warmth of old friends telling old tales.

A man with a kind face, in a nondescript suit, of medium height and average age, who might break you into little pieces and leave them outside for the wind to blow away, Dessel stood in the rain, unseen.

♪

It was a breathless day, the heat making even sound seem heavy, the glare of the sun forcing his gaze down towards the grass between his toes, where the soft green blades appeared to shout their own shrill intensity.

He knew this place but – like waking suddenly without having planned to fall asleep – it was strangely disorientating, familiar made strange, distorted in the heat's humming haze.

The feeling wouldn't leave him and the sun pressed its advantage, leaning hard on him...but this served only to liberate him.

He began to run, cautiously, hesitantly at first but with each step the grass cooled, and as his legs became greedy participants in a ground-hungry sprint carrying him faster and faster and as the weight of his body became negligible, he accelerated into what could only be an expression of freedom.

He looked up, into the light and it was everywhere and he no longer felt his legs and it was cool and it was everything.

♪

tick
    tick
        tick   tick
            tick
                        tick

        tick

Chapter Two

Sing because you like it and you will succeed every day; sing because you want someone else to like it and you will fail most of the time.

Similarly, the best music is mostly written by those who really don't give a damn what an audience might think.

The music industry, by definition, however, really does.

This being their guiding principle, The Fifth Season had always remained fiercely independent, consistently achieving for a considerable time in a crowded field where being good was never enough or even, for that matter, a basic requirement.

How Powdermouth managed to keep the band viable, let alone on tour without the benefit of the industry infrastructure and promotional support mechanisms, was a marvel to Kick.

They had benefited in part by never really appealing to the fickle attention spans of a young audience for whom everything was new and exciting even when it wasn't. A more discerning – and more loyal – listener found them and tended to stay.

It was the eve of the tour and they had just completed the last of the warm-up shows in the small coastal town that was home to The Hesitants.

So called because of their instinct to consider and reflect before acting, The Hesitants weren't even proud of the sustainability of their lifestyle – only taking from the sea and land that which would sustain them, wanting little more than what they needed, tending toward generosity and kindliness, understanding and empathy – it was simply simple, they felt, and the way to live.

Often affectionately referred to as The Un-Shore, a horseshoe of mountains stretched up to snow above the town but with its buildings made mostly of rugged local stone, it managed to resist the apparent attempts of the steep slopes to tip it into the waiting sea.

It was an ideal place to iron out the last of the show's teething problems and, sitting backstage, Kick felt that it had been a qualified success. There was still some work to be done but he felt good because he knew that when work solves the problem, worry is a waste.

There had been the odd technical spit and sputter that had needed dealing with but Slopehound, the onstage engineer, had finally banished them to somewhere else, marking his satisfaction with a contented utterance of his only two words, 'Cool beans…'

Rumour had it that he knew other words, even that he had spoken other words (though Kick hadn't personally witnessed that) but if anyone could convey the full spectrum of human emotions and communicative exchanges with just two words, it was Slopehound.

Crunch, front of house sound engineer, currently deep in conference with Slopehound, certainly showed no signs of frustration or concern as they walked past the dressing room, the latter nodding or shaking his head, rolling his eyes and offering gestures only, until, parting to the call of separate duties, those two words, 'Cool beans...' by way of salute.

Bat Fantastic, observing his old friend, was also relatively pleased with how the gigs had gone – he was mostly pleased that Kick hadn't taken the receptiveness of the audience as an excuse to recite some of his poetry.

Lyrically Kick could cut it, held tight to melodic phrasing and rhythmic requirements. But his words unfettered and let loose to run around unchecked in the form of a poem...? Well, hell, who said free range was best?

It was just plain awful and seeing Kick opposite him with that slightly bemused, good-natured look (Kick always looked slightly bemused and was, in fact, good-natured) on the face that so many wanted to kiss and almost as many wanted to mother, Bat wondered what hidden part of this beautiful man was so corrupted that this turgid prose would seep out on occasion.

Despite these thoughts, when Kick glanced his way he saw only an expression of sincere affection on Bat's face.

Zip was usually somewhere talking as though his only hope of stopping was to run out of words.

Right now he was striding alongside Mangler (Head Roadie, today's T shirt reading 'Guilty At Birth') as he cleared the stage, each speaker cabinet an over-sized, inflexible dance partner willing only to be led backwards towards the tour bus in an ungainly two-step.

As they passed the open door of the backstage area, Zip's urgent pressing of the yet-to-be-convinced Mangler was made clear with the overheard, 'All I'm saying is that if Darwin wanted us to take him seriously, he should have allowed for his theory to change with time,' and Kick knew that they would be at it for hours now.

Zip, apparently oblivious to everything – including the fact that Mangler was currently very busy being very busy – found the awareness to break off mid-sentence on seeing Riot with a wide-eyed, excited fan, to say, 'Hey, you drummed well tonight, you must be a guitarist,' before returning to the drumming of his own tattoo into Mangler's ears.

Yo-Yo, the band's publicist, had been with the band for several tours now and Kick would have it no other way – she was so good at what she did that he wasn't even sure it was difficult and she maintained a calm so total as she did it that he wasn't sure there were ever any problems.

Powdermouth, all dark features and composure and Yo-Yo, all dark features and composure, broke from their personal conference and turned Kick's way, reminding him that tonight's work was not yet done.

Kick Vivid was, in many ways, too cool to be a rock star – he simply didn't need that much attention.

In coming together with Zip, Bat and Riot he had achieved a rare thing – four points of a diamond, strong enough to prevent breakage, transparent enough to pass the closest inspection.

Not least of the things they had in common was a wry distrust of what it was they actually did – as passionately committed as they were to their music, they all found it faintly ridiculous that people, anyone, a paying audience, would applaud them for it.

It was a constant source of discomfort that they – at least superficially – resembled those performers who played to an audience of uncritical sycophants and who liked it that way, needed it that way. The Fifth Season would be far happier having to win the crowd over each and every night and saw no value in being worshipped by anyone who might be prepared to worship someone.

'I'm most definitely superior to the people who are prepared to think I am,' was how Riot had put it in an early interview which at the time was not the most controversial thing ever said by a musician but displayed a knowing disregard for media savvy and went a long way towards thinning out and defining their audience.

In fact the audience being there, whilst a crackling trigger for the adrenaline shot of performance, was not essential at all – an attitude that in itself was seductive to a general population saturated to de-sensitivity by the tireless marketing by Major Labels of their moulded, compliant, Employees Of The Year, those often transient sales reps for the corporatisation of art.

All the Major Labels were owned by Universal Services anyway and it was to Powdermouth's credit that the band had been able to sustain a career without succumbing to the endless and increasing U.S. offers.

Though Kick had a sense of wonder, he was a hard-headed realist with a sense of wonder and, in

Powdermouth, the band had found the joiner he knew they needed, who had the skills to dovetail their needs with the world beyond them.

Powdermouth and those employed by his promotion company, Deaf Fret, spent a lot of time holding Kick to the tour timetable.

Being an empath, Kick found it hard not to be helpful – he filtered most things out as a means of self-protection but Powdermouth had learnt to become adept at reactive re-scheduling in response to Kick's irresistible desire to help out with some local or private problem at almost all tour stops.

Protective strategies in place or not, those with needs found an open warmth in Kick that invited them to share and his fundamental kindness responded so often without hesitation that Powdermouth had even begun factoring spare days into the tour itinerary.

For this tour, however, Powdermouth had been firmer with Kick, insisting enigmatically that this one 'is all about you' but mostly he would indulge Kick and the band wherever he could.

But only so far.

Zip had once expressed the band's discomfort with merchandise on sale at the gigs:

'Look PM,' he began, the rest of his words addressed to a Powdermouth with raised eyebrows at the abbreviation, 'if you had a friend, whether it be at work or at school and they invited you to their place and you got there and there were posters of you all over their walls, that would be just plain weirdy and stalky and for no reason other than the obvious you'd be sure not to answer in the affirmative next time they invited you anywhere but because we're in a band, that's okay…?'

Powdermouth let his eyebrow drop and, leaning conspiratorially in towards the impassioned Zip, said, 'You know, if you could just raise a tear now, you'd be a cert for Best Actor.'

So the band sell merchandise. But no posters.

♪

And, of course, they did press which, in the early stages of the tour – and especially with The Hesitants – was more knockabout banter than serious promotion.

The band had been invited for a late dinner in the elegant house of the venue owner, one of the conditions Powdermouth had agreed to – a gentle, unstructured meet and greet for competition winners and local press.

The crew had also been invited but politely declined, claiming the need to iron out the last remaining technical problems. Crunch, articulating the earthier dining preferences of his colleagues, had confided to Kick, 'I'd rather steeplechase on a tightrope.'

On the subject of technical problems, Kick had canvassed Slopehound who, with a couple of subtle nods and eyes that had narrowed slightly, had offered a reassuring 'Cool beans…', so it was only with his fellow band members, Powdermouth and a sense of calm that Kick now sat with the other guests, post-gig, post-meal.

An earnest young reporter was trying to keep his arms around the band's responses to his questions, with mixed results.

Unaware that any question would make Zip's verbal horse bolt, leaving the listener with little choice but to hold on, he had made the mistake of asking him directly what he thought of the latest male ensemble act to be the breaking news of the Major Labels.

And so it was that the other band members sat in serene, sated silence as Zip began by explaining that he had actually quite liked them until he realised that, damn hadn't he just gone and fallen for the marketing, had gone on to ponder more generally the morality of selling songs to an inevitably young audience in which four or five grown men sang about the same romantic experience with just the one girl and anyway, what emotional turmoil did they have to moan about when, surely after that, she would be the one that was sore, before moving on, unprompted and unstoppable to a more thorough evisceration of the music industry itself.

The candles grew shorter and the yawns grew longer as the night ebbed away; the shadows cast by the flames smudged listless over the stone floor of the dining room, yet, as though defying gravity, deepened high into the staircase that hugged the wall and the balcony overlooking the last of the diners.

Kick knew she was there, somewhere on the balcony where the light was past its bedtime, way past her own, that everyone called her Eventually Kelly because she was so shy and that Tasco's left paw was saturated.

The host of the evening, Kelly's father, sensed Kick's distraction, noticed his glance up to the balcony.

'Kelly? Is that you? Are you okay honey?'

Eventually, Eventually Kelly emerged from the shadows a feature at a time, as though surfacing through oil, her eyes a little puffy, her sandy blonde hair spikily testifying to a toss-turned bedtime restlessness.

With her left hand holding the banister and her right hand holding her teddy bear close enough to continue chewing on its lower left limb, she padded gently down the staircase and fixed herself in her father's lap, never once taking her eyes off Kick.

'A cugan sheep,' she said…eventually.

'Honey, take Tasco's paw out of your mouth.'

'I couldn't sleep.'

Kick knew that she was not lying but also that this was not quite true, that she had intended to sleep but had been unable to ignore the need to tell him something and had actually been waiting until the room had been vacated by enough guests for the subject matter to be afforded what she considered to be enough space.

'Was it the floorboards creaking again?' asked her father.

'Lissel bik.' And despite addressing her father, she was still peering openly at Kick.

'A little bit? Sweetheart you've got to stop eating Tasco,' a father's love evident in the smile he was giving Kick over her head.

'Remember those floorboards only creak because the invisible guards I put around your bed to protect you sometimes forget to tread lightly, that's all.'

Suddenly emboldened and with brown eyes black by candlelight, wide and focussed, Kelly spoke straight at Kick, mouth Tasco-free, her voice so pretty, so insistent.

'My friend Ben Tempo is missing.'

'I'll find him,' said Kick without hesitation, without choice and in the beat it took him to register surprise at his response, Kelly fell asleep in her father's lap and Tasco fell to the ground.

Powdermouth, typically, betrayed no reaction.

With a night sky so clear and of such endless depth that Kick felt he might fall off the Earth and into it, this was, right now, the best place to get away from everywhere else.

It was much later and he was alone on the shoreline where the sea engaged a tranquil encounter with a gliding river, the calm elder to a turbulent younger self, borne high in the mountains in the tiny violence of raindrops landing, before tumbling an urgent twisting thrust through rocky descents.

Rain had been limited in recent weeks so, in addition to the full moon's glowing scrutiny, Kick was fitfully lit by tracers as non-feeding migratory fish sheared through bioluminescent plankton, going through the motions of predation, restless for more water in the river and the chance to relieve the burning imperative to spawn.

He thought about the journey the river took and how disproportionately often the ratio between the overall length of a sea-bound river and the direct line from source to sea approximated pi – and the significance of that within the geometry of the expansive night-time view he now sat before.

No doubt U.S. would prefer the efficiency of the straight line; he, for one, preferred the arbitrary, the art of the river.

'Beautiful isn't it?' she said and laughed as Kick's realisation that he wasn't alone with the fish and the bats and the stars manifested in an involuntary exclamation, followed by an embarrassed, sheepish grin.

'You know, for an empath, you're rubbish at knowing when I'm around,' observed Tempra Kay distractedly, sitting on a flat rock a little upstream and just behind him, hair being rolled around fingers in faux-innocence.

'Thanks for reminding me,' said Kick without sincerity but they both knew that he loved it that she could surprise him so they sat for a while and shared the sky.

Around Kick's age and – to him – everything good, she always arrived bearing a sober simplicity, albeit on an unpredictable schedule. He had originally thought she was a fan of the band but along the way had found no evidence of that.

Only later, when he realised she was never around unless he was alone, did it dawn on him that she might even be some kind of imaginary friend and he'd laughed a little nervously to reassure himself that, surely, that couldn't be true.

For this and other reasons, however, he chose not to discuss her with the others – and not to wonder too hard who she was.

Knowing would make little difference to how he valued her or what he valued her for – as usual, she was here for a reason, one not immediately apparent in the evenly modulated voice that asked, 'How was the gig?'

'It went pretty well,' he responded, conditions apparent in his tone.

'No poetry then?' and the smile was as much in her voice as the tease was in her tone.

Opening his mouth to respond before realising he had no words to actually do that with, Kick and his facial features wrestled with too many unknowns before Tempra brought him back in from his isolation.

'You've done this before Kick, your team's good and you know that the deep end will get shallower. Something is troubling you other than the tour.'

'A boy has gone missing from The Hesitants.'

'He's been taken? By U.S.?'

'No, I don't think so, although the philosophy here has always been a threat to U.S. He's growing up and I think he wants answers. I think he went looking for an understanding of what makes The Hesitants safe and what he can do to consolidate that.'

'They told you this?'

Kick turned to her, a small gesture with open palms – he had been picking up fragments of thinking from everyone local, those who had attended the gig, the meal. It was only Kelly who had used words.

'Kelly is afraid that he might be dead,' continued Kick, 'but I don't think so. I don't think anyone wants him dead.'

After a pause, Tempra Kay, her voice as though trying to focus on something in the distance, said gently, 'Death is what happens to those left behind when someone they love passes on.'

She paused again before brightening and adding, 'Trust your instincts Kick, there's a reason you have them after all.'

Staring at the stars – or possibly the reflection of the stars in the untroubled surface of the sea – Kick placed, 'I promised Kelly,' into the space around them and Tempra broke a beat of incredulous silence with:

'That's right, on the eve of a tour you make an almost impossible promise to a girl…you're all bullshit and balancing acts Vivid.'

Aware as he was of the truth in this Kick sighed, smiled and turned to her.

'I know,' he said to the space she was no longer in.

Chapter Three

He was late but he was compelled to stop all the same, the decaying light of the sunset to his left teasing in and out of the car, an errant child insisting on his attention as he drove the sensuous curves of the mountain route to his destination.

And for just a moment it felt as though the road fell away, that he had parted company with his own anchored reality as a particularly bright shaft of amber soothed its way through the car, leaving him with only thoughts for company, planet Earth temporarily erstwhile, uncaring.

But there she was again before he could fall, supporting him in a mother's embrace and it was now that he chose to stop, the place that he had chosen to do so no more or less anything than anywhere else along this route, just the place to stop.

The gravel by the side of the road protested a crunchy satisfaction as the car came to a halt, delivering him unfettered to stare at the panorama below; the urgency he had felt at the beginning of the journey now starting to lose focus, to lose its imperative, as his senses drank in Mother Nature at her finest, indulged in the forest below, the sky, the colours, the aggressive, undeniable life in the view he was witness to.

Yes, he was late – and much of him was still in the car, still in a hurry, still trying to convince himself that he could get there on time if he just pushed things a little harder, pushed the combination of plastic, alloy and rubber into an increasingly dissatisfied haste, its engine revving higher and higher, an appropriate soundtrack to the urgency of his driving.

The lighter wouldn't work and it didn't matter. There was a calm here, even the car seemed charmed, offering nothing to break the silence. Or perhaps he was too infused with the sepia sedative of the sunset to hear the tick as the engine cooled.

For he too was charmed, absorbed so totally in and by the landscape that it was difficult to say whether he was experiencing this or was part of the experience.

It felt right to move away from the car, further and further – yet a sadness so total threatened to step between him and the vehicle, a living thing closing off his return.

He took that one step away; this time the gravel offered no commentary, the silence of this allowing room for that fear to grow larger behind him, conspiring with the car to force his hand. He had to keep going now and it was down a path that he found himself, stoically supported on either side by the at-ease-sleepy sentries of the mixed trees.

Still, he wanted to return to the car, get going and be there for her, his love, when the 'plane landed and every step was a step away from her.

And it hurt, it really hurt but there was no choice here for him; he had to keep moving.

The lighter may well have been working by now but he had left it behind at the car so he couldn't light the cigarette that he had looked for and not found in the packet he thought had been in his pocket but wasn't.

It didn't matter. What mattered was that the path was getting longer and longer behind him, forging itself as his new partner with each step he took to an indefinite destination somewhere in the forest around him.

But that was not how it felt; it was as though he had always been here, always known this place, was always going to end up here at some point.

He laughed uncertainly – the path ahead forked, creating an almost comical choice of route, like some laboured symbolism; yet that's how he experienced it, each fork having a different quality…

To the right, the light was resonant, embracing, the path seeming to open into a meadow not far from the fork; to the left, darker.

Right or left, he thought, he must choose one. Or so it seemed. Really? Surely he could go back to the car, forget all of this, deny it, get in and drive away, continue his journey, meet his love from the 'plane.

So it was this that he did but as he turned to do so he realised that he couldn't – he was late, very late, too late and knew in that moment that he would never see his love again and the sensation was evocative of childhood, of summer days that decreased in their endlessness, darkness settling earlier and earlier, the taunting inevitable harbinger of autumn and another year's evening freedom put to bed in the shape of the reluctant little boy he once was.

But the sensation was stronger than that, so much stronger than that – so strong that he almost physically recoiled from the impact of the memory, the bright vision of himself as that youth, that irretrievable youth.

His body shivered and he started back towards the car but without conviction. He stopped.

He was here now and this had always been inevitable; the car would take him nowhere and he knew there was no reason to return to it.

He laughed at the stupidity of this moment, a barking irrational splutter that brought with it tears.

He could do nothing but turn back towards the crossroads in the path and suddenly he did not want to be here; the dusk, that had warmed him so totally before, now edged towards darkness and the mood of the moment was set as such.

Light fading.

And in resistance, he turned down the left-hand crossroads, not wanting the welcome of the meadow, not wanting to be seduced by this moment, not wanting to be here, so without choice, without will.

In the darkness of the option he chose, he found the will to return to the car – once more, all was well in the world and it was with this in his heart that he turned back and found that the light had faded so completely that all he could see was the crossroads behind him, viewed from this perspective as a vaguely luminous continuum in the gloom, the route to the meadow now imperceptible.

He fell. His face hit the ground, the flaw in his choice now clear. From his ground-level perspective he could see the ankle-traps all around, broken tree stumps and branches gripping up from the ground, clutching intentions of harm and disruption.

He wasn't ready for this. He had never been ready for this. Not so soon.

The floor of this heavily-wooded path was littered with more than this and maybe it was his mood, his circumstances, but it seemed to be his floor, the litter personal to him; the bike tyre that so reminded him of his own, the one that he had dragged all the way home from school, howling for Daddy and the puncture repair kit, the rain of that day landing an unnoticeable impact on the cheeks of a little boy whose world had disappeared along with the air of that treacherous tyre.

But Daddy would not fix this tyre. It was not so old, not so broken but it was clearly beyond repair, surrounded by a litter of empty beer bottles, like the alien offspring of some peculiar mating that had occurred in this path at some point between the tyre and some unknown surrogate, now long gone.

A drink would be good he realised and the thought suddenly became paramount, the only thing in his rapidly receding world. There was a drink in the car and as he clambered to his feet, he craved the cold water that he knew to be in the car, knew to be his friend.

But in getting up he fell again, the gloom obscuring the low branches above him like some sadistic magician and as he hit the floor of the path once more, he thought he caught a glimpse of the car. It was a long way away, much, much further than he remembered both in distance and in time. It was aflame and the flames, distant as they were, smoothed a golden glow over his world, lighting the path just enough for him to notice a tiny sparkle to his right, blinking at him in the periphery of his vision. He turned, all thoughts of thirst now back-benched, and stared into the eyes of a magpie.

No more than ten feet away, the silence of its arrival and its regard of him, unblinking, did not trouble him as much as the tiny delicate bauble in its beak. Tilting its head to one side slightly, as though to offer one last look at his wedding ring, it mocked the failing light by flying deeper down the path, into a tangle of branches, darkness and danger. Instinctively he began to follow.

But he slipped and was again treated to a view of the ground at its own level and it was only now that he noticed the shed skins of the condoms. It crossed his mind that this was an obscure place for young lovers to find their thrills, to pursue their adulthood, their learning. But what struck him more was the amount of life that wasn't here, this tasteless littering of carnal by-product serving no purpose other than to emphasise a prohibition of life.

He thought of all his loves, not just the one who would wait for what would feel like forever in some airport terminal, at first angry, then concerned, then worried. He thought of it all again, what it had meant to him and he had had no idea at the time of its true significance – not as he did now.

Tears fell from his eyes, down his cheeks and on to the leafy floor of the path and his vision offered a prism of multi-colour as they caught, for just one moment, the flames from the car, so far away and ebbing to their own natural demise, slowly darkening the route back to the crossroads.

He knew he had to go back to the meadow but it could wait. It could wait just a little while.

He raised myself to a sitting position and rested his head on bent knees, the backs of his hands a makeshift headrest. And that is how he stayed until the light returned, this time with the burgeoning stridency of early morning.

And without fatigue, without regret, he stood and returned to the crossroads in the path, this time negotiating an effortless passage through the scatter of bike tyres, bottles and branches.

He did not look back in any direction; there was nothing he would see again.

Only the meadow.

Chapter Four

With The Hesitants diminishing behind them as the trip across The Spaces began, Kick sat up front with Bat, the silence between them an appropriate companion to the tranquillity of the surrounds.

Both of them were experienced enough to know that this would not last so for now offered each other interactions as sparse as the population between their current position and their destination, The Partisans.

They knew that they would only encounter Out-Of-Towners, an occasional superimposer who may or may not be working for U.S. and the heavies who most definitely were.

It wasn't in the interests of U.S. to persuade anyone to return to The Hesitants but everyone in The Fifth Season's travelling party knew that before long they would be encouraged by one means or another to head for a population centre and sure enough, just at the point where it would take longer to return to The Hesitants than it would to go on to The Partisans, they encountered the first soft-touch enforcer.

'I think he's new to this,' Bat said, leaning into Kick as the insistent stranger came alongside them imploring them to hurry on to The Partisans since a devil of a storm was behind them and closing fast.

Kick laughed along with everyone else as they accelerated away, the crew feigning terror at the prospect of being hurt by weather in this most temperate of seasons. Both he and Bat grinned as they looked back to see the man once again casually sitting on a rock eating a sandwich, waiting for the next travellers to pass his post.

And in this way, the tour truly began.

♪

Whilst Kick could always tell what Riot was thinking and could only ever hazard a guess at what Zip might *not* be and whilst he valued them both, it was mostly in his own company or Bat's that he found himself in the long empty hours that came with the work they did.

Steady, considered, lean in thinking and tone, Bat brought to the table – along with an unconventional humour – a selfless, blended offering of generous and curious.

Not as intimidating as Powdermouth (Kick was always slightly surprised but mostly very glad that he was on *his* side), Bat none-the-less had an intellect to stimulate and inspire. Kick was only just realising how much he had missed it although, typically, it was to an old subject that Kick returned now.

And because this is what they did at this point in any tour, their smart minds engaged through discussion of The Event and what had happened since.

It was after The Thinning and before their time that The Past had ended. What were at first thought to be visitors from another world had arrived in a great city of a free land, millions witnessing their descent from the sky and the initial startled reaction of the authorities. The press conference held two days later was apparently scrambled together by government but more likely – Kick and Bat and many others believed – by Universal Services.

U.S. was science, energy, life-saving drugs, diseases cured, broken things fixed, communications, entertainment. It was universal services and it was the science of reproduction. It was the science of science.

And science was trusted.

And it was from this position that, as governments and leaders found the floor moving beneath their feet, the Chairman of U.S. had addressed the world.

The two beings, he was proud to say, were visitors not from another planet but from the future, that U.S. had been working on time travel and the two beings – seated calmly (many thought sedated) behind him as he spoke – were messengers from the future, essentially employees of U.S. here to tell the world that this is the future to look forward to.

U.S. had tried to return, the Chairman continued, several times in other times including a time when their ship may have been mistaken for a star to follow but, only now, with you, the generation that will be spoken of in history books, are the people educated and informed enough to be able to absorb the message that they bring.

That message was that, in the not-too-distant future, U.S. would discover the secret of eternal life.

And in a blink, what was left of the Great Religions died.

'Like I've always said, it was just too convenient that less than a week later U.S. had deals on offer to freeze and store you until such time as their science department could bring you around to the smell of coffee and a life without end,' opened Bat.

Kick, whose skills as an empath were lost on past events, volleyed that one back over the net, with enough pace for it to be easily returned and the two fell into an easy rally.

'Not everyone believed it.'

'That still means millions did Kick. Enough to end The Past and give us Now. And you've seen the footage – I know it strikes you as odd that they never actually spoke.'

'You know that at the time U.S. explained that language had evolved and that, anyway, they were only authorised to communicate through the strict protocol of an established U.S. code.'

'Or they were doped up and paraded.'

Kick used a brief silence to express how receptive he was to this idea before going on, 'They were beautiful though weren't they?'

Bat turned to Kick before following his gaze somewhere into the mind's eye's middle distance where the image of the two beings, one male, one female, still remained, clear and precise.

Humanoid for sure, taller, the skin a fluid caramel over long limbs, they were to humans what a leopard might be to a pampered domestic cat.

They were awesome, evolved.

'I always thought it was strange that they looked so different before they left.'

Bat was referring to how they looked tired, vulnerable, weak even, the next time they were seen, the last time they were seen – at the windows of the U.S. Head Office, images beamed across all lands.

'U.S. said there was an intense physical cost to time travel and that this would be evaluated more fully when they returned to the future which was, superficially at least, pretty credible. Or maybe the future is just more gentle,' said Kick with a cynical smile, 'but I did find it strange that no-one saw them leave.'

'Perhaps the one giant stunt of their arrival was all that U.S. were capable of.'

'Or needed.'

Kick wasn't sure what was more difficult to believe, that the future had come back to the present or that U.S. had staged the future coming back to the present.

Either way, U.S. stole the moment and had used it to further consolidate their dominance of everything since, monitoring its customers through their purchases, customising its marketing to fit the individual, knowing the fears of each and soothing them with 'this product will...' in personal tones, providing a waking sleep for the digital daydreamers, drifting drowsily to that ultimate of consumer goods, life without end.

Bat and Kick never reached any conclusions – that really wasn't the nature of their discussion; they both knew, however, that in the times after The Deal began, no-one behaved any better towards each other. After all, they had guarantees of eternal life – what did it matter how they behaved?

And for those feeling insecure as a result of the fractured links in society, well, U.S. had the ideal solution – at a price to suit your budget. U.S. knew that if you found a fault in any of their services, they would have another that would be the perfect fix.

Kick wondered how long it would be before they would see Dessel, whose own behaviour suggested that he was confident that there was no Hell.

But then, considered Kick, if you're the kind of person who's going to Hell, the chances are you're going to love it.

♪

The Tavern never failed to surprise – several hours from any significant population centre and nestled hillside, overlooking clean land on most sides, it always came into view suddenly and was somehow always busy.

It had become a familiar and welcome rest-stop since the band had been touring at this level but as Kick entered, he sensed that something was wrong. Nothing much, just something.

So, as the band and crew rattled shambolically into the remaining free tables – and Bat took responsibility with a sorry-folks-we'll-be-quiet-very-soon glance around the room – Kick's attention was unable to focus as fully as he would have liked on the almost erotic come-hither succulence of the food menu.

And then he knew. And was very hungry. So, after Slopehound had placed his order by pointing at a burger on the menu that really should have been ashamed of itself, Kick placed his own with the striking waitress whose cheekbones, he was sure, could separate whites even after a particularly long wash and then excused himself from the table.

'Keep an eye on Riot,' he said fondly to Bat, turning his eyes briefly to the waitress and Bat understood this to mean that not all objects of Riot's attention necessarily wanted to be, or experienced it with the light touch that Riot assumed was obvious.

As he passed the bar he said to a young man waiting to be served by a moody barmaid, 'You're a lucky guy, she clearly adores you,' and moved on to the bathroom.

Once he had shaken off the surprise at being spoken to so directly by a stranger, the young man, who had in fact been wondering why his girlfriend had been so disinterested in him this evening, concluded that maybe he had just been misreading her in some way and returned to their table with two drinks and a more contented disposition.

His girlfriend – who had been troubled by trivial work issues all day and had been struggling intently to keep them from affecting their time together, hoping that he would not notice, sensed the new mood and for the first time that day, was able to relax.

Soothed and without being aware of it, her boyfriend no longer tapped his foot anxiously beneath the table, close enough to the leg of the adjacent table for its insistent, irregular pulsing to disrupt the concentration of the young man seated there.

Opposite him, beyond the bumping's reach, a friend discussed nothing much in particular but the tap tap tapping that had been taking part of his friend's attention had caused him to become distracted himself, wondering why he wasn't being listened to.

Consequently, that part of his concentration which would ordinarily be concerned with sending an occasional glance and smile to his girlfriend working behind the bar, had been otherwise engaged by the subtle conundrum of his friend's apparent non-committal participation in their conversation.

Released from distractions, they both relaxed and, instinctively, he glanced towards his girlfriend behind the bar, whose feigned frosty indifference melted willingly as she wondered vaguely why he had taken so long to acknowledge her tonight even as she now realised nothing was wrong.

Her manner immediately softened with her colleague, Emma, who dealt directly with the waiting staff and who had been catching the crisp irritation of the barmaid's frustration with her boyfriend.

Emma had – as is often the way with things – been unwittingly passing the hostility down the chain of command but was accordingly reassured enough such that one of the newer waitresses, who had been hot-thought resenting being spoken to like that, was therefore able to concentrate on Table 12, a small party who considered themselves patient but for whom the wait had simply become too much.

They had finally asked another waitress who had not been impressed that she had had to pick up the slack, serving a table outside her station but who could finally pay attention to the increasingly-agitated attempts to pay the bill by a table that was.

This party was in a hurry, so much so that one of them had already been at the door, swinging it in a failing attempt to temper his impatience. The waitress's consequently swift conclusion of their transaction allowed the two tradesmen sitting at the table nearest to the swinging door, who had been anxious and braced for some kind of confrontation, to relax.

Their faces, which had been fixed and attentive, giving the impression to those standing nearby that they were looking for, rather than expecting to witness, a fight, instead softened into their break.

Those of a certain disposition who had assumed defiant or passively belligerent stances in response to the tradesmen's own manner, making the life of the glass collector that much more difficult, with no-one moving to allow him to work, also unwound, although some did only with a sense of anti-climax such was their way.

The glass collector, in turn able to travel more freely through the bar, could desist with the sporadic slamming of clearly insufficient numbers of glasses at the end of the bar, which had previously added to the barmaid's fractious mood.

So when Kick returned from the bathroom, the room felt much better and he felt a moment's relief – practised in this though he was, he had not always been so.

On a previous tour he had stood, hands behind his back, head down, smudging the ground in front of him with the tip of his right shoe, a naughty boy in front of Powdermouth's chastising Headmaster, as a rolling fist fight broiled in the bar behind him.

His mumbled explanation, mostly lost in the sound of breaking glasses behind him, that it had been the right thing to say but perhaps not the right person to say it to, had fallen on the unimpressed ears of Powdermouth who had suggested he stick to the singing in terms Kick still couldn't forget.

It was as close to angry as Kick had ever seen Powdermouth; he hoped never to see it again and for this reason was eternally grateful that Powermouth had never found out about the time with the monkey and the bowling ball.

As they left to continue their journey to The Partisans and as Kick sensed that Bat really wanted to tell him something, the entire group froze at the sound of a shrill scream, its proximity difficult to judge accurately in the dark but it was surely not far.

Some superimposers go mad and Kick, whilst knowing that U.S. let this one roam to scare people into the population centres, took this as a warning never-the-less. On a number of levels.

The intimidation manifested less subtly directly outside the city boundaries of The Partisans with thuggery, random beatings and muggings employed – this time as a means of keeping people in.

A funnelling myriad of posters, placed roadside on vertical surfaces, presented a variety of lurking faces, nameless all, but under the banners 'Wanted' and 'Beware', laying a heavy hand of encouragement on those intent on passing by to not do so but, instead, seek the safety of the city.

It only made Kick smile, this last superficial gauntlet, before entering one of his favourite places.

The Partisans reminded Kick of restless children, good-natured for the most part but exasperating, exhilarating, argumentative, questioning, dumb, inspired, daft and as likely to say 'Yeah, but...' as 'Why?', or, for that matter, 'Why not?'

Not for the first time he reflected on what life might have been like in The Past, before Now, when the population centres were occupied by disparate peoples, all thinking differently and wondered if that would have been more thrilling, more restful, more or less.

Bat had once expressed the view that if you held the same opinion about something ten years from now, then you hadn't been paying attention – to which Zip had immediately responded, 'You won't be saying that in ten years' – and Kick understood the sentiment.

It was why he enjoyed The Partisans, who had taken that philosophy and crunched the time-scale to the extent that, mostly, you simply couldn't tell who had what opinion or for how long, aware and uncaring as they were that they didn't know what they didn't know.

Delighting in this, The Partisans didn't care for such subtle details. A place where what little reason there was settled fewer debates than a chicken winning an egg and spoon race – it was a great place to have an argument.

Not one informed by the generalised, intolerant tribalism and lazy stereotypes of thoughtless conditioning that so often meant that the participants didn't have the imagination to see the other side's point of view, rendering a bad-tempered, judgemental and self-righteous impasse the only outcome, with no hope of effective resolution. No, here, everyone recognised that – for the most part – everyone else pretty much wanted the same thing as they did but differed only in how to achieve it.

In this way, it was perhaps the most grown-up of all places despite wallowing in its own recalcitrance.

They were greeted where they were staying by Powdermouth and Iodine, an immense man who had been co-ordinating security from this point on for years and whose skin's dark glossiness rivalled Riot's.

Whilst both were big men, the comparison fell apart at the eyes – Riot, who could be heard somewhere saying to his new centre-of-attention, 'I don't care what I *am*, is it *attractive*?' had a light in his eyes that worked to make you aware of him.

Iodine's made you aware of you, made you act a little different maybe, made you behave.

Kick had liked him the moment he had met him.

♪

Backstage, first gig at The Partisans and Kick was struggling on the choice of the jacket for the show; currently a scarlet frock coat auditioned for the man with the slightly furrowed brow reflecting back at him in the dressing room mirror.

His restless face-on-profile-face-on fidget maintained an unrelated dance to the sound of Riot speaking from the shower, recounting loudly to anyone who cared to listen, the reasons for his separation from his wife.

'I'm not saying she was possessive but she used to answer the phone with, "He's mine!"'

Bat sat calmly, having seen all this before so when Kick asked him, 'Should I wear this jacket?' he responded distantly, 'Well, it doesn't seem to be very good for you – ever since you put it on, all it has done is made you look in the mirror.'

He knew that within minutes, Kick would throw it off onstage.

'Mmmm...' said Kick, frowning.

'Our sex life went from nothing to lose, to nothing to prove, to nothing to look forward to,' continued Riot.

Bat sat calmly, having seen all this before. He looked to Zip, only ever close to placid just before stage time, reading.

He called through to Riot, 'How come you always leave it so late to shower?' and got a 'Don't worry my friend, I will be dry in three wipes of a mewling kitten' as an indicator that it was time to focus Kick.

'Kick, it's time,' he said and Kick, watched by his three band mates, opened a door and strode resolutely into a cupboard.

'How many times have we played here anyway?' asked Bat as Kick, struggling to regain his composure and authority, led them through the actual door to the stage.

'It would seem Chocolate Bollocks here isn't perfect after all,' Zip suggested, neatly marking his page before following the others.

♪

Kick was a powerful empath, relentlessly peppered with mood and truth inflexions in any situation and just as relentlessly filtering and screening, blocking and parrying – more instinctively as he got older.

In this way he could reach the essence of a situation with unrivalled precision and it was this insight that he brought to his lyrics. By touring and performing and listening with sincerity, he unwittingly acted as a carrier of truth from region to region by putting what he was experiencing into words.

However, his poetry was awful. Truly awful. Which, for an empath, was both a mystery and – to his fellow band members – very, very funny.

They had struggled to comprehend how he was able, on the one hand, to avert a riot with one careful word yet could not pick up on what must be an audience's deep, though reluctant, dismay at having three quarters of their favourite band provide only silence as accompaniment to his wayward word plays.

It didn't always happen; it was as spontaneous as mostly every other action on stage and they could only assume that Kick misunderstood their mischievous glee and bitten-down giggles as positive endorsements of his decision to 'take a moment out'.

It had to follow that he also misread the audience's despair as confirmation that the rank doggerel about his 'love being water crashing against the rock of her indifference' was reaching, truly reaching, into their hearts.

The Fifth Season's audience always clapped him, perhaps, in the moment, the polite grown-ups in the relationship, Kick bowing slightly, actually humble, whilst Zip, Riot and Bat desperately attempted to keep it together.

So as not to hurt their friend.

Despite being one of those nights when Kick punished the innocent in this way, the gig went well.

Zip, in particular, had really enjoyed the support band and the quaintly old-fashioned irony in their name – Product, whose members compounded the statement with the stage names Voca List, Lee D'Guitar, Bay Slines and Drummond Perc.

Naturally, Zip chose Mangler's busiest moment of the day to discuss the matter, Mangler's T-shirt reading 'You believe in UFOs? What planet are you *from?*' and whose opening gambit was that Product were essentially metal.

Zip considered this an excellent place to start; tiptoeing over cables as he countered an industrious Mangler, bobbing up and down to an irregular beat behind speaker cabinets and onstage lighting rigs.

Zip maintained that the lyrical content, such as 'Ain't no Miss Right, Ain't no Miss Wrong, There's only the Miss with whom you get along' placed them outside the traditional birds, booze, bikes and Beelzebub orthodoxy of metal.

Mangler, wrestling with the continuous co-ordination of his team and their wordless routines, offered the suggestion that there was more to metal than just the lyrical content and whilst Zip agreed, he still felt that, on this matter, Product's sound was, not unlike the Fifth Season's, more hips than crotch.

Mangler accepted this position with a nod but argued some more anyway.

Meanwhile, backstage, Kick and Bat wrestled with post-performance adrenaline and the last of the press commitments for the day. Riot was nowhere to be seen so it was just the two of them left to field the usual questions with the usual answers.

It was as Bat was patiently answering 'What's your favourite sexual position?' with, 'Wherever I happen to be at the time,' that Yo-Yo came in with a sheepish Riot and coolly, almost without anyone noticing, terminated the interviews.

Kick's, 'Need we ask?' subjected Riot to his own kind of usual question and like a naughty schoolboy he stage-whispered, 'Confession is gonna take forever.'

Yo-Yo, not entirely without humour, glared at Riot enough to prompt him to expand upon his theme for those who had taken press duties in his absence.

'Easy to please, pleased to be easy,' he offered, palms up and considered this said it all or at least enough.

Kick, as usual when they were in The Partisans, had other business on his mind and having made his excuses, found himself striding up Feisty Canyon, the main street through the centre – he smiled as he went, seeing the posters of one of his favourite bands, Point Counter Point, who had been there a few days ago with their 'When There's Nothing Left To Believe In, What Do You Believe In?' tour.

The first sensations of post-gig adrenaline crash made the short journey a little harder with each step but as he knocked on a familiar door the effort provided its own reward as he was struck all over again by the beauty of the woman who opened it.

They had met on an earlier tour. Kick was glazed somewhere backstage somewhere as she passed by and said simply, 'Notice me,' without slowing or stopping.

Stirred, alert, it took him ten minutes to find her again, standing alone on the balcony of the venue.

Kick had gone and stood next to her, shared her view for a while and playfully, casually, said, 'You know if you ever have a spare kiss you don't know what to do with, I'll take it off your hands.'

She turned to him, the second time he heard that beautiful voice, 'How can I resist?'

'If I knew, I wouldn't tell you.'

It was as dawn was breaking on the other side of a long night's conversation of discovery that Honeytongue found that spare kiss.

It wasn't easy to forget how beautiful she was, to him at least – yet each and every time he returned his gaze to her he was astonished anew, surprised again, even if he had looked away only briefly.

But it was her mind and her voice as the expression of it that captivated most – he had believed he could have some beautiful moments with her and this had proved to be true.

'Hey Vivid, really nice of you to make an appearance. I heard you were in town,' flowed over him like cooling water, the vowels pooling in intimate lingers and Kick shivered deliciously.

Despite this, Honeytongue, inviting Kick in, knew how this would end, tonight at least.

Struggling now, desperate to keep his eyes open, not wanting to miss a moment, Kick made his way to the bedroom, artlessly kicking his shoes off as he went, scattering Nottienuffroomtoswinga, Honeytongue's sanguine tomcat.

And as he fell face-down onto the bed, one foot out of

his trousers and a sock clinging to the big toe of the other, he attempted a mumbled, 'It's gonna take more than nine lives to save your pussy tonight,' into the sheets before sleep took him.

'I should be so lucky,' said Honeytongue, kissed him on the forehead and went to the spare bedroom where she had, knowingly, made up the bed.

Once Nottie adjusted to these new circumstances, the house silenced into a happy overnight.

♪

Kick spent as much time as he could with Honeytongue whenever he was in The Partisans – they liked each other, making the fundamental nourishment they gave each other intellectually, spiritually and physically resonate with a giving honesty.

Uncorrupted by agenda or circumstance, liking each other, it seemed to Kick, was a stronger basis than the unpredictable excitement or lust-filled headiness of what was often described as, or mistaken for, love. It was with a rare interference-free communication that Honyetongue had made love simple again for the first time since love was simple.

People treated him like a good man and he was fairly sure that he was but she was the only one who made him feel like one.

He was Honeytongue's to pick up, put down or throw away – there was never anyone on the road. Perhaps in the early days but not since he had met her.

For some, having a child offered the ultimate fulfilment,

for Kick things were less easy to achieve and he recognised, everyday, what he had been lucky enough to discover.

That they could spend months not seeing each other without fear, longing or creeping distrust bridging the distances between them was something that neither of them took much time to think about; this situation worked for both of them, the balance found as casually as Kick now prepared breakfast.

Nottienuffroomtoswinga, a discarded fur hat, slept in the middle of the kitchen table, reflecting Kick's own sense of serenity and as Kick turned to see Honeytongue coming through the kitchen door it struck him again that, yes, it helped that she was so nice to look at.

'I'm surprised the cat's still talking to you,' she said.

Not quite sure what she was referring to, Kick flighted, 'We both woke alone and unburdened by any sense of wrongdoing,' and hoped this covered most possibilities at least.

And then they held each other. Standing in the kitchen, they just held each other.

Staying in Kick's arms, Honeytongue stepped back slightly and, with a defiant look on her face asked Kick, 'So have you met Miss Right on your travels yet?'

Staring into the middle distance, deliberately fluttering his eyelashes in a mockery of mournful tragedy, Kick whispered, 'I don't think I would find Miss Right even if there was only one Miss left.'

They laughed and they kissed and Kick said, 'Breakfast?' and Honeytongue said, 'In bed,' and Nottie slept on.

♪

Not many sports had endured from The Past to Now but the universal appeal of kicking a round leather ball into a net was one of them, resembling the old game only through the rules.

The application of those rules had become increasingly gymnastic, players of astonishing physical prowess and flexibility mixing with superimposers able to read, respond and utilise pockets of localised and temporary atmospheric conditions to influence the flight of the ball. Telekinetics were banned from the sport for obvious reasons but the spectacle didn't suffer as a consequence and if ever a crowd could create an atmosphere, it was at The Partisans.

Today The Stickle Brick Superstars were playing The Beautiful Losers who were anything but, given that they had, in a closely-fought race, beaten The Psychobunnies to the Title on the last day of the previous season.

Kick, along with Honeytongue, Yo-Yo and some of the crew, was enjoying every moment and he couldn't help the smile on his face as the crowd changed their allegiances from moment to moment, a feature unique to The Partisans.

The joyous festival, the good-natured barrage of noise and Honeytongue next to him was as good a way as he could imagine of relaxing before the last of the two gigs here tonight.

Along with the rest of the crowd in this tiny amphitheatre he gasped in delight as Curve Ball, The Losers' star player zapped the ball into the net, somehow executing an accelerated impact on the ball at the full extension of a back flip.

As Kick jumped up and down with those near him (who were currently supporting The Losers), smiling into the eyes of Honeytongue, he began to sense something was wrong. Very wrong.

Her own concern now beginning to blossom, she sought clarification in his eyes but he looked instead to the pitch just moments before the celebrating Curve Ball put his hand to his temple.

His smiling face slowly loosened into one of mild confusion and then into a fixed rigour of alarm and as he sank to his knees, the first blood began to flow from his nose.

The crowd, engaging with each other in elation or disappointment, were unaware that, on the pitch, his team mates had stopped a few paces from him, several backing away, a primitive fear now very evident.

Curve Ball twisted and writhed on the floor in cruel contrast to the flexible fluidity of just moments ago and as the crowd gradually silenced, before realisation and horror thrust them into an altogether different type of fervour, he began bending backwards into a brutal curve, his head at first touching the back of his heels, then the top of his legs before a loud crack signalled his release from agony just as his head reached the base of his now broken spine.

The crowd rapidly evacuated the arena, with even the team doctors standing reluctant to approach the snapped athlete but through the thinning crowd, Kick became aware of one set of eyes looking at him.

He turned to see a plain man with a kind face ignoring the fleeing mayhem around him and staring straight at him.

'Dessel,' said Kick involuntarily.

He hadn't felt The Maze but he knew, as he was meant to, that Curve Ball was all Dessel's work and as Dessel ambled over, he wondered where Tapper and Drumbeat were. Before he could be sure, Dessel was standing in front of him, his back to the rattling confusion he had created on the pitch.

'Through other people's eyes, I horrify myself,' he sighed and shrugged his shoulders in a time-honoured, aw-shucks…me?

He turned briefly to take in the dazed Beautiful Losers searching for comprehension in disparate aimless meanders around the pitch before returning his attention to Kick.

'Holders of trophies, Champions of nothing,' he said, pausing for a moment before spitting overtly on the ground between them.

They both knew all of this was a display of power for Kick's benefit, little to do with team loyalties, although it wasn't unheard of for Dessel to refresh his hatred through any means.

'Winners are determined, skilled, lucky perhaps but champions have a dignity. They understand the responsibility of their position,' continued Dessel, apparently for his own benefit but Kick, to his surprise, found himself loosely agreeing with him.

'Join U.S. Kick,' Dessel on point once more.

Iodine appeared at Kick's shoulder and even amidst the tension, Kick marvelled not only that he had not even been aware that he was near but also that Iodine was so swift to act.

Unmoved, Dessel continued, 'The Board Members have got plans for you Kick…big plans.'

Before Kick could reply, Iodine cut in, 'They'd shit down each other's necks if they thought it would come out the other end as pennies.'

'You have a lot of being quiet to do,' countered Dessel with a tone in his voice that made the watching Honeytongue's concern edge towards fear.

Sensing this and never one to forget his brief, Dessel smiled gently at Honeytongue before resuming evenly, 'Kick I'm here with the best intentions and I mean no harm,' stressing the last words slightly and spreading his arms wide like his smile.

'You could have fooled me,' spat Iodine.

'I know,' said Dessel flatly.

'Don't patronise me,' flexed Iodine, stepping forward.

'If you think that's patronising, you should hear how I speak to grown-ups,' escaped from Dessel, his behaviour now becoming less voluntary and Kick intervened with a hand on Iodine's arm.

This was escalating dangerously.

'Dessel, you know I'm not going to join U.S., we've been through this,' and whilst Kick's words were chosen and delivered carefully, they were fuelled by contempt.

'But Kick, we can spread your word to a wider audience, provide you with the better things in life. Provide you with the future.'

Kick noted Dessel's choice of words and irritably recognised the impatience with which U.S. urged him to sign up to their immortality package, with him being an endorsee they had pursued relentlessly.

Allowing that irritation out – and before his will could withhold it – Kick said, 'I don't believe a word you say and those are just the ones I listen to.'

'And that's about the lick and taste of it,' added Iodine definitively.

Dessel, wanting to react in kind, thought better of it, instead adopting a faux-playful tone.

'I think you'll find I always tell the truth,' he said, widening his eyes, scratching his ear, 'but that I may not always mean it literally...'

Amused, he trailed off as Tapper and Drumbeat made a belated appearance, Kick noticing from the little twists in Dessel's face that they would be spoken to about reaction times once they were alone with him later.

Tall men with small haircuts, big men with little on their minds, their short fuses allowed long leashes, Tapper and Drumbeat had, since an early age and with percussive timing, started or finished each other's sentences. Enforcers of the highest order, their job was often completed – to their acute disappointment – with intimidation alone but their reputation was built on firm-ground violence; a breed always ready and willing to kill you and if they did, it would add to their sense of self instead of destroying them from within like it would most.

Occasionally U.S. would remove a middle manager from the payroll, sometimes for minor aberrations, sometimes to set an example, sometimes for no reason at all.

Powdermouth had once told Kick about the time when, in an underground car park, these men had taken a thick rope and looped it around a vertical supporting strut. One end they tied to the rear tow hook of a car idling next to the strut, the other they fed through the sunroof and around the neck of the quivering manager in the driver's seat.

Nothing if not meticulous, they had measured the rope – allowing for the lost length when knotting a noose – to be a few feet shorter than the length of the car park but long enough to build up some decent speed.

Leaning in through the driver's open window and slicing the manager's lower lip along its length with a razor to demonstrate the full extent of the options now available to him, Drumbeat said simply, 'Drive.'

And as the manager accelerated away and as the noose pulled out red from the sunroof and as the car hit the far wall and all through the gathering up of the rope, their footsteps scuffing echoes off the concrete and tile, the expression on Tapper's face told of his sulky resentment that, in that last action, Drumbeat had not provided him with a sentence to complete.

They didn't like Iodine. They never had.

Addressing him directly, 'We could tear your head off…'

'…to the sound of cheering thousands.'

Iodine, his blood up, was no respecter of reputations and threw, 'You'd better actually be tough, 'cos if you're not, I'm going to find out,' at them.

Now it was Dessel's turn to calm things down.

'Gentlemen please,' and turning to Iodine, 'From what you are saying, I assume you're here to see me lose my temper…which I won't do.'

Yet as he reassured with his civility, Tapper and Drumbeat twitched with frustrated aggression behind him, unable to back down from Iodine's boring glare.

'Every time you wake up…'

'…count your teeth.'

'You'll be sifting through your shit…'

'…to clean them.'

'Is it because you don't have many words each?' asked Iodine.

'I think fighting is going…'

'…to become happening…'

'Gentlemen *please!*' stressed Dessel in a tone beyond argument and in that moment, with dead athletes behind him and absolutely no light in his eyes, Dessel looked at Iodine like prey.

'These two are just for show, it's me you have to worry about.'

Iodine wouldn't back down and spotting that Tapper had missed a clump of hair on his cheek so totally when shaving that he might have been Picasso's Hitler, mocked some more, 'They're so thick. How have they survived? Who feeds them?'

'If you keep turning over my stones, you can't complain about what comes crawling out,' Dessel's composure struggling for balance.

Kick had had enough of this and attempted humour to diffuse the situation – someone needed to ring the bell for the end of this round.

'Dessel, I don't wish for the future, I am all for the active participation in the joyful sorrow of humankind's natural life-cycle.'

Dessel sighed deeply, came very close to Kick and said in a soft tone not reflected in the flint of his eyes, 'Can you hear me ticking?'

♪

That evening, the last of the two gigs served well to distract Kick – there had been much to reflect upon after his encounter with Dessel.

Certainly, he had been impressed – but mostly alarmed – at the ferocity of Iodine's protection, a lack of composure not seen on previous tours. Iodine was not unaware of how dangerous that situation had been and Kick couldn't help feeling that this was escalating on all sides in a way that needed cooling.

Iodine had always been of the philosophy that you should never wrestle with pigs because you will both end up covered in shit and the pig will like it. Kick had found comfort in this history, Iodine's track record and that Powdermouth could be trusted to make the right judgement call on all matters, especially security.

However, he still couldn't resist an 'Easy tiger' to Iodine as Dessel had walked away with the muttering Tapper and Drumbeat throwing insults over their shoulders at them as they went.

'The more he teaches them, the dumber they get,' was all that came out of Iodine's mouth, his eyes still fixed on the retreating subjects of his contempt.

What Kick couldn't have known was that this was the first frayed edge of a greater unravelling but at the time it was the fact that Kick had not sensed Dessel until it suited Dessel that troubled him the most. He felt sure that this was part of any message that Dessel had intended for him to receive.

There would be time to reflect more fully on that; right now it was close to show time and backstage he again found himself face-profile-face in front of the mirror, modelling the same scarlet coat.

'What do you think?' he asked the room.

Bat sighed patiently.

'Looks good,' he said, 'just not to me.'

'Uh-huh,' said Kick.

Zip read and Honeytongue – a welcome guest to all – picking up on the prevailing mood, said nothing.

Riot, on some kind of repeat loop, continued his soapy soliloquy to single life from the shower, cheerily championing a new acquaintance to a disinterested audience.

'She was the kind of girl who took what she wanted – I was just lucky enough to get in the way.'

Bat checked his watch and called through to Riot, his tongue half in his cheek, 'How wet is the kitten?' which seemed to shake Kick away from his own image, a vague recollection struggling to form; he turned to Honeytongue and asked cautiously, 'Did I do a nine lives thing last night…?'

He wrinkled his nose as she gave him a look that made him search for a distraction that no-one was going to give him.

'Mmmmm…' he said.

♪

Post-gig, the crew packing down more extensively this time, ready for a morning departure, Zip and Mangler (today's T-shirt reading 'A Tension Seeker') discussed the support band Chaos Feary.

As Mangler grunted and grimaced, by a lengthy wordy process they concluded that, heavy as they were and as difficult to get into as they were, the muscularity of their music and the intensity of the performance meant that, if Chaos Feary were an animal, it might not be pretty but it would be pretty damn impressive.

Around them the crew had gone through their checklists, the last of which traditionally being everyone shouting for Guilty, the tour's dog.

No one was really sure if Guilty actually existed but on the last night in each venue, the rear door of the equipment bus was left open to allow him to hop aboard.

If anything went wrong, from leads breaking to speakers falling, it was never the crew's fault with everyone collectively and affectionately shouting, 'Guilty!' whenever these things happened.

All the crew went through the ritual on the last night and anyone missing on a bathroom break was reminded to go out and shout for Guilty when they were done.

Slopehound held up a sign.

In this way, for all his apparent misdemeanours, Guilty was the tour's lucky charm.

For his part, Kick wanted to drink Honeytongue in as indulgently as he could in the last few hours before the tour moved on.

They were each other's and that travelled across vast distances, often enough to be considered always.

As he lay there in bed with her deep-rhythm breathing colluding with his own fatigue to draw him into joining her in sleep, he remembered something from the gig.

At a point where everything came together, the band, the song, the audience seeming to vibrate at the same frequency, he had experienced an intense image, almost a vision.

A boy, in sunlight, in a field and though it had lasted only seconds, it had been both beautiful and a little sad.

No, not quite. It had been beautiful and maybe the boy was a little sad. He wasn't sure.

And as the understanding of it cartwheeled lazily away, he joined Honeytongue.

Waking to her poking him in the shoulder to get him out of bed, he had joked, 'You're the woman of my dreams but only when I'm awake okay?' but the morning was bitter-sweet. More time with Honeytongue but goodbye too; they had given up on finding the right words for this situation so Honeytongue didn't even try.

'Careful,' she said as she kissed him goodbye, 'God isn't alone out there…'

When he was with her he didn't need the rest of the world and up until now that had been a trade he had been unwilling to make but the wide orbit that she was in around him always made her susceptible to someone else's pull and he could feel his position on the rest of the world changing.

Kick smiled and as he walked away one more time from everything, all that she was, all that she offered, he promised himself this would be the last time.

It didn't help his mood that next was The Mean City.

Chapter Five

The boy bathed early, the rising sun doubling as alarm and functional friend, drying the clothes spread out on a flat rock next to the river, a bodiless dreamer.

He had chosen his spot – had continued to choose his spots – carefully; the river, having squeezed through the discomfort of a narrow rock gorge, shouted relief as it landed from the height of a man into the deep, wide, relative hush of the pool below.

By necessity he had to bathe at the edges away from the implacable current – plus the pool was remote so, as he lay on a rock, absorbing the gathering energy of the sun, his clothes a drying fabric shadow next to him, he was secluded from anyone passing by on either bank.

And though he picked his way across rock, field and forest like a cat on tiptoes, he welcomed the burble and gurgle of the falling water that would cover any noise he might make to anyone approaching from upstream. Downstream he could see.

He was sure that so far he had remained unseen, even in the great open spaces where this boy on the edge of adolescence, still young enough for five years to be a long time ago, had often stood out against the horizon.

Alert, watchful, he had always found cover or a ditch to keep him from others' eyes.

There had been a group of Out-Of-Towners that he had almost approached, a travelling canteen selling fried and grilled foods, the sign over the serving hatch reading "With prices like these, your dog isn't your best friend, we are!"

It wasn't the food that appealed to him – a grease-dealer seemed out of place to him in such fresh lands despite his hunger. No, there was a boy with a red cap, younger than him, sitting laughing in the front seat and seeing this as he passed discretely by, he had missed his friends acutely and had craved company.

In the end, he did not know why he had not gone to say hello; these people were no threat to him he knew.

He didn't question it too hard as he lay on the rock, his light brown hair drying against his forehead, the tips golden from the sun; this journey – whatever it was he was doing – was his to take alone.

He lay still but not without a sense of potential, like a tide at its lowest or highest point, until, with the weightlessness of youth, he stood.

His trousers dry enough, he left the rest of his clothes to release their remaining moisture to the sky and – the coast clear – went to check on his traps.

Two held enough fish for breakfast, the third a fish so small in comparison to the bait that he could only assume it wasn't so much looking to eat as pick a fight.

He saluted the small fish's verve with a smile, watched it swim away, killed the other fish quickly and humanely, removed the heads, tails and guts and returned them to the river.

Good for drinking, good for drowning, so the river feeds, so the river is fed and after a small moment of reflection, of respect, the kind given to a species only by those who hunt it, he ate the fish, raw and real, knowing that they understood.

He had no plan other than to keep travelling in the direction that drew him – he was unaware that he was heading towards Maskelyne and he would not have understood the significance had he been so. His intelligence, manifest as a tempered curiosity, was, as yet, uncluttered by the distractions that intellect might later indulge.

He carried only what he needed and left no trace wherever possible, a mixture of instinct, luck and listening to his environment keeping him safe. And fed.

The land gave and in exchange, in the end, all shall be returned to the land and he knew this in an abstract sense – it might be said that childhood is over the moment you truly realise that you are going to die and his childhood was not yet over.

Despite his actions being an investment in an unknown future, for now life was in-the-moment and a direct engagement with immediacies. The adult world of struggling to pick out appropriate from an ocean of strange was yet to encroach upon his thinking. It might never.

Enjoying the last of the fish, he spotted some berries on the far bank, high above the river on an over-hanging branch.

Already tasting the sweet reward of the fruit, he made his way cautiously across protruding boulders in the gorge at the head of the pool and was soon scaling the tree.

From the far bank he had had an inaccurate perspective, the branch being much higher than it had first appeared but this inspired only the briefest of pauses, more a reassessment of the task, and before long he was high above the bank, the berries a juicy handful.

It was then that he heard the voices coming from upstream. The sharp learning that the water falling may have covered his own sounds but also those of anyone approaching hit him frustratingly late as he realised that, while he might pay no further price this time, all he could do for now was stay where he was as the two men passed by on the riverbank below him.

His instinct told him that these were men most often on dark business; holding himself as still as possible, he heard them talk as they came closer…

'…that's great, another vague job,' a sulky tone in the younger one's voice.

'Hey, don't blame me, I just follow orders. Regional says. I do.'

'Oh man, that guy talks like he was at every meeting.'

'He's under pressure 'cos this one came down from the big man himself apparently.'

'What would Dessel want with a kid?'

'Beats me but when was the last time you didn't do what he wanted?'

The older man stopped directly beneath the boy and jabbed his finger into the other man's chest to make the point.

'Ours is not to question why, ours is not to question at all.'

He started walking again leaving his exasperated partner to throw his hands in the air and exclaim, 'So we're keeping our eyes out for a *kid*?'

'*Everyone* is keeping their eyes out for a kid – the info from HQ is that they can't read him, can't get a bearing on where he is.'

'A *kid*?! What the – ?'

His stomping footsteps faded off as he hurried to join his colleague and resume their reluctant recce.

'Listen, word has it that he's already simmering that this hasn't been dealt with so you want to just rein that attitude in,' was the last thing the boy heard clearly.

Peering through the leaves, he watched as they continued on downstream and sat on the branch until they were long gone, their voices becoming lost in the sounds of the moving water, his confused thoughts stilling him along with his caution.

Were they really talking about him? For no reason he knew that this was true. Why would they be looking for *him*?

His gaze, unfocussed in thought until now, alighted on a point further along the branch, a clutch of berries swelling to burst their skins.

Sure that the men had gone, he edged his way along the branch, the berries he already had forcing an awkward one-handed grip.

He was high above the river, the rocks and stones on its bed blurring and distorting as the clear water swelled and rolled beneath him.

Good for drinking, good for drowning.

And just as he reached the berries, and as he struggled to hold the branch as he stretched for them, his fall tipped over the edge of inevitability and into the moment of happening and he landed hard on the water.

The silver thrusts of migratory fish scattered as he tumbled without control, bubbles in all directions giving no hint of upright.

'I don't remember rain,' he thought randomly as the river continued to make decisions for him and the air was squeezed out of him like an unwanted guest.

Today, the river would be kind, making of him a graceless deposit in a shallow, shingled eddy close to the bank opposite the tree.

He sat, gulping for air, thankful again for the noise of the waterfall, masking the explosive smack of his landing on the water from the men who had passed just a few minutes ago.

He had had enough berries. Now he had none.

Hanging far over the river as the second bunch had been, maybe they had always been destined for the river but as he made his drenched way back up the bank the thought did not make him feel any better about being the middle man.

The fact that enough never fulfilled the restless dissatisfaction of the giant process he was a part of, had never done so, would have given him no succour even if he had such awareness.

To his surprise – and mild alarm – he returned to where his shirt was drying to find next to it, laid carefully and obviously, a bunch of berries, picked by a boy in a red cap that he would never know.

Wet trousers or not, he travelled on that day – that day of much learning; he knew now that his instinct for caution had been correct. He was troubled that he was being looked for but also that someone had been watching him, benevolently or not.

Maybe it was just someone passing by he told himself, he had not sensed anyone following him.

And he was troubled by what he had heard the men say.

Mostly he was troubled that their mouths had not moved as they had spoken.

I AM WATER

Chapter Six

The Mean City looked better behind them than it did in any other position, not that they would ever turn around to confirm this. They never had.

A dark, cynical place, not entirely evil as such, it considered itself brutal and prided itself on its hard edges.

In many ways it was little more than a collection of insecure wannabe tough guys, the names of whom offered testament to a kind of adolescent posturing, inappropriately feeling its way, one might hope, to a better adulthood.

However, under the showy veneer and the strutting fist fights over the ownership of names such as The Dark Dude, Black Havoc, Black Black, Black Black Black, The Darker Dude, Black Infinity (and so on) lay a very dangerous environment.

Those short on options, tired of life, or both, regularly found their way here in search of the right bar in which to say the wrong thing, a crass but effective form of assisted suicide, satisfying the various needs of all the participants.

It wasn't called The Mean City for nothing.

Psychopaths and sadists naturally found their way to this place, any rules that might contain their tendencies being monitored and managed by those unlikely to enforce them – fellow psychopaths and sadists.

Although, these sadists were, of course, different to those found at The Indulgence Junkies.

The support acts for the three-night stay (Suffer the Blow, The Mucho Machos and Death's Contentment) each sounded like they were auditioning for Hell's House Band and whilst few bands told their tales with such consistency over the years, The Fifth Season never particularly liked their stories. None of them wrote songs so much as chiselled them out.

No-one called for Guilty as they packed up to leave since no-one considered for a minute that he would leave the trailer in a place such as this. Slopehound held up his sign just in case.

Bubon had once requested that U.S. provide permanent night to complement the rock and stone twists of the buildings in this angular, uncomfortable city; however, enough biological processes changed to make the management of the city possible but difficult and expensive, by which time the city had discovered that permanent darkness could be adjusted to, that fear blossomed better in the cyclical anticipation of darkness coming. So natural daylight hours had been resumed.

For all the scientific advances, the basic premise remains that without light there is no shadow.

The Fifth Season always played this city. As lucrative as the gig was, past experience never prepared them or softened its impact so it was fortuitous that geographically it could come psychologically early in the tour.

The U.S. thugs outside The Mean City were, as you might imagine, of the most convincing type given that so few would want to venture in voluntarily and so many might want to leave if they ever did so, but a trade status allowed The Fifth Season – each band member deep in reflection, processing their experiences – to leave through this human minefield.

That and Bubon's influence.

As Kick had dined with him, post-gig on that first night, Bat had been with Zip, Riot and some of the crew at a bar, The Strychnine Kick, trying to stomach something of his own.

The screens around the bar were – in theory at least – possible to ignore; in actuality, this wasn't true at all, being an endless loop of executions, beatings and murderous natural disasters.

So, whilst the regulars in the bar – apparently indifferent, maybe desensitised to the churning flesh-red on the screens – limited their gaze to lingering but frustrated scowls in the direction of the colourful new arrivals, Bat had to escape to the air outside.

He closed his eyes in an attempt to wipe clean the images pressed against their lenses and at first didn't feel the blow of the metal bar as it doubled him over and rapidly introduced his cheek to the cold stone floor.

Only once he had cognitively established what had just happened did the pain turn up, as though needing the invitation of realisation.

As Bat lay on the ground reflecting that, had he been struck in the head, not the stomach, this might not have hurt at all, the second blow, a full-hip-swing kick of delicious abandon, invited pain in on a significantly more residential basis.

Bubon guaranteed safety in the city but clearly not everyone was paying attention.

Bat could only focus on his assailant up to chest height, protecting his face as he was; he could see as far as the logo on the sweatshirt which read 'Damn, These Clothes Are Comfortable' and his own anger stirred through the pain for the first time at the corruption of that message by the wearer.

A third blow never materialised, the mystery attacker standing still and soundless a couple of paces away and having heard the disturbance, Zip and Iodine burst into the alley looking for their friend and charge.

Bat's anger turned to a reluctant curiosity as he sensed the uncertainty in their movements.

Without hesitation, although with differing degrees of enthusiasm and ability, they would both have fielded physical violence to protect Bat but now didn't know what to do with the young woman lazily regarding them as they came to a inelegant stop.

She wore a tattoo across her cheek that meant she wasn't going undercover in the straight world any time soon and a look on her face that said she knew the best way to a man's heart was straight through his chest with a knife.

She stood waiting for Iodine and Zip to make a move but, even here, even Now, they were part of the vast majority for whom hurting a woman, even a violent one, was still low; very low.

'Pussies,' she spat and wandered off.

The pain still dictating his terms, Bat threw, 'At least we're happy with our bums,' after her, a retort fresh out of the 'girls smell' school of boy-dom and one he would be surprised by and a little embarrassed about when he was reminded of it later.

The words had come out of his mouth like they owed him nothing and instinct had considered it acceptable to let them leave.

'You would have thought evolution would have weeded that out by now,' said Zip, crouching to help Bat, the irony in his voice designed to lighten the mood.

They all knew that evolution was proving to be a successful driver for the expanding expression of female violence and whilst this incident was not too unusual, it was enough for Powdermouth to react and hire a local female to work alongside Iodine for the rest of the tour.

Entenne was added to the security detail from the second morning in The Mean City and right up until the time he met her, Kick considered that Powdermouth may also have brought her on board to provide a stabilising balance to Iodine's recent and increasingly blunt physicality.

However, what Kick encountered was a woman of such poised urgency, a physical specimen so relaxed, yet taut and ready, that he was sure that if he got just a little bit closer to her, he might hear her body faintly humming.

He had glanced briefly at Powdermouth with a look on his face that asked 'She knows she works for us, right?' and said, 'Welcome aboard.'

'What do I call you?' she had asked and as Kick extended his hand it struck him that she could call him pretty much whatever she wanted and get away with it and her handshake confirmed it.

'Just call me Kick,' he offered hopefully.

'Women liking each other is more often a pretence than men liking each other,' she responded enigmatically and though Iodine had been considering his new pint-sized peacekeeping partner with the same caution as he might the prospect of cuddling static electricity, when she added, 'Nice poetry,' she became a fully-fledged and welcome member of The Fifth Season's family.

Over the next couple of nights, The Fifth Season would witness the demoralising spectacle of The Mean City's gig-going public.

Eye-gouging, scuffles, stabbings; though there were enough genuinely interested audience members to fill the modest venue and the gaps between songs with appreciative sounds beyond grunts and struggles, these were really private gigs for Bubon.

He placed himself – surrounded by his own security – just in front the sound desk, in what could be mistaken for a metallic, over-protective high-chair, its clear dome of acoustically invisible armoured glass serving only to emphasise his delighted antics in the spotlight he had trained on him.

He rolled his head, smiled, closed his eyes, spread his arms in rapturous appreciation of his favourite band, under their own spotlights a crowd's length away in front of him.

Bubon knew that his visibility was a key element in his control of this most unforgiving of towns and though these gigs were as welcome to the band as a hip-high barbecue at a nudist colony, it was Kick that had the greater burden: dinner with Bubon.

As Bat was struck, Kick had flinched only slightly but just enough for his host to notice.

'Are you okay Kick?' asked Bubon, spray-flecks of saliva and half-eaten food escaping as far as his own chin, a gross display at odds with what Kick knew to be genuine concern.

'Something. Somewhere,' said Kick and returned to paying deliberate attention to his food.

He might not ordinarily have picked up on Bat's plight amongst the thousands of stories that he spent so much of his time actively desensitised to but whenever he dined as Bubon's guest of honour, he filtered as little as he could get away with.

He was always safe with Bubon but when a senior U.S. executive in charge of the cruellest place in all lands, surrounded by his own army of superimposers, invites you to personally dine with him, it pays to stay alert in his presence.

Despite this being far from the first time that Kick had been honoured in this way and despite Bubon trying to hide his child-like delight at seeing him on each occasion, Kick had witnessed enough casual, unexpected explosions of violence across the history of their meals together to stay wary.

Here, high above the city, cut into a rock face, they dined, surrounded on three sides by flat stone surfaces, a panoramic total view of the city below them afforded by the vast glass wall at Kick's back.

Bubon faced the city.

Kick, with no such distractions, was left with nothing but Bubon to look at and the waves of goodwill beaming off Bubon towards Kick served only to clash with the vulgarity of his table-manners.

Bubon was a big man, his love of the finest, richest foods adding a considerable, shapeless bulk to an already-immense frame despite – Kick couldn't fail to notice – food actually getting further than his mouth being little more than a possibility.

He was covered in cuts and sores, seeping and glistening – Kick had occasionally witnessed these being dabbed at by assistants with wipes at Bubon's request but more often they simply went ignored.

Bubon had once told Kick that he didn't trust doctors – and certainly not doctors in The Mean City – and this, combined with the sweat produced by any small movement, gave Bubon the impression of rotting.

Bubon heaved, regardless of the extent of his movement and the only subtle variation from this was the wheezing he did as his chest heaved as he breathed.

One eye gave the impression of being abnormal although both were normal in their own way so Kick was never sure which one and had settled long ago for simply being disorientated and the red hair, receding at the temples, gave form to the furious flame that was Bubon's essential being.

Bubon missed nothing.

He turned to the only other person that was in the room on this particular evening, a figure so unassuming that Kick had almost forgotten that they were there.

She stood very still, a few feet to the side and behind

Bubon, gazing through the window from behind dark-rimmed cheap glasses.

She wore head-to-toe, all-black stretch fabric clothes for comfort, her body so shapeless that at first Kick had thought that he might have been looking at a dab of black paint on the wall that had dripped to form two skinny legs before pooling into foot-like blobs.

Breaking the illusion, she moved towards Bubon and, as she applied an antiseptic wipe to the worst of the troubles on his face, he, in turn, stroked her cheek.

She had a pleasant, amiable face – disengaged – a housewife from The Big Nowhere perhaps.

Bubon made the smallest of gestures with his head and she reached into her ears to remove the ear-plugs that had deliberately isolated her. Her head snapped to the side, hard, as Bubon struck her open-handed, the sound made loud in the stone tomb they were in.

'I wanted you to hear it my darling,' he said to her and her smile, with the fresh red swell on one side of her face, was a touch crooked – adorable, Bubon might say.

She cautiously resumed her position, behind and to the side of Bubon, this time on one foot. Bubon watched and wheezed his approval.

Kick concentrated on his food, feeling her pain, feeling her pleasure, the love in the room.

'Mister Five,' said Bubon to the room and Kick had an instinctive shiver at the mention of Bubon's eerie assistant.

He had greeted Kick for years and had taken him to Bubon on each occasion. Dressed in long, dark, fluid robes, Mister Five used his height to emphasise his elegance and could speak normally if he chose to. On occasion, however,

Mister Five would speak directly into your ear – though he might be standing five feet in front of you and you could see his lips move, his breath, the tickle of his lips, touched intimately against your ear.

Kick couldn't see what the point of that was – or how Bubon could find a use for it – but it didn't half creep him out.

'Now get out,' added Bubon and Kick realised that Mister Five was – perhaps amongst other things – a mind reader and had just been given orders by Bubon, the imperative to leave being instruction to now get out of Bubon's thoughts.

Bubon shivered and rubbed his ear and finally Kick knew how Bubon used Mister Five's skills – an exchange of sorts having just occurred between the two of them.

Reaching under his jacket to scratch at an itch, Bubon returned his attention to Kick and as he then wiped his hand on his shirt – adding fresh blood smears to the established body-fluid tapestry – he spoke to Kick like a favourite son.

'Something, somewhere, indeed,' he glinted before asking mischievously, 'So… how's Dessel, Kick?'

After a thoughtful pause, Kick replied, 'Various.'

Bubon smiled, 'Ah yes, try as he might, he falls a little short of charming.'

He attacked an indiscriminate forkful of food and stared blankly at Kick, his grinding chewing almost serene, the mouthful almost fully swallowed before he spoke again.

'Don't underestimate the commitment he has to the work he does for us, Kick. He's no fool and he believes in what U.S. has to offer. A man like that is better to work with than against, eh?'

'I think he's so full of shit because there isn't enough moral fibre in his diet.'

Bubon smiled again – he was dining with his favourite singer and would indulge Kick as far as he could.

'Kick, I find you as refreshingly candid as usual,' and then, glancing first left, then right, he added in a conspiratorial stage whisper, 'For some reason, most people are careful what they say around me.'

His chest heaved as he struggled to contain his mirth, a failing attempt to fortify the humour with a deadpan delivery.

For a moment a tension was relieved in Kick and the moment it was, Bubon threw a glass at his lover who had touched her raised foot down – he had seen it in the reflection in the window behind Kick. The glass missing her was of little consequence although it clearly disappointed them both.

'Don't. You. Dare,' Bubon said deliberately and she raised her foot again and Kick felt that tension, her discomfort, the love, return to the room.

Bubon, now to Kick:

'If you look around my beautiful town – and even I have to concede that the gene pool here is more of a jacuzzi – you will, no doubt, find frontal lobe deficiency on a significant level. Of course. And it would be fair to say that you would probably find the same in some of those that Dessel chooses to associate with.'

Without affection, Kick thought of Tapper and Drumbeat.

'But not Dessel,' continued Bubon, 'His motivation comes from a considered belief that what we are doing is for the betterment of humankind.'

Kick ate mechanically, treating the meal as work, aware that he was the subject of the good-cop, bad-cop approach U.S. was applying with Bubon and Dessel; well, the psychopath-who-liked-him, the psychopath-who-didn't approach more accurately.

'It's not as simple as good and evil, Kick,' stated Bubon and, perhaps suddenly feeling a touch pompous, added, 'I know you know this,' sheepishly, gesturing with his eyes towards his lover's current delicious discomfort.

Laying his fork down on his empty plate, Bubon slapped the wooden table twice with his palm, cueing the entrance of several waiting staff through a sliding trap door in the stone floor.

'Dessert Kick?'

'How can I resist?'

'If I knew,' said Bubon bypassing cutlery and scooping a handful of creamy pleasure straight into his mouth, 'I wouldn't tell you…this…is…delicious.'

And as his actions dawned on him and as he wiped his hand on his jacket, picking up a spoon and muttering sincerely, 'Excuse me Kick, where are my manners?' Kick realised, with no humour at all, that Bubon really could be funny with a straight face.

Not that he would ever tell him.

Then Kick's mind left the room.

Something Bubon had said, he'd heard it before. Or said it maybe. Somewhere. With love. Elusive. Sadness. Leaving. No time for goodbye. No time.

'I said, have you heard of censors Kick?' asked Bubon.

Returning, organising his thoughts, 'Sorry?' said Kick.

Bubon teased him, 'Don't worry Kick, I'm good enough at conversation for both of us.'

Another pause, before he prodded, 'Kick…censors?'

'I've read about them. In The Past, they were state-employed to filter harmful or corrupting images and words from public media. Even in a…'

'…democracy,' Bubon finished the sentence for him, opening his eyes wide in a can-you-believe-it expression of astonishment and a delight that Kick was fully engaged again.

'So if we follow the logic, those who claim to be protecting us from images which may deprave or corrupt are the ones actually exposed to those images…and by their own definition they will become depraved and corrupted…but still be in a position to decide what will deprave and corrupt us…'

Bubon went back to corrupting his dessert in a depraved way, leaving Kick a little space to unpick the thread of Bubon's point.

'What I'm saying is, that evil can be found in the best intentions; it walks with good,' Bubon provided helpfully.

'You'll also know from your reading [was there a touch of mockery in Bubon's tone?] that The Great Democracy in The Past kept on voluntarily voting in The Devil!' and with this Bubon did laugh.

'Do you think they went to the moon to explore?' he continued, warming to his theme, 'I'd bet any money that those astronauts stood on that lunar surface, looking back at Earth for no other reason than to get a sense of the job in hand and that their report form simply stated – *will need more weapons.*'

Bubon's laugh sprayed obvious white flecks in pinpoint patterns close to Kick's plate, making him self-conscious, calming him down from explosive, through active, to almost dormant.

'Don't,' he said gently, turning slightly with a finger raised and the foot went up again and Kick had no relief.

They ate in silence for a while, Bubon occasionally rumbling although through disquiet or satisfaction, Kick found hard to assess.

At one point he stopped, again as though listening and Kick picked up only that information was being exchanged.

'Out,' he said gently and rubbed his ear.

'It's different Now, Kick,' Bubon resumed once the plates had been cleared, the table wiped down, the coffee had been served and they were (almost) alone again.

'Take female violence,' Bubon began knowingly, enjoying Kick's reaction, his barely perceptible cautious alertness.

'In The Past – probably a long time ago in The Past if truth be told – women might have colluded with violence. Maybe turn the other way if they had a violent partner, justify their behaviour as protective…bless. Maybe they would encourage and enjoy being fought over, be disappointed if they weren't.'

'Some women,' Kick corrected. Despite feeling in the dark, he still felt morally and reflexly compelled to stymie the momentum he knew Bubon could build on this subject, an old one that seemed to have new twist tonight for some reason.

Bubon held up his hands in a no-doubt gesture of agreement before carrying on.

'I always thought that men got a particularly bad press on that one anyway. I had a teacher once...'

Bubon's sentence trailed off and his eyes focussed somewhere in the distance, perhaps hoping to see where it had gone.

'Do you know,' he said, 'I don't remember where I put her.'

A shake of the head, a private smile and Bubon continued, 'She said that all men should be castrated, that sperm should be kept in the fridge for reproductive purposes only. She said that there would be no wars, no violence.'

The look on Bubon's face suggested that he had taken issue with this in some way.

'That would be a fridge that a man had conceived of, designed and made one would assume, the raw materials for which were dragged out of the earth by a man using tools that another man had conceived of, designed and made. I imagine she was aware at the time that she had arrived at a school building and in a vehicle that had both been conceived of, designed and made...well, you get my point Kick.'

Juices ran down Bubon's chin.

'We are not without our flaws,' he offered unnecessarily, 'Let's face it, most men are no more than fresh out of school every day of their adult lives but...but male aggression builds, creates, protects, moves the species forwards. It HAS to. It's all that's left over. Women got the plum job – they create LIFE for fuck's sake.'

His head lowered and he muttered darkly into his coffee, a one-way argument that Kick could not fully hear, the thoughts too scattered to read effectively.

Brightening, Bubon waved his teaspoon lightly in the air.

'Anyway, we know that the notion that women aren't violent is as out-of-date as thinking they didn't like sex. Perhaps you have come across that old notion in your… reading.'

That tone again.

'Now, for better or worse, all of us can be who we are. Evolution, don't you think Kick?'

'We have a greater responsibility to each other than to simply indulge ourselves in this way,' countered Kick. 'It's a cliché but it's also true – with personal freedom comes personal responsibility.'

Bubon paused for a moment.

'Maybe. And I know you believe that the majority live by that code. But to deny our essential selves is dishonest and I would argue that this is the evil that walks alongside that particular best intention.'

'We owe each other a society that doesn't descend into Hell,' Kick found himself engaging more passionately than he knew was prudent.

'The individual is responsible, as you say.'

Then, beginning to grin, Bubon went on, 'After all, if society was to blame you'd have a bunch of super-violent grannies terrorising the neighbourhood having been exposed to it the longest,' and began to giggle.

Kick spoke before the eruption could gain momentum.

'You're saying that life is harsh and cruel, let it be what it is? Sounds the same as letting the bad guys win to me.'

'And there you go with your definitive notions of good and bad again…' said Bubon, his laughter settling into a bubbling restlessness.

He stared fondly at Kick.

'Don't,' he said, turning slightly.

And the tension in Kick remained.

♪

'So why do you come here Kick? Apart from the immense fee I hand over to Powdermouth that is?' but there was no spite in Bubon's tone.

'People listen everywhere, here is no exception,' said Kick diplomatically, knowing Bubon would not leave it at that.

'And we try and drag a few away with us, invite them to later dates on the tour…in other cities,' was the bone he threw to avoid being mauled, knowing that, despite everything, Bubon valued honesty.

'Oh…my…saviour!' Bubon teased, clasping his hands together in mock exaltation before smiling, sighing and adding matter-of-factly, 'There will always be more.'

'If we drag one out with us it will be worth it. Even Riot gets involved on that level.'

Bubon stared into space above Kick's head.

'It's true, some here are lost,' said Bubon wistfully before he added, 'I'll arrange for the usual safe passage out of town for anyone joining your convoy as a sign of my respect.'

He offered a seated, heaving bow on the last word.

'But many belong here Kick, I know you respect that too,' dangled Bubon and when Kick didn't bite, instead merely tilting his head in acknowledgement, he smiled widely, fondly.

'That's what I like about you Kick, your endless belief in the goodness of people. No. No. That's not accurate. It's your refusal to be affected by the bad. Yes...'

Bubon paused, tapping his chest with his palm, while he considered his next line.

'Yes, that's more like it. In a less thoughtful man it could be a naivety but you're too smart for that; yours is a deep commitment to optimism.'

The waves of respect coming from Bubon in Kick's direction never did make him feel any better about being here.

Bubon threw a sugar cube at his lover, avoiding the heavy frames of the glasses and catching her just above the eye so that Kick's response stumbled in its first steps.

'I...believe...that...love and respect should be motivation, not fear...that fear should not be manipulated for gain...'

Bubon put down a second sugar cube – finally the conversation was in the territory he had been hoping for.

'You think that U.S. manipulates the fear of dying for their gain Kick. I know that. I understand that. But don't forget that fear itself is essential. Fear of starving puts food on the table, fear of freezing led to fire and fear builds a house. Fear of failure makes you strive for success.'

He sat still, the silence in the room broken only by the scratching of his breathing.

He knew that Kick knew this, knew that he had wandered slightly off course. He returned to it.

'Dessel would argue – and he would believe his argument – that U.S. is relieving the most profound of fears and charging only a nominal fee to do so. Did the Great Religions do any different?'

And at that point, Bubon's rage ignited. Always a slow-burn ember, it now fanned into flame, hungry and hating, his voice tightening around his words to keep them from spreading indiscriminately, making of them sharper points to penetrate.

'The arrogance of those fuckers...'

He paused and Kick fancied that he was actually counting to ten but then picked something up from Bubon's thoughts that startled him.

Bubon took a deep breath and smiled – the genial host once more – before Kick spoke.

'Do you believe in God, Bubon?'

The directness of the question took Bubon by surprise but the momentary widening of his eyes expressed delight not anger.

'I've just described the Great Religions as arrogant fuckers and that's the question you ask me?'

'You haven't signed up for the life-after-death deal,' Kick, following his instinct, not sure how far he could go without rattling his host.

Bubon threw another sugar cube at his lover, striking her lower lip and making a muffled 'kuk' sound against the teeth underneath.

'Well now, there's me forgetting about your little skill,' Bubon said, tapping his head as he eyed Kick.

'I didn't mean to...'

'I know Kick, I know.'

Surprising Kick, Bubon revealed a little reading of his own.

'You know, don't you, that empathy wasn't included in the dictionary until 1909 in The Past?'

Regarding Kick frankly, he continued, 'Sure that's still centuries ago. But you're New. Maybe you're the Future. More evolved perhaps.'

Returning his attention to his food, they sat in another silence broken only by his muttering something about knowing when Mister Five was there but Kick, clean as a whistle apparently. Kick understood what Bubon didn't quite – whereas Mister Five, as a mind-reader and telepath it would seem, was an obvious intruder, Kick, being an empath, could only pick up signals being sent, a non-invasive process.

Bubon's signals were regularly stronger than most but now he resumed a more direct communication.

'It's hard to believe in a God when more people have seen that…what do you call it…that…monster…in that lake…somewhere,' began Bubon, his hand waving away the exact geographical details as though not particularly relevant, 'and besides, science has proved beyond doubt that being top of the food chain is somewhat more complicated than some fucker simply being able to build an ark.'

Kick listened. Breathing scratched. Lovers hurt.

'The Great Religions asked us to believe that the notion of good – this vast concept – needed a figurehead? Look around you, Kick. A Devil is believable but a God less so if that's your persuasion – certainly I think he should be seeking *my* forgiveness, not the other way around.'

Bubon's voice hardened as he continued, the anger flaring again, 'If God answers your prayers, then he is also the need for them. Do I believe in a God that lost His influence that got superseded, replaced, forgotten? When all he had to do was show us Heaven? The arrogance! He just expected us to *believe*.'

'Like Dessel believes in U.S., Bubon?'

Kick had been unable to resist throwing this spark into the head of pressure Bubon was building and now sat braced for an explosion, not least because he had interrupted his host.

Bubon, however, addressed it as a valid point, rather than undermining provocation.

'Science,' he said, regarding Kick with a steady eye although which one that was, Kick was still not sure.

With his voice sounding a little weary now, the extent of his hospitality reaching its limit, Bubon continued, 'Despite the depth of your own thought, Kick, most people are just getting through the day. The extent of their thinking rarely stretches beyond eat-shit-fuck-don't-die. I don't believe in a God that so ineffectually mishandled such easy criteria to satisfy.'

A biscuit crunched in the yawning maw of Bubon's mouth, its crumbly punctuation at the end of his sentence a blameless mini-landslide over his lower lip.

He went on, 'But if you believe that God is the name given to coming to peace with dying then, yes, I believe in God.'

A little startled by the last of Bubon's words, Kick was slow to respond but eventually asked, 'What will you do?' which sounded clumsy in his own mouth, the interrogation of Bubon's existential belief system narrowed to a question of function.

Bubon knew what Kick was getting at.

'I'm going to explore Pluto,' he said and raised his eyebrows as if to say 'How do you know I won't?'

He appeared suddenly very tired.

'Kick, as usual I loved the gig but you have worn me out. In my own home! You devil you! Mister Five will take you back to your accommodation. While you are here, as usual, you will be under my protection and will be when you leave the city limits as far as my influence can reach.'

Kick knew this was significant influence but without meaning to – maybe a little off-balance because he knew that something was wrong with Bat – must have shown a moment of hesitation on his face.

'What I say I do Kick. It's what I bring, it's what I expect.'

Kick knew this to be true and wished he had not betrayed a reaction that meant Bubon felt he needed to say so. But Bubon understood.

'You have my word,' reassured Bubon and as though wanting to make a point, added, 'and if you don't have your word, what *do* you have?'

♪

And with The Mean City behind them and a few struggling vehicles full of those they had managed to convince to leave, they made their way – cautiously, despite Bubon's assurances – towards The Indulgence Junkies.

Bat sat alone. Everyone left him for now – they would be there when he needed them.

They had seen, at the last gig, the sweatshirt with the words 'Damn, These Clothes Are Comfortable' draped across the front of Bubon's high chair.

They had seen the uneven slash of blood across it where the throat above it had been cut from behind, naturally deeper on one side than the other.

They had seen Bubon, in-between his ecstatic seated contortions, look to Bat onstage, nodding his head and ostentatiously winking.

And when he did catch Kick's eye on that last night and he saw Kick's discomfort, his wayward eyes widened incredulously as if to say 'Did you forget who I am?' before he lost himself once more in the music of his favourite band.

♪

Kick's was an especially jagged sleep on that last night – a fragmented wreck of images pervading him without permission, the consequence of having let his defences down on that first night with Bubon.

He dreamt, or imagined from a shallow consciousness, of a time in The Past long before he was born.

Of The Thinning.

As a reaction to an earlier, perceived pandemic that was benevolent enough to allow world leaders time to um and ah as to what to do about it, the human race – panicked by a ruffle in the glide of their safe existence – chose an increasingly anti-septic society.

This weakened the fierce immune system of the species that had made it to the top of the food chain long before there had been modern medicine.

Yet, despite the warnings of those who saw this, the scared won the argument with the policy-makers, who welcomed the opportunity for greater control.

So, a generation later, came The Thinning – the real pandemic, the one that had taken the human population of the planet and made it its plaything for a while, toying with it long enough to squeeze the life out of it.

Whether this was through malice or clumsy over-enthusiasm made little difference – the human race's bottle-necked population, numbering in the tens of billions and bloated on its renewed sense of invulnerability, plummeted to millions in the six months it took for its hubris to be crushed humble.

And then, having reminded an arrogant animal that something might actually be bigger than it, whatever it was, it was gone, leaving a shattered people feeling around to re-establish priorities, direction, systems.

There was loss for everyone but once this had been accommodated and processed many privately felt – but never said – that with fewer people now sharing the same technology, the same resources, the same knowledge, the same land, it was not unlike a good friend getting out of the car having shared the back seat with you; you missed them but it was also kind of nice to have the extra room.

Universal Services took a firm hold in the aftermath.

Prior to The Thinning they had been almost exclusively concerned with the extension of female reproductive viability.

Many had expressed concern that a woman's ability to bear a child up to and beyond 80 served a woman's needs but very few of a child's; that U.S.'s presumption to tweak the terms of conception – nature's binding contract – was the arrogance of calling Mother Nature wrong.

Boredom, fear of being alone or simply creating a carer for their dying years – many had questioned the motives of these women who had been able to resist the urgent hormone call of their natural fertile days yet suddenly, really, simply must have a child.

With being a parent still the one thing not deemed beyond anyone's competence, Universal Services cared little for the morality debate surrounding their work and as The Thinning struck, as the human race teetered on potential extinction, it took the first of its tightening grips on the world, ideally positioned as it was in the science of repopulating this frightened species.

Of course, there was money and influence but it was more than that – U.S. was a totem, a sober, cogent, believable authority in alarming times.

Kick woke. He knew with startling clarity that Bubon was awake too; he felt directly connected to him and in those moments as he stared at the ceiling, somewhere above him in the darkness, he heard Bubon and knew him.

Bubon could love. Bubon could laugh. Bubon could have moments of great pleasure, Kick knew.

But Bubon was hollow. Bubon was helpless – it was only now that Kick understood the jumbled dark mutterings that had been so hard to read at their dinner.

Bubon, in his own way, adored women but he also despaired at them. That they would ever think they were the only ones without choices when he knew as fact that they had more than he did.

And like all choices, you could have one or the other, rarely both and if you did have both then, most usually, at least one would suffer.

Why would they want a career, why would they consider it a failure to not have a career and if they did have one, why would childbirth ever be described in terms of being an interruption?

He dreamt of his career being interrupted by childbirth. He fantasised about not *having* a career because of childbirth. To have that choice. He craved it, it informed his every thought and action.

Bubon had not signed up to the life-after-death deal because an eternity of this emptiness would be unbearable for him and dead was as happy as he felt he would ever get.

Because, except for the few when he suffered in silence, Bubon cried himself to sleep each and every night, alone with the implacable reality that – even with U.S.'s scientific advancements – he would never be able to bear a child.

♪

Tick

    Tick   Tick

      Tick   Tick

        Tick

Chapter Seven

As The Indulgence Junkies shimmered into view, its implicit promises seductively expanding to encompass the entire horizon and an infinite suite of desires, the spirits of The Fifth Season's touring party raised.

By definition.

To say that The Indulgence Junkies was all things to all people would be exactly accurate – so much so that many might call it Haven, others The Me-Time Town, others Reboot Central and of course a healthy proportion (or at least they were healthy when they arrived) might refer to it as their very own Sodom.

All descriptions would be credible.

It was a place where you sought and (always) received what you really craved – for a busy executive, this may be peace and quiet fishing an isolated river, for others dancing through the night, for others the opportunity to discuss esoteric hobbies with like-minded people.

But, of course, it was mostly a place where things were done to excess, a deliberate, total break from the norm, whatever that might mean to each visitor.

It was a place where people came to find themselves and too often lost themselves, not so much an easy place to stay, more one that was very difficult to leave.

At once it was a caricature of vulgar over-indulgence, more ow than wow, yet at the same time, if approached right – and with respect – it was deeply and profoundly spiritual, a place offering learning, serenity and peace.

This was not immediately apparent as the tour vehicles entered the city limits, the gaudy fronts of the party houses serving only to bathe the stumbling revellers outside in a flickering neon wash, even in the early evening semi-darkness.

These hollow things. This part of town held no interest for the band…well, maybe the first time they toured it did; naïve, young and curious as they were.

That time, Kick and Bat, both fired by a degree of drunken panic, rolling eyes and inefficient slapping footsteps, had finally found Zip and Riot in the toilet cubicle of one of these hedonistic outposts.

Zip, on his knees in front of the toilet bowl, turning blearily to address their bumbling arrival with an unconvincing attempt at defensive indignation and an index finger pointing at nothing in particular, had stated, 'I'm not throwing up, I'm looking for Atlantis.'

With Riot there, eyes closed, leaning against the wall, one hand holding Zip's hair clear, the other flat against the wall for support, it made for an oddly tender scene.

Although not one that was ever repeated.

Not at The Indulgence Junkies anyway – this behaviour could be indulged anywhere and it was the last time they had behaved like tourists, like those who had come without an aim, who came just to get wrecked, who didn't know better, of which there were many.

Zip came for his tattoos now. Zip came to fly.

Nothing was too outlandish, everything was acceptable and if The Indulgence Junkies had ever had parents, they had never uttered the words 'Now enough is enough' to their unbridled offspring.

The city ran on its tourist income, a huge part of which came from the sex venues and events, such is the way of these things. Commerce always bloomed in the permanent spring of shows participated in by those who think there is nothing wrong with what they are doing, watched by those who hope there really might be and criticised by those who are certain there is.

Voyeurs, exhibitionists – Kick knew that some of the bar owners considered their customers as the freaks that frequent the freak events but he also knew that such thinking was steeped in a self-aware irony given that bar owners were often either the voyeurs or the exhibitionists. Or both, depending on how quiet the night was behind the bar.

Besides, tolerance was the word at The Indulgence Junkies – without co-operation it would descend into the joylessness of The Mean City and the city planners were sensitive to this.

They had, for example, suggested to the suited middle-aged father of three that to place his bouncy castle next to the innocuous-looking house that just so happened to contain ancient blow-pipe enthusiasts might not be prudent.

The feeling was that having a grown man, his shoes sensibly side-by-side in front of his inflatable fantasy house, tirelessly bouncing all day offering a relentless, 'Wheeee! Wheeee!' might test the patience of the otherwise reasonable neighbours who just so happened to possess game-changing weapons.

Let's be sensible with our silliness was their sage advice to the suited man at the time and Kick felt that might be a motto to grace any coat of arms.

Over the years Powdermouth had tried ordering the tour in a variety of ways.

Leaving The Mean City until the end had brought a sense of dread across the entire tour; leaving The Indulgence Junkies until the end was too long to wait for the band and crew.

There was little for it – inevitably the price of performance and travel was a numb fatigue towards the end of any tour regardless of the order of the venues, so playing The Mean City then wiping the mess up with The Indulgence Junkies early in the tour became the chosen operation, conveniently fitting snugly geographically.

The outskirts of the city were all show, fizz and – for those seeking lurid tales to either take home or keep very much to themselves – the bang and the wallop.

Fun-rides, bars, lights, a host of gig venues and, of course, entertainment of an adult persuasion.

Always, at this point, the band left the vehicle and took the remaining distance to their destination on foot, gleefully absorbing the atmosphere.

The truth is, they loved the chaos, the joy in the streets, the sales pitches. As soon as they disembarked it started – an apparently disinterested Madame ambled down her establishment's stairs and tottered uncertainly towards the band, her talent for walking not quite compatible with the height of her heels.

Stopping right in front of them, she took a moment to place what appeared to be a toffee between the red smudges of her lips, her jaw working slowly at first before gaining the advantage over the chewy sweet, her face like slo-mo speeding up as though building enough momentum to catapult her words from her mouth, an impression only added to when she spoke in a voice so loud that Kick felt it may well be trying to escape her apparent boredom.

'Genelmen! Welcome to my lovely establishment,' she said optimistically, standing in the street as she was. Pointing to the neon sign over the doorway in which she had previously been standing that read 'Stabbing The Cat', she added, 'City Council approved, all extensions given instant planning permission,' and gave what she no doubt hoped was a mischievous wink to none of them.

Unconvinced but entertained, the band listened to the rest of her spiel.

'All of my girls offer more than before, skilled enough to lick the tan off any man. I assure you that you will not be able to tell your arse from her elbow and all come already bumcomfortable,' and just in case the inference was lost, 'Doctor Bloodmuscle is more than welcome to take their temperature... We have even thoughtfully provided a dictionary in every room so that you can find the words to describe what my lovely girls have just done to you.

Tighter than Sunday nuns, they are the best in their... genre. My girls bunny!'

She stood absently waiting for a response and when there wasn't one she made an almost straight-line return to her perch at the top of the stairs, hooking the last of the toffee from between her teeth with a shout-coloured acrylic nail.

She didn't look at them again.

The band walked on, with Zip – as unlikely as it seems – rendered speechless by a passing girl's whispered-in-his-ear description of how she would like him to render her speechless.

This part of town was particularly lurid but it was still oddly joyful, as hard as they found that to reconcile – no-one was here against their will, by definition.

This was The Indulgence Junkies.

The Madame they had just encountered, the girls she recommended, the boys recommended elsewhere, were either here because they worked here willingly or were holidaying in a fantasy.

Kick thought again of her walk…definitely holidaying…

However, as they passed the desultory quintet of fatigued employees outside the Happy Five Times brothel – who were clearly not the inspiration for the title – the irony was unavoidable and the casinos and bars, likewise, were less than inspiring in this part of town. Each to their own in Fun Town.

Small gig venues hosted bands in keeping with the environment.

As he passed, Kick regarded the youthful, thrilled musicians of amongst others, Rubbing the Pearl, Blowing the Joker and Thrust Buttock and hoped their motivation was positive. He had known too many who had come to The Indulgence Junkies, over-indulged, become junkies and died a pointless rock 'n' roll death.

Put a guitar in the hands of an inconsiderate drunk and he will be romanticised as a hell-raiser but Kick was sure that most fatal over-indulgences were fired by a different need, not selfish but desperate.

He felt that, in so many instances of obvious self-destruction, either slowly or as an empirical suicide, fame didn't so much kill people as not keep them alive in the way they had hoped or expected, fraudulently masquerading as the great solution to an internal desolation time and again.

It was of no great note that another front man had died only last year during and despite what, at the time, appeared to be two groupies attempting to blow air into him at both ends.

The girls had been so wasted that they had taken to pleasing each other in response to the lack of reaction from their back-seat partner and simply hadn't noticed that he was no longer – and would never again be – performing on a stage of any kind.

Stoners are to drugs what drunks are to alcohol – there was doing drugs and there was doing drugs like an idiot and Kick knew that most here weren't idiots, that most would party and go home, start saving for next year. More than most he could feel that the majority were overjoyed and there was little undercurrent of anything sinister. The Mean City it was not.

A greater degree of sophistication battled for dominance the further they walked, the two naked elderly ladies playing free-standing one-armed-bandits by the side of the road perhaps the last resistance of the random and by the time they reached Single Malt's bar, there was a degree of social sobriety.

As they approached the door, at the top end of a quiet cobbled cul-de-sac, the name of the bar 'XX + XY = XXX + WHY?' tastefully framed with sympathetic lighting, they were greeted by security. As expected guests, they were led through soft halls and into the main atrium where Single Malt reclined on an oversized sofa.

On one side a long, unobtrusive bar hugged the wall, the muted clinking of glasses the tick-over of its smooth-running engine. Subdued lighting and elegant waiting staff oozed through the gaps between tempting sofas and chairs, all private though none secret, and a small, beautifully lit fountain refreshing an ornate circular water-feature provided the ideal centre-piece.

Single Malt fully understood that, for many, this environment was an indulgence and the burbling conversations around the room proved him right. He sprawled across the sofa, his other indulgences clearly including food, most definitely not exercise, and Kick wondered what it was about City Leaders that meant they had to be so…heavy.

But Single Malt was not Bubon by any means.

Apparently in no need of a significant other, he had never had a boyfriend for any length of time, hence his name. Although it was rumoured that this was more to do with a talent for going down well 'on the rocks', it didn't really matter, certainly not to Single Malt.

His affectionate and indulgent tolerance of the foibles, mistakes and morals of straight relationships inspired the construction of this bar – a place for all, away from it all – and had informed the wry cynicism of its name.

Malt ran the bar discreetly for a discrete clientele and – as far as anyone knew – had only had to intervene on one occasion.

Still indulged as a festival, one Christmas, a mid-level U.S. manager, not without influence, drank himself into over-confidence and an inappropriate friskiness. With his ding-dong merrily on high he had approached an ambitious young female singer, who, whilst receptive to exploring new platforms to promote her songs, had found his fingers meandering all over her body to be a digital distribution of an unwelcome kind.

Malt dealt with the situation so that no one was offended or embarrassed and it said much about the nature of The Indulgence Junkies and specifically about how the bar was run that this minor incident might count as any kind of event at all.

Spotting their arrival, Malt welcomed them with a 'Hello Gentlemen' in a rich, warm voice that reached them easily and disturbed no-one. The band scattered lazily around him, each achieving a satisfied inertia almost the moment they sat, barely needing to rearrange the generous cushions.

'Don't get too comfortable, you're playing later,' teased Single Malt and for a moment, just a moment, the band members felt a little bad for the crew, by necessity currently busy making sure everything was ready for tonight's gig… and not relaxing here.

They didn't feel too bad – this was The Indulgence Junkies.

'They know the venue, they know the system. We'll sound check in an hour, onstage in 3. We're all yours until then,' said Bat, throwing the tease back at Single Malt who had always had a particular soft spot for him.

'One day Bat,' he said, heavy with affected longing, 'I will find out just how fantastic you are.'

At that moment a flashbulb went off from an area

close to the bar and the ambience of the room was lost for a moment.

A small, chaotic figure made its way over to Malt, the language of its body apologetic even buried beneath a dozen different old-style cameras on neck-straps – the awkward, scruffy-haired figure stopped sooner in front of Malt than the bustling clatter of his paraphernalia.

Buzz Paparazzi, fidgeting from one foot to the other said, 'Sorry Boss, didn't check the flash was off.'

With the room settling back into its ease, Malt saw no reason to further upset him, rolled his eyes in a kind of paternal tolerance and Buzz hustled away a few paces before returning and addressing the band, 'Oh, hey guys.'

Each gave their version of 'Hi Buzz' before he went away again, immediately settling at the bar, his attempts to inconspicuously continue taking photos somewhat undermined by his thumbs-up pointing to the 'flash off' button.

Single Malt indulged his ego – Buzz was employed by him as his own private press hound and had little interest in the band. Malt never knew if Buzz had any medium in his camera. He wasn't even sure you could still get film for such old cameras; for that matter, he didn't know where you could even get the cameras.

It didn't matter to him, his indulgence was fed and all was well.

Malt was of the opinion – and it was hard to disagree with him – that everyone was born with a hole in them.

In some, that hole took the form of a butterfly collection, maybe the shape of a significant other or one that would do. In others it was renovating furniture but it was this belief (and his understanding of it in others) that made him such a great Leader at The Indulgence Junkies.

In others that hole may remain empty with no great consequence but from his own bitter experience he was aware that it might also get filled with the wrong things, destructive things that at first appeared to fit the space but ultimately served only to obstruct what actually needed to be there from taking its rightful place.

Malt was very familiar with the anxiety that resulted from this and wise to the fact that, mostly, people's response was to feed the anxiety with something that was good for the anxiety, not something that was good for the person.

Whilst the irony in his own maturing from taking pills and joints to taking pills for his joints was not lost on him, nor was the understanding and it was this, combined with a learned discipline, that allowed him to feed his need but never sate it.

He recognised desire, dissatisfaction and need as motivators, forces for good if harnessed on a correct-length lead. He fed these working animals enough to keep them from frustrated biting, never so much that they were content.

Over years, Single Malt had focussed his considerable intellect on diligently reconfiguring the elements in his life, professionally, socially, chemically until he had enough of them above to keep reaching for, enough below to catch him when he fell and enough alongside to support and encourage.

He had struggled with debilitating depression as a younger man, hours spent staring at walls, mouth open, a mind entirely unable to define the problem let alone find a solution. Over time the depression did not so much go away as become something he learnt to live with; some people walked everywhere on flat surfaces, all of his were uphill.

Sometimes the hill was too much but mostly, over time, he got used to it – learnt to do so – and was able to start constructing his world in a way that worked for him.

He knew that depression and mental health were not necessarily linked with weakness or fragility and had a fraternal respect for those who, like him, achieved beyond any reasonable expectation each day by the simple act of getting through it and on to another.

Depression offers no benign compromise – more a parasite than an illness, it uses isolation to encourage its host to need it, reducing both the ability and the desire to fight it, settling in, wanting nothing more for its host than to have a future of looking back fondly on nothing.

It wasn't about unhappiness or life's reasonable setbacks – it was about mentally pulling a weight behind you, dragging its inflexible bulk everywhere you went over all terrain, every day, all day.

This weight that was impossible to describe to those who had never encountered it because – sly as it is – it teases the sufferer with the intimation that if they could just accurately explain it to someone then it might just go away, the betrayal being that any verbalised explanations so often sound flimsy, as though the individual might just be feeling a little down that day.

But still that sneaky promise, with suicide or an attempt at it perhaps being the last resort of a desperate urge to articulate this and be free – a high-stakes body-language statement (this…THIS is how it feels) when words fail with a total, bitter regularity.

Or maybe depression is contemptuous enough of its own qualities that it occasionally rids the world of itself at the hands of its own host.

He had deliberately worked to find a way not to resent those who did not have such obstacles.

Even Now, with the existential grip on mental health eliminated, there were still many who had not signed up for The Deal but seemed unaware and unconcerned that life was a ride in a car that was definitely going to crash, a blissful state of denial beyond his reach.

Whatever peaks he had experienced, in whatever form or duration, served only to drop him from a greater height into the troughs and he had learnt over time that to diminish one was to reduce the other – he now embraced a world to managed evenness.

He could even pay the price for laughter on occasions after all – in the moments after, as his smile would fade, a sadness would replace it, a despair, a little crash, shadow cast by light on the smallest of scales, moments of unnecessary cruelty that he never expected and never failed to resent.

He had found a way to work through his problem – if nothing else, he had rallied enough, mostly, to deny his stalking Black Dog the satisfaction of ruining his day. Experience helped but with the kind of small victories that brought no celebration – over years he had learned that the only reason to get out of bed each morning was that, simply, it was worse if he didn't.

He defied his depression wherever he could, grimly marvelling at the monotonous consistency with which it delivered.

Talking therapy had contributed to the solution but, ultimately, he considered it the process by which your glass went from being half empty to half full by way of your wallet going from full to half empty and this sentiment indicated to him at the time that it had usefully served its purpose by making itself obsolete.

He had at one time assumed that company would fend off the loneliness, that therapy was surely for those who didn't have the right friends. But the wrong kind of company served only to throw a harsher light on his sense of isolation and separateness and the right kind was supremely hard to find.

With a black irony he felt sure that he was not alone in experiencing a kind of loneliness that made him want to be alone, forced him into being alone; a loneliness that, surely, in company, was as apparent and as hard to hide as an open wound. Something for any company he kept to notice, worry about, see as a reason to leave.

It broke his trust in himself, defined his interactions. He had had a serious love earlier in his life, one that made these feelings almost entirely go away and had made him actually feel like the person he would like to be.

Yet always, the roiling spoil at his centre contrived to convince him that this love – who brought out only the best in him and reacted to that version – would be less enamoured by the dark, wordless ghost that might turn up unannounced as was its wont and insist on guest status on its own terms, offering no interactions and as many explanations.

In a sadistic twist, Malt had also discovered that contentment was as uncomfortable as a lack of it. Whether his sorrow was simply too reliable a companion to ever fully leave behind or not was a matter for debate but what was true was that he experienced whatever satisfaction he had actually achieved as a bitter stagnation, a claustrophobic constraint, a window-less jail with only an unpredictable, coiling restlessness for company.

His depression, he realised, was sewn into the hem of his soul, making him what he was – if it was removed, he would be as ill-defined in function as a stick of rock with no writing in the middle.

So Malt had become used to being alone rather than bear to diminish in a loved-one's eyes and had never fully mastered that side of him that convinced him he was unlovable. In another disingenuous twist, he often found that those who actually understood his feelings also had an interest in him keeping them, with their own needs, as carers or enablers, being fulfilled – their need to 'be there' and 'understand' dying on the vine of any happy mind.

Yet whilst he may never have a going-to-bed-in-order-to-get-up rather than a get-up-in-order-to-go-to-bed mentality, he had raised himself up out of depression into simply being relentlessly dissatisfied and he wasn't sure that this – being happy enough being happy enough – was any longer a mental health concern.

A permanent dissatisfaction and striving for better was the status of unlikely stability that he had worked hard to provide for himself.

He felt only a slight solace that this he shared with evolution.

He did, however, keep a close eye on himself, aware as he was, that he was able to live quite casually with patiently waiting to die and this made him a skilled watcher for signs in others.

He believed that, in many cases, depression and its siblings, despair and desolation, were a practical case of needs unfulfilled and to take something as mundane as a Sunday walk away from someone who loves Sunday walks would, bit by bit perhaps, gently but firmly lower the individual into such unwelcome mental space. It may have happened early in life – or an essential need may never have been identified – and a negative state of mind might then have become established.

And whilst thinking that so many were merely looking for a home, he himself found no reward in feeling welcome, having never experienced any accompanying sense of belonging.

Yet still his belief was that many simply need to find their need and though he found his own joy to be elusive, his appreciation of its value to those who were actually able to feel it made him an ideal and deeply committed City Leader of The Indulgence Junkies and whilst he wasn't strictly on U.S.'s payroll, they allowed him to get on with it.

They just collected the taxes.

An astonishingly good-looking waiter – who surely hadn't come out so much as fire a starting pistol – delivered the drinks, skilfully managing to place them in front of each band member whilst keeping his rear-end aimed…

firmly…in the direction of Single Malt and as Malt stared at its hypnotic, alternating lift and drop as the waiter walked away, his gaze strong enough to give the impression of trying to help in some way, Kick broke his distraction.

'You have such a dirty mind.'

'He didn't really give me much choice,' was Single Malt's accurate response, one that conveyed that often unsaid understanding between the observer and the observed, before adding:

'Besides, if you don't have a dirty mind, what keeps you company when you're alone?'

Kick smiled and Malt pressed the point, 'Anyway, what's so bad about being bad?' and the 'Amen to that' offered by Riot neatly rounded off the exchange just as Gee Whizz arrived.

Small, sober, sensible, maybe sixty, he had been The Provider for as long as they had been touring. For all they knew, he was ninety and had a chemical solution that made him appear sixty. Or maybe he was a hologram, an idea not so outlandish given that he dealt in virtual realities so virtual as to virtually be actual.

He was a high-end Provider, his product clean, most probably from the labs of U.S., at least a matter for their attention, definitely subject to their taxes.

'Good evening gentlemen. So nice to see you again,' he said cordially, politely, 'May I take your orders?'

Tomorrow Zip would fly and all that ever changed was the terrain over which he did it. The following day he would have no need for Gee's services although the flying would heighten the anticipation for his tattoo, for him a passion not a fashion. Zip loved getting tattooed, the planning, the designing and, yes, the pain. He loved the process and whilst he got a tattoo at this stage on any tour, his skin, apart from his Gods, was tattoo-free.

Inks had been developed to react to specific exposure to UV light; in The Past, they would fade, Now they had a time-scale.

Zip wanted an elaborate depiction of 'Eat and Be Eaten' on his right forearm for the duration of the tour, a literal not philosophical statement, more of a description and one that he considered likely to become permanent at some point.

Bat would spend most of his time here 'not thinking' and only Gee knew what that meant and how it was achieved but it worked for Bat and when Riot said, 'The usual,' no-one ever asked what that meant. And Gee would never say.

Kick, they all knew, would indulge his love of water one day and his love of speed the next.

'Then I shall bid you goodnight and safe carriage until the morning,' said Gee, leaving them to finish their drinks before they headed off to the sound check.

As they left, Single Malt held Kick back for a moment and in his view-finder, Buzz would have caught him placing a hand-written note in front of the singer. If there was film in the camera – and we will never know – it would have captured a series of images showing Single Malt pinch Kick hard on the arm just as the words 'They are watching you very closely' came into Kick's focus, the momentary pain designed to distract and scramble his thoughts.

The camera would not have known, however, that Kick reacted very quickly to what Single Malt was doing and instantly threw his thoughts into the gig tonight, the practicalities, the words on the note gone from his mind.

'I'll be joining you tomorrow,' said Single Malt as Kick turned to follow the band.

'I'll look forward to it,' said Kick, neutrally, already acting on the advice.

♪

As the band assembled the next morning in the reception area of the hotel and as Crunch, Slopehound and Mangler attempted to slink past them on the way back from their own all-night indulgences, the arriving Gee Whizz blew their cover.

'Hey guys,' he enthused to the tip-toeing trio, 'great show last night.'

Alerted to an opportunity to grind on the road crew, Bat accused them of being dumb schoolboys, behaving like they had broken a curfew when –given where they currently were – no such curfew applied.

Mangler (today's T-shirt reading 'Actually I *am* all that') and Crunch wandered off, struggling with smirking grins, having deployed their best weapon of response, Slopehound, who lingered a moment longer, composed his features in as thoughtful expression as he could before simply stating, 'Cool beans,' in a tone that said 'We are the road crew' yet really said so much more.

Bat narrowed his eyes.

'Nice move,' he said and Slopehound's expression suggested that he agreed.

As he ambled off to join his fellow conspirators, none of whom would miss a beat in their professional attentions, which is ultimately what made the exchange such fun, Gee brought the focus back.

'I especially liked the new songs you did…which is unusual in a live context don't you think?'

He went on before anyone could respond.

'Great support act too I thought. I think Powdermouth has outdone himself this time. Tonight too, I believe.'

Kick couldn't help but agree – for some time he had been really looking forward to seeing Maniacal Menace and last night they did not disappoint.

Almost as colourful as The Fifth Season, deeply committed to their music but with as much commitment to having fun with it, they were always good value.

Like The Fifth Season, they had formed through Art Not The Industry Music (ANTImusic). At first, an underground jamming forum, ANTImusic had connected musicians across all lands; guitarists from The Great Waters and, say, bored drummers sulking around The Big Nowhere, could collaborate in latency-free real-time virtual rehearsal rooms.

Eliminating the safety-first approach to the selection and presentation of creative talent by Universal Services, ANTImusic ignited and began to branch out to a vast listening audience who were – contrary to all boardroom marketing assessments – entirely able to accept that level of eclecticism streamed directly to them.

The almost infinite combinations of differently skilled and influenced musicians created its own problems when searching for something you might like, since so many new genres were created and disposed of instantly and continually, but mostly people found what they liked or were at least prepared to keep looking.

Others simply listened to the streamed rehearsal room output, listened to creation as it happened.

Universal Services had decided to let it be, instead circling overhead, waiting to pick off an idea or even a fully-formed band although those bands, having succumbed to the financial security and material comforts on offer, instantly lost their audience on ANTImusic. An audience that, despite drinking U.S. water, watching U.S. TV and living almost entirely on U.S. products still found a line they were unwilling to cross when it came to creative expression.

Maniacal Menace were not one of these bands – so dedicated were they that Kick suspected that they might actually be permanently playing and that engineers simply walked them towards stages on occasion or placed microphones around them to catch an album's-worth of work at a time.

If they weren't already around, you would surely have to invent them; each darkly-charismatic member very different to the other but somehow carrying a uniqueness common to the whole, as though they might all have met in prison but were in for different crimes.

Last night they had delivered another one of their everyone-will-be-talking-about performances, the lead singer grasping the microphone with both hands close to his mouth with such rolling-eye intensity as to give the impression of sucking molasses through a pipe, apparently foregoing any consonants in the howling expression of his art.

Music might press the right buttons but often it is the performance of it that makes the hair on the back of your neck stand up and Maniacal Menace were amongst the very best at this – The Fifth Season would have to be on form to follow them.

Powdermouth must have smiled to himself when he had booked them, knowing that The Fifth Season would relish the challenge and as inclusive as he was, Kick was also competitive and had, in fact, looked forward to their performance last night almost as much as he did the day that lay ahead of him.

Gee handed each band member a small inhaler with a red button on top for releasing vapour customised to the individual.

'That door gentlemen,' said Gee pointing to what appeared to be a laundry room at the side of the reception area.

'One at a time as usual if you will,' he continued politely but unnecessarily before bidding farewell.

'See you later,' said Zip once Gee had gone, the urgency in his tone testament to his desire to be flying. He inhaled the vapour as he stepped through the door, Riot following about 30 seconds later, then Bat after a similar wait. Kick had an image of his fellow band members passing out cold on the other side of that door and collapsing into the arms of burly colleagues of Gee's but the truth was he had no idea how this worked. As usual, he spent little time wondering.

Instead, he stood alone a few moments longer, deliberately breathing deeply, relishing anticipation for the delicious appetiser it was.

He pressed the red button, inhaled and stepped through the door.

♪

The smell of the sea hit him first, the warmth of the sun running a close second, one carried, one softened by the light breeze teasing its way across the jetty.

Several small boats, styled in The Past, the likes of which no longer got commissioned but ones Kick knew well from these trips, rippled gently against the jetty, patiently waiting release from their moorings, some apparently for fishing purposes, others, like the one he was standing on now, serving different needs.

'Hey Vivid, some help wouldn't go amiss,' said Single Malt standing on the jetty, the diving equipment a dense, uneven spill around his ankles.

Adjusting to his new circumstances, Kick made his way to the side of the boat, the Psychopomp, and helped Single Malt bring the equipment on board.

'Didn't Gee provide crew for this?' asked Kick as he grunted with the air tanks.

'Didn't *you* want a full diving experience, old-style? Well, this is it. Don't worry, we'll have crew when we need them.'

With the equipment all on board, Kick held his mask against his face to check the fit, checked the flow of both regulators, smelled the air, inflated and deflated his jacket to check its buoyancy control and prepared his weight belt.

'Kick,' said Single Malt, smiling, 'do you really think Gee hasn't done all those checks?'

Humoured by the irony, Kick responded, 'A full diving experience remember?'

He went on, 'You ask me that every time my friend. I like to do it. Maybe you think Gee should figure out a way for me to dive without actually diving too, eh? Maybe get someone else to do it for me?'

'Maybe he should figure out a way to make you look good in a wetsuit too while he's at it.'

'I'm deeply hurt by your comments and will be making a complaint to the management in the form of a strongly-worded letter.'

Malt laughed, turned the humour on himself, instead of his lithe, athletic friend.

'I'm a fine one to talk. Sometimes I feel like I accidentally sat on something and then realise that's just the shape my arse is taking today.'

The boat began moving, trundling gently away from the jetty's bustle at the hands of a previously-unseen captain, now issuing orders to a previously-unseen deckhand in a language Kick didn't know.

'Like I said…crew when you need them,' offered Malt as he sat on the padded bench seat of a small table at the back of the boat, Kick joining him as the deckhand scuttled around securing ropes, with the effortless balance of those used to being on water, before disappearing somewhere at the front of the boat.

It wasn't a big boat – any more divers than Kick and Malt and the boat would feel crowded – but as it powered to an open water destination, there was room enough to recline and relax.

Within half an hour, the boat's only company was the

deep blue surface of the tropical sea and it struck Kick once again, as he lay lulled into a companionable silence, that large expanses of water tended to simplify things. The immensity, the history, the unknown, the weight all combining in an insistence to comply with its wishes; if the sea wants, the sea will.

Engaging with it always made Kick feel wonderfully small.

And viewed from high above, the small vessel ripped through the vast blue fabric, leaving temporary white frays almost instantly repaired and absorbed back into the whole as though never having been there.

♪

The pressure of water is only ever fully appreciated once experienced; air halves in volume with every ten metres you descend below the surface, its exuberance compressed by a life force even greater than its own.

A lung-full of air twenty metres down is the equivalent of four at the surface. The pressure crushes any body to an extent – at enough depth, the human body, or anything else, would be crushed flat.

For recreational divers following the rules for survival, the result of this crushing would be a change in reactivity of inhaled nitrogen and the squeezing of it into body tissue, leading to an effect called nitrogen narcosis, a condition that feels not unlike being pleasantly drunk.

Although significantly more on deep dives, this may occur anywhere from around 20 metres down depending on factors such as fatigue, hydration, the number of dives on any given day.

New divers quickly become aware of water as a living thing, each metre down amounting to another metre of water pressing down from above with the additional insistence of gravity – at a certain depth any attempt to surface would be doomed, the weight of the water above simply being too heavy to swim against.

Many a narked diver, made dozy and inattentive, realised the peril they were in far too late as they sank deeper and deeper into a liquid tomb that offered no explanation and had no conscience.

Likewise, surfacing too quickly and not allowing nitrogen to reabsorb fully and at its own pace, might lead to it bubbling in the blood and tissues, ultimately manifesting as the potentially lethal 'bends'.

Deep dives – anything around thirty metres and below – increased the chances of getting bent and the physical demands of the increased pressure inevitably involved gulping through air, in larger volumes at depth, making dives shorter by necessity.

Both Kick and Single Malt wanted as lengthy an experience as possible today so both dives would be around 20 metres, the deepest first.

The boat coasted to an informal stop an hour after leaving the jetty, the deckhand appearing from somewhere unseen to moor it to a buoy.

Turning the engine off, the captain invited the return of a silence broken only by the lapping of the water against the side of the rolling boat.

Single Malt and Kick faced each other, checking each

other's equipment, the deckhand having handed them their fins as they stood, ungainly, on the backboard of the boat.

'I'm ready, steady. All I need is go,' said Single Malt and laughed, realising that the deckhand – who had disappeared again – had no authority to give him the go anyway.

With one hand over his mask and the regulator in his mouth and the other over the clasp of his weight belt, he took one big step off the back of the boat, sank in the maelstrom of bubbles his landing had created, resurfaced, tapped the top of his head and shouted through his regulator something along the lines of, 'Guff shoo brig ee ewa funt.'

'Uck foo!' shouted Kick through his reg and took a leap of his own, his fins hitting the surface of the water in a single liquid gunshot.

Kick and Single Malt only ever dived in warm waters, the detail in Gee Whizz's designs extending to natural and credible underwater visibility.

The quality of Gee's designs meant that, for example, his Ice Waters had so little life the visibility was infinite and disorientating and the sea bed would resemble the eerie surface of a barren alien moon.

As the water closed over Kick's head and he began a lazy descent on this more tropical dive, the integrity of the experience was as exquisite – the wreck lay clearly visible twenty metres below, fluttering with life.

With one index and thumb pinching his nose to help relieve the pressure building in stages as he sank and the other index and thumb offering the universal 'okay' sign to Malt, Kick felt the world narrow down to the immediate.

It had been a while since he had dived so as they levelled themselves just above the deck of the wreck, he didn't immediately find neutral buoyancy but he was experienced enough to use his breathing to steady his depth until he had allocated the right amount of air to his jacket.

Once weightless, a peace held him, the effect enhanced by the steady rhythm of his breathing.

In front of him Single Malt signalled the start of the exploration of the wreck and he finned towards him until he was alongside.

About forty metres long, the wooden hull of the Ad Astra lay snapped in a loose dog-leg, its deck a metre or two below them, the sandy sea bed four or five metres below that at around 25 metres.

The dark corners of those internal structures that had survived the tugging and pulling of storms and tides stood in mysterious contrast to the clear spaces of those that had been unable to resist, giving the impression of an unfinished project lying in a very wet dock.

Whilst little of any real structural detail remained, the wreck teemed with life and as they approached it aft, they could be forgiven for thinking of it as a sunken yacht such was the density of the glittering shoal of fusilier that rippled above it like a sail in a restive wind.

The shoal ran the full length of the wreck, ever-changing in its form, sometimes two metres deep, sometimes four metres wide depending on the enthusiasm of the cruising trevally which seemed to want to intimidate rather than actually hunt as they periodically fired through the body of fish.

A porcupine fish rose out of the belly of the wreck a little to the left of Kick. Its innocent, surprised face showing no signs of fear, its comport in the water curious but cautious. As Kick became distracted by it, he noticed, very late, the intimidating, bad-tempered head of a moray eel slowly edging its way out of the dark hole that he had unwittingly drifted too close to.

The moray would take no time to consider why Kick was drifting too close with 'why', like 'fair', being human constructs of no relevance here where everything was fair. Kick inhaled and held a breath, long enough to lift himself up and over the defensive moray, letting his breath out slowly as he passed, assuming his previous depth.

Kick looked back at the porcupine fish, now joined by another and did he imagine that it was gently admonishing him?

Curious. Cautious. Get it? Kick accepted the reminder.

Kick had known one diver who had failed to respect these terms, an over-confidence that he had a relationship with the sea and its inhabitants being his downfall. Had he actually been able to communicate with the fish in the way he had assumed, he might have heard the stingray he was getting way, way too close to tell him, perhaps repeatedly and with increasing imperative, 'Any closer mate and I am going to fucking kill you.'

On this occasion, Kick thought it more likely that the porcupine fish was laughing. *He* was. He delighted in this, the domain where the locals really were in charge.

The unforgiving nature of their existence made them naturally careful but it also meant that their instincts were quick to learn and adapt. As Kick and Malt glided into the great shoal, at first it parted; then, as the shoal recognised that these lumbering creatures posed no threat, it closed around them, encasing them in a sparkling blizzard of silver and yellow.

The breath-taking kaleidoscopic display, metres deep in all directions, hid the surface, the wreck and the divers from each other.

The shivering life permanently changed shape around them, making Kick and Single Malt, despite being perfectly still, feel as though they were accelerating and slowing, sinking and rising.

Deep in the shoal were smaller shoals of slightly larger fish, bannerfish and snapper, taking refuge from their own predators behind the protective wall of fusilier.

Given long enough, the trevally would figure out that the divers were of no consequence but for now the fusilier enjoyed their reluctance to come too close whilst they were under the protection of such large, unknown creatures.

Kick fancied that he could hear the fusilier closest to him mocking the trevally whilst at the same time staying just out of reach of their new protector, clearly of use to them but not yet to be trusted.

Curious. Cautious.

The shoal washed off to their left, making Kick and Single Malt feel suddenly exposed and as they looked at each other and slowly shook their heads to express 'Wow!' they caught the attention of a shoal of batfish ten metres ahead and slightly shallower in the water, facing into the current.

Perhaps a dozen of them, they contrived to let the current carry them back towards Kick and Malt until they were alongside them, whilst giving every impression of doing no such thing.

Of course, they held a safe distance and for a minute or so they regarded the two friends before, almost imperceptibly, resuming their position ten metres ahead, their tall, slim bodies turning just enough on occasion to glance behind them and keep an eye on the divers' whereabouts.

Single Malt gestured to the wreck, most of which they had yet to explore; Kick checked his air, circled his index finger over his left wrist, held up two fingers, then pointed at the shoal – now drifting back their way – and held up ten.

Malt understood fully and after two minutes of glancing almost dutifully over the rest of the wreck, they once again buried themselves in the shoal, rapt and meditative in the funnelling, rolling cascade until it was time to surface.

The deckhand and captain, having been so involved in getting them out of the water after the dive, were once again nowhere to be seen, leaving them alone for lunch.

'Where do they go on a boat this size?' asked Kick, knowing full well that only Gee would know the answer to that. Well, Gee's chemists might also.

The only company they had was another boat, which had arrived whilst they were underwater, maybe a hundred metres away and across the silent sea surface Kick could hear a distant clicking whirr suggesting that Buzz took his job very seriously indeed. The look of 'What? You expect me to give up my indulgences?!' in Malt's eyes confirmed what he already suspected.

Addressing the bigger picture, Single Malt squeezed, 'Don't worry, no-one can hear us here,' around a mouthfull of creamed potatoes.

Like a comfortable bed at the end of a day's honest physical activity, little was as satisfying or, as anticipated, as a boat lunch after a dive. There were only two of them and a feast was displayed before them, yet both would struggle to politely offer any last spoonful to the other.

'That,' said Kick, pointing seriously at a roasted chicken leg, 'is mine.'

'Uck Foo,' said Malt and they sat a while in silence, absorbing, assimilating, understanding their role in – and their insignificance to – the swelling shoal still tirelessly mobile and alive beneath them.

♩

'You took a risk last night. You still are,' said Kick.

Single Malt finished his mouthful.

'I've had a lifetime of bending more rules than a bored kid at the back of class Kick…it's become habitual.'

He stared at the glinting water surface, its restless speckles of changing light.

'Besides, look where I work. There are more laws I'm happier breaking than upholding. Generally-speaking.'

They both smiled, lazy with food, unhurried, the enforced safe surface-time between dives a natural curtailer of any urgency.

Kick let Single Malt begin.

'They think you know where the boy is. Or, maybe they are going to watch you until you do.'

Now it was Kick's turn to stare at the sea as Single Malt continued.

'I get a lot of wasted, indiscreet people around my way so you never know quite what to trust but I wouldn't be here if I doubted the information.'

Kick had a good idea what Single Malt would say but he asked anyway.

'Why would they be so interested in this boy?'

Single Malt let the question hang in the air.

'He's beyond their reach. He simply doesn't need them.'

'That's not so unusual, why...'

Before Kick finished the question, Single Malt interrupted him, 'Hey, my assumptions are a non-exact science,' but his tone hinted at a deeper understanding than the words suggested.

'It's fine if he stays with The Hesitants. They avoid the rest of the world up there and no doubt what they have is a nourishing meal in a fast-food world but they can be treated as odd-ball eccentrics. Localised. Minimised. Harmless.'

Single Malt took a mouthful of water to wash down the last of his lunch.

'That ideology, though...that...how would you put it? That ideology can't go on tour. Can't spread.'

Kick thought about it for a moment, for the first time needing a question answered.

'Bands, poets, Out-Of-Towners...they all have this philosophy, they all spread the word...'

'He's different...'

'But he's just a boy…'

'Kick you don't think he's just a boy. Maybe you don't know why but you are searching for him yourself.'

Kick, typically, tested the comment. Usually, he only responded when he had a response but, 'I made a promise…' was what he came up with rather lamely and Malt let him wrestle with his thoughts for a moment before expanding.

'He has no plans Kick. He's hungry, he eats. He's tired, he sleeps. What he takes from the land he returns to the land. There are no traces and they can't even find his thoughts, let alone affect and control them. They can monitor bands, even you.'

'They think I can find him, lead them to him?'

Single Malt was less sure of this.

'Well, on this your guess is as good as mine,' and as if to express his mild discomfort, a seventh wave nudged the boat a little heavier.

'My feeling is they're confident they'll find him. Ultimately, he will have contact with people and they have spies everywhere. You finding him might help but I just have a feeling that knowing where you are will allow them to actually keep you apart.'

Single Malt turned to Kick to emphasise the point.

'I think you finding him is what they fear the most.'

♪

Kick large-stepped into the second dive with much on his mind. The water was having none of it, the impact relieving him of distraction, holding it at the surface for his return.

The reef, entirely invisible from the surface, bristled alongside them, its vertical surface a scattering of crevices, corals and anemones, their furious colours brilliant despite the reduced light at this depth.

As Kick and Single Malt held their depth, gliding effortlessly with a gentle current, they resembled two beings orbiting a distant planet.

Below them, an eagle ray sailed effortlessly into view before gliding back into the tempting bruised-blue of the deeper water, the elegance of its movements belying the harsh reality of its world.

Humans often speak of the thrill of a life and death scenario, relieved in those moments of the burden that is the awareness of their own mortality, the basic imperative to survive connecting them to the moment with unflinching insistence.

It is both the luxury and the cruelty of an animal's existence that they are in this state at all times, endlessly living in their moments.

The human has a different responsibility.

Even in a world of U.S. immortality deals, humans are vulnerable to life-threatening peril. They owe it to life to live it urgently, to live its limited span with passion, not let it stagnate or tread water, comprehending, as only they do, its finite nature.

Kick's mask got bumped by an adult clown fish and as usual with these feisty protectors of their nest, Kick smiled and found himself saying, 'Don't worry little one, I am not here to harm you.'

He always felt like the clown fish knew this and were, in some way, practising on him. Which made him smile more.

Ahead of him, the sea bed shallowed, the foot of the reef visible for the first time at the top of a sandy beach that fell away to their right into the blackening unknown.

Both Kick and Single Malt saw it at the same time, a sense of wonder filling them bit by bit as the unmistakable profile of the thresher shark cruised its dominant presence out of the dark towards the reef.

They say that if you think you might have seen a shark then you haven't, the assertive, economic directness of its movement leaving no room for doubt, the implication of explosive power unavoidable.

Kick and Single Malt held their position, finning gently against the current at their backs, facing the reef over which the shark was now circling.

Maybe four metres long, about half of which was its elegant upper tail fin, it became surrounded by cleaner wrasse which immediately set about eating the lice and deep-sea detritus off its skin.

The bolder – perhaps the more experienced – wrasse knew the real rewards were in the mouth and between the teeth, the thresher opening its jaws in compliance, occasionally spitting out the wrasse for over-enthusiasm or poor table manners.

Kick watched this sea's routine, one that had been repeated for millennia, since before man, this ancient rhythm making a mockery of all things mankind.

The tiniest pieces of the shark, the wrasse, the sand, the small hairs on the back of his hands, say, all might have been disparate particles in separate far reaches of The Universe. Almost certainly they were, each and every thing elsewhere, part of something else and before that somewhere else and something else. And might be again.

Right now, in this briefest of moments, they happened to combine into this event and as the shark shook off the last of the wrasse and ejected the chancers from its gills, Kick fancied that he saw an understanding of this vastness, this endless time, in its eye as it coasted fearlessly back into the lightless depths.

It left him euphoric but strangely lonely and his thoughts followed the fish involuntarily. What do you see? What do you do? What do you know? Not for the first time, he felt that an animal knew more by knowing nothing.

Once the shark was well out of sight, Kick turned to Single Malt, expecting his dive partner to be expressing his own thrilled excitement if only in his body language.

But he turned to find Single Malt facing him, unreadable. A prowling unease brushed him – he could not even be sure that Malt was looking at him, unable as he was to see his eyes behind his mask, its glass surface a mirror in which he saw only a reflection of himself, behind him a midnight maw of deepening water.

Kick realised that he was sinking, that he was too deep, getting a little narked.

And it was nice, really easy to succumb to, and as he sank away from Single Malt, impassive – angelic – above him, the glowing light beyond him at the surface became less and less desirable, less important.

He looked at his hands as though for the first time, wondered how they worked, what they did, and laughed into his regulator that he was definitely wetter than Riot's kitten right now.

And in that moment Single Malt was alongside him again, his eyes through the mask a little concerned but mostly curious, the humour in them apparent.

He gestured to the surface and Kick, shaking off some of the effects of the narcosis as he went, joined him in their controlled ascent.

Back in the boat, gear off and safely secured for the return to shore, Single Malt enquired with a smile on his face, 'Where did you go?'

'I think I must have got distracted watching the shark, sank a bit without noticing and got myself a little narked.'

'If you say so,' said Malt enigmatically, 'but don't go sinking too far just yet. You've got work to do.'

Kick knew there was more to Malt's words than the words themselves but any understanding of which seemed to have followed the shark into a place he couldn't reach.

He was still a little fazed by his lapse. The sea forgave him this time but it rarely gives you a second chance when it considers you lucky to have been given a first, and he knew this.

'Here,' said Single Malt, placing a friend's arm around Kick's shoulder and an inhaler in his hand, 'let's get you back.'

Chapter Eight

He watched her from across the room as she intermittently sipped her coffee and read her book, taking care that she didn't notice his gaze, breaking it regularly so as to limit the possibility of making her uncomfortable.

Yet his gaze always returned, his drink going cold in front of him as, not for the first time, he found himself helplessly enchanted.

She was of medium height and average age, an everyday woman and the way she periodically tried and failed to brush away an errant hair that had fallen free from her hair band to tickle her chin – even the way she moved her feet once in a while – made him want to fight all of her causes.

Occasionally she would look up and out of the window as though needing a moment to assimilate what she had just read, perhaps to regard her ghostly reflection in the glass as it lay transposed over the scene outside.

He wondered how she would see herself, wondered if the slight asymmetry of her face, as in all of us, meant that she never liked photos of herself unless the lens had somehow caught the mirror image that she was used to seeing.

He wondered if there were other ways in which she saw herself as the world did, whether she was happy with what she saw, what were her concerns, did she like the sprinkling of freckles across her nose that drew attention to what we rarely focus on, the actual surface of our skin – made us look properly – or did she see them as unwelcome guests?

He wondered what else she thought, how this might be the same or different to other women and this mystery seduced him further, had always done so. He looked away, stared out of the window himself for a while.

His focus shortened and he regarded her reflection. She, the effortless centre of creation yet so much more than merely the custodian of the wealth in her belly, which is a measure of youth and we only ever have youth for a while.

Powerful and influential every day in a multitude of ways and more deeply and more profoundly than could ever be weighed in pay scales and public status.

This he knew as a truth, a truth across all stages of their lives and relative to his own – the older woman to his child, the fearless peers of his youth and the sweet child that he needed to nurture and protect when he himself was the elder.

Each special – though not all nice – but wondrous, otherly, different.

Wise men know, amongst other things, to seek a woman's counsel and understand that, to truly enjoy women, they have to like their minds and be curious about and accepting of those parts they don't understand.

Because, as he sat and watched her, he realised that men had little to complain about – to share a life occupying the same space with such a perfect fit for all that they find attractive, that satisfies even as it fuels a delicious hunger for more.

Men, flawed, powerless in the face of this, the transience of their achievements – so often testaments to women or of their desire to impress them – making so many mistakes along the way, their love of women often being that which gets in the way of loving them.

No Mother, no family tree and, despite the mistakes, nothing is eternal; things change.

If there were words to describe how he felt as he sat in simple awe then he didn't know them but from the first moment a girl had made him sensitive to their difference, had made him celebrate it, everything he had done, conscious or otherwise, had been for them.

Chapter Nine

Kick put the inhaler in his mouth and for the first time there was a sense of apprehension mixed with the vapour and expectation.

The gig last night had gone well, but – unusually for one of Gee's trips – he had been unable to settle after his time with Malt.

Images of the shark, wafting shoal fish and light framing Malt from above misbehaved at the edge of his thoughts.

He had put it down to a touch of touring fatigue – despite the point of The Indulgence Junkies being refreshment – and tried to put his discomfort aside as he watched one of his favourite support acts.

A.C. Calamity had, as usual, brought the whole band to the side of the stage to witness his pastiche of old-style country music stars.

The over-sized cowboy hat shaded eyes that – when you could see them – were backlit with humour and a genuine love of the genre he considered himself as paying homage to.

He introduced the penultimate song of his set with the time-honoured, 'For those who haven't seen me before, this song is called The Reluctant Lovers,' before adding, straight-faced, 'For those of you *have* seen me before... this song is called The Reluctant Lovers.'

Kick and the band had always wondered how he could sing at all with his tongue so firmly in his cheek.

With his unique drawl A.C. introduced his last song by explaining to the audience that, despite his appearance, he wasn't particularly cut out for the life of a cowboy since he was no good with animals and had apparently been very lucky not to get kicked that time he tried to feed sugar cubes into the wrong end of a horse.

As the crowd laughed at the image, he added, 'All I could think was, this dog's breath *stinks*!' before bursting into his final number.

Yet, as his three friends grinned their way through A.C.'s dead-pan delivery of, 'I've got five bullets left in my six-shooter, 'cos I just said goodbye to my girl...' Kick still felt removed, off-balance.

'She's been shakin' her ass at the Friday dance class, doing more to the beat than just twirls...'

Kick looked over at the smiling faces, the nodding heads of the audience and, for a moment, had the intense sensation of not actually being there.

But as A.C. continued with his strophe of dry-wit reasons as to why he now had four, three then two bullets left in his six-shooter, leaving one that could only be for himself, Kick finally began to relax.

So by the time A.C. was holding a replica gun to his own head, a trail of dead girlfriends, dance instructors and chasing policemen behind him and by the time the crowd screamed, 'Shoot!' and there was the sound of gunshot and the lights went out signalling the end of A.C.'s act, Kick was ready for show-time.

The gig had gone well.

Making it all the more puzzling that, as he now opened his eyes to find himself on a wide seaside promenade, he still had a distant, nagging anxiety at the back of his mind.

Putting it aside, he surveyed Gee's latest construction.

Many found a perfect virtual reality to be missing the point. They had reality for reality and needed something quirky or surreal, a flaw, to confirm a sense of otherness. Not Kick. He wanted his immersion to be total and found Gee's designs to be seamless.

He stood alone, a summer's day sun spangling on the shallow crests of the sea, as a community of couples and kids kept contented company with courting teenagers, collapsing deckchairs, solo swimmers and cold ice-creams.

No-one knew him here and that suited Kick.

In some circles being famous – even on the limited level that Kick was – might be considered desirable but he recognised that mostly it was just weird, a position only willingly occupied by weird people who considered it normal or by people, at one time normal, now made weird by its effects.

The cost of fame was always high in workload and dedication but the price was often very different – the level of fame was directly related to the level of personal freedom you voluntarily gave away and there was only so much of that Kick was prepared to surrender.

Besides, fame became a very dangerous game late in The Past. A fashion sparked, ignited and burned long and bright for individuals to define their own fame by the famous person they murdered; even the public records and digital histories immortalsed them in a blended name format.

It became so rife that celebrities even used how many times an attempt on their lives had been made as part of the publicity for their next project.

However, this odd badge of honour ultimately tarnished irreversibly. Ending up as a frazzled and paranoid inhabitant of a highly-guarded home prison, employing food tasters hired from highly-vetted specialist agencies became the new price of fame and made the years of working towards success less than worthwhile for many.

Instead, it became more desirable to seek fame another way – by killing someone famous.

The Thinning seemingly extinguished that fire but Kick still had no intention of allowing someone the opportunity to become John 'Kick Vivid' Smith. Kick's current level of recognition was just fine by him.

Apart from being successful enough to be on U.S.'s radar he was quite happy with where The Fifth Season were, respected and financially sustainable. It wasn't lost on him, however, that, despite their independence, U.S. could stop them in their tracks on a whim with influence alone.

He didn't think they would do that – their dark pragmatism knew not to send Kick into a martyr's exile, giving a name, a figurehead to any anti-authoritarian sentiment. Everyone, after all, was a potential future customer.

It had taken a lot of hard work but at this point in time, with the sun on his face and the rattle of the sea-front roller coaster off to his right, Kick felt that the balance in his life was just about right.

The modern genes that formed him and other superimposers (mind-readers, telekinetics, seers and so on) were almost mundane Now, having been rare at best, more usually mythical in The Past; Kick could not remember a time when there were no superimposers. Several generations before him couldn't either and across this time The Maze had been managed respectfully.

Opinion was divided as to exactly what The Maze was.

Maths and art were the languages through which the Universe gave sentients the responsibility of defining what they saw around them. Maths spoke with flawless precision whilst art, when on its most instinctively accurate form, achieved a wordless perfection; The Maze was more than both.

Some thought that it was knowledge, immense knowledge thrust into the minds of those most receptive. Everyday minds, even brilliant minds, simply didn't have doors wide enough to let The Maze in so it bounced off them harmlessly.

Yet most superimposers had a direct line to it, were in some way more connected to the ageless, universal beating of the original heart.

Most had learnt to manage this connection – them being merely the newest expression of the Universe's creativity – utilising its power into the skills and functions that made them superimposers whilst careful to maintain a respectful distance. The Maze, whatever it was, if left to its own devices, would simply crush the individual and absorb them into its whole.

Many superimposers could channel it effectively, letting a quick clip of it run through them on occasion, usually to seek out other superimposers who would feel it (as a kind of drowsy disorientation) and recognise one of their own.

Kick wasn't sure what it was but thought that if superimposers were an expression of the Universe's creativity then many, Mister Five included, were from its avant-garde period.

In his case The Maze might threaten his existence were he to, as an empath, let too much information in or seek to know too much – his filtering systems protected him from the jabber and chat of daily life but also, much more significantly, kept him from stepping too close to the precipice that was the endless everything of The Maze.

Which is why he liked Gee Whizz's constructions so much – Gee understood this about Kick and his designs incorporated a supporting cast of happy, good-natured participants; Kick's fantasy-land of nothing to think about, nothing to fix, nothing but his indulgence.

On this occasion, speed…and as he took his seat at the front of the roller coaster, two grinning kids in the seats to his left, their legs bouncing and jumping in giddy anticipation (he knew how they felt), he closed his eyes and let out a long, relaxing breath.

'Ayeeeee!' exclaimed the kids (or was it Kick?) as the car lurched alive into a grinding slow climb, the dragging beat of its clack clack providing an is-this-really-safe heightening of senses already primed with dread-love.

The tracks stretched upwards and away, ahead of them only sky and as the car reached its highest point only then did the sea come into view, swinging up from beneath them, impossibly far away, as the car levelled out and stopped at the edge of an almost vertical plunge.

The crowds on the beach far below might have looked up to see the car begin its descent and might have heard the screaming as the car went over the lip and immediately stopped, leaving everyone in it facing straight down, straining against the safety harnesses and wondering if this was the day they were going to die.

Kick had just enough time to think a thousand thoughts but nothing at all before the car was released, beginning its journey with a ferocious acceleration earth-bound.

At the bottom of that first deep plunge the tracks screamed back up into the sky, Kick shouting at his fellow passengers (who really weren't listening) that he didn't need his stomach anyway.

The track rolled up and over to the right, the car upside down for a second or two in the first of many inverted sections before righting itself for a split second ahead of a sudden lurching drop into an underground tunnel, the darkness within broken only by the evenly-spaced lights on either side mechanically accelerating in the opposite direction, accentuating the car's rattling speed, the enclosed space making the thrilled screams louder.

The track veered up and out again into daylight, the car thrown up into a loop-the-loop section, its speed deliberately calibrated to slow almost entirely at the highest point, the most upside-down, the most vertigo-even-in-your-third-eye moment, picking up a forward momentum only when each and every one of the passengers had actually expected to drop.

And as the car resumed its pelting urgency, Kick felt it for the first time: The Maze.

It might have been the ride. But it wasn't. And as the car jammed a harsh left, adrenaline throwing fuel onto a swoon rapidly becoming nauseous, he felt The Maze come at him from another source.

It was coming from behind him in the car and from at least one place on the ground and this shouldn't be happening.

He began to lose consciousness, the kids next to him fading into the distance, his head rolling on his shoulders with each muscular change of direction.

He fell forward against the restraints, all of his remaining energy focussed on just getting to the end of the ride, his mind a mangled mix.

As his eyes rolled and saw nothing, he had visions of Tempra Kay; a boy in a field, his light brown hair sun-kissed. He saw Honeytongue and wondered why he ever left her arms. He saw a car, its engine revving but going nowhere and light, so much light reflecting off its broken lines.

Instinct fought to stay conscious, his skull apparently shrinking, compressing his temples in a crushing grip, a shrieking headache starting between his eyebrows, knifing behind his nose and through the roof of his mouth.

He felt the car stop, The Maze retreat. Gradually, he came back to awareness, slowly reintegrating, breathing deep against the receding pain, vaguely aware of the kids stepping over him, this silly grown up who couldn't handle the ride.

The ride attendant engaging him with an 'Are you alright Mister?' roused him. He rose from his seat and looked around, blinking through the lingering pain. The seats behind him were now all empty and there was no-one on the beach or promenade who was acting…well, acting how? Like they had just sent The Maze to an empath on a roller coaster? What did that look like anyway?

'Here, take this,' added the attendant offering Kick an inhaler.

'Unless that's a painkiller, I'm not sure I can trust it,' said Kick, his voice still thick with discomfort.

He inhaled all the same.

♪

Kick sat reflecting on the day. It was post-gig and late was a long time ago.

The gig had gone well – the band on form, Zip preening with his new tattoos. Yet despite no intrusive images, no Maze, he could not relax.

The Maze never got used like that but the fact that it intruded into a personal virtual reality troubled him more. It made him wonder who he could trust.

He had said his goodbyes to the support act from this, their final night, Frotty Pan, a leather-clad solo act whose band, Busy Cutting Funk, had been exactly that throughout his set.

Like every front man, Frotty was part hero, part bullshitter-at-the-bar. As Zip was prone to tell Kick, all front men were arseholes, it's just a question of whether you like them or not and Kick liked Frotty Pan.

He admired his commitment but also his ability to contrive an ear-worm of a chorus with the lyrics: 'Get born, get fed, get drunk, get laid, get kids, get fat, get dead, but don't for-get, to get remembered.'

How *did* he do that?

Zip also enjoyed pointing out to Kick that, when he wasn't singing, he was just some bloke standing on a stage with musicians.

Usually Kick accepted this deliberate prod to keep reaching for better and better performances but tonight it had a different resonance, Kick feeling separate, distracted.

He'd left the crew undressing the stage, loading up and calling for Guilty.

Zip, typically, was slowing Mangler in his duties.

Mangler, today's T-shirt reading 'All I Got for My Birthday Was Mental Arithmetic. It's The Thought That Counts', patiently, methodically went about his business, nodding, rolling his eyes and mmm-ing as Zip inflicted today's subject on him.

In between glancing at his new tattoos like a proud new parent, aware of the irony but considering it worth mentioning anyway, Zip had wondered openly about the thinking behind genital piercing, expressing an appreciation that whilst it might heighten the sexual experience, if this is what you needed to make sex interesting, then maybe you might want to admit that sex really wasn't your thing.

Zip, pressing the point in the spaces left by Mangler's periodic grunting exertions, offered that he had tried crochet once and felt even that could be made a more interesting experience by shoving two or three metal bars through his genitals but that a more natural solution might be to simply find something that he found more interesting than crocheting.

Leaving this behind, Kick found himself in Single Malt's bar, not sure if he was looking for answers, less sure he wanted them.

He sat in the cool atrium next to the water feature, feeling bleary and more fatigued than he should have done. The absence of Buzz Paparazzi was a blessing – any image taken of him right now surely destined to feature the word 'Before' beneath it.

But no Buzz meant no Malt and with his old friend's absence adding to his despondency, Kick eventually left the bar and headed back.

He was alone in the streets in this part of town, the only moving shadow in the cobble-stoned network of small alleys that surrounded Malt's bar.

When he woke the next morning, he wondered if he had dreamt it, the slow glide of the girl out of the shadows ahead of him.

For some reason on this tour, Kick – more than usual – had been marvelling at women, each and every one a delight of the unknown, as though he had never seen one before.

Yet, even in the limited light of the moon and scattered curtained windows, Kick was struck by how attractive this particular girl was; her movements, whilst not overtly sexual, convinced him that the two of them were close in some way, his lyricist's mind instinctively reaching for, yet failing, to find any appropriate words.

He knew why. As she passed in front of him and looked coolly into his eyes, it was nothing less than a primitive thrusting urgency that he felt – a feeling older than words, making them redundant and futile.

She was thrillingly attractive, not a catnap short of her beauty sleep; the kind of girl men regularly embarrassed themselves in front of, her form almost too much to accommodate in the confined space of the alley, her eyes giving the impression that her lips were slightly-parted even though they weren't.

Despite being a few feet ahead of him, there was something right-next-to-you about her and the lithe temptation of her body, her breasts keen and competitive beneath her fitted top, rendered Kick's desire to its basest level.

Even as a horny teenager, Kick had never experienced such a reaction and as she moved on into the shadows, he closed his eyes and let out a long, shivering breath in an attempt to get his adrenaline under control.

Opening them, he was grateful to be alone, that she hadn't returned to torment him more, the almost painful imperative to breed, jarringly unwelcome and fading far, far too slowly, leaving him desolate and entirely spent.

♪

Too many fractured images accompanied Kick as he left The Indulgence Junkies the next day.

He never left this place anything other than uplifted and refreshed, at least on some level. Except this time.

Bat, typically, had noticed his friend's troubles but would wait until Kick was ready to talk, such was their way. Meanwhile he busied himself tending to a straggler.

Mint Breen, a young man they had tempted away from The Mean City, had fallen foul of the temptation of The Indulgence Junkies, hadn't eaten or slept in days.

Whatever dissatisfaction had led him to The Mean City in the first place had clearly insisted on being over-fed with chemical, narcotic destructives during the three-night stay.

Bat patiently fed him fruit and water, Mint's eyes struggling to focus as Bat played nursemaid.

Gently, tenderly, Bat attended to Mint.

'Drugs are the place you go to only if you can promise to come back.'

Bat had no idea if Mint would ever be able to take this advice but hoped he would keep it close in case he ever could.

Bat was also hoping that Mint wasn't lost already, rendering his, or any advice, glib and naïve.

From the milling chaos surrounding the departing band and crew, Single Malt appeared and caught Kick's eye. Mint would be safe with him he seemed to be saying and as he held him by the shoulders, he spoke as though to him but looked straight at Kick.

'Don't ever tire of their behaviour; never tire of them reminding you who they are.'

♪

Out into The Open Spaces again, Kick sat at the front alone.

In his right ear, suddenly, the unmistakable flicker of Mister Five's voice, the tickle of his lips, insect wings against his skin.

'Don't blame Gee. He didn't know…or maybe he did? Join us.'

I AM LAND

Chapter Ten

With The Indulgence Junkies some way behind them, the terrain softened into undulating meadows on either side, sprinkled with small natural ponds that would outnumber the human population for the next few hours.

Bat Fantastic, none the less, had much on his mind.

He hadn't always been the composed, thoughtful individual that now sat next to Kick, his proximity assuring Kick of his availability, his silence an appreciation of that option being taken up, or not, in Kick's own time.

He was once a cock-sure and – let's be honest – irritating young man, his intelligence and eloquence being weapons routinely and unnecessarily released on a world that was just then beginning to turn on him in response.

Whilst most were considering that a touch more humble from him wouldn't harm, he was nurturing an attitude that took from the respect he showed other people and gave to that which he showed himself.

The day he learnt to learn was not unlike any other in the life of this particular pubescent pain in the proverbial, a slouching shuffle bringing him late to another class at school. It should have been a subject to engage him, the use of sound in the regulation of arrhythmic heart conditions and the disruption of negative circular thinking but his sense of entitlement, that the future was his to do with as he pleased, acted as an effective obstacle to anything that Dev Menton was telling the class.

Dev had learnt long ago how to react to this kind of challenge to his authority; long enough in the tooth to have seen it all before but also knowing instinctively – as good teachers might do – that education was often about timing.

Today, though, he felt that – right moment or not – Bat needed a little warning shot across his bow.

'I worry about you Mr. Fantastic,' he said, his neutral tone disguising his irritation and a sincere frustration that a smart mind was slipping through his fingers.

Bat, sensing wrongly that he was being patronised, regarded Dev with as much surly contempt as he could and responded, 'No, you're just worried that I'm going to grow up and realise you're only a teacher.'

'Until you understand the value of a teacher then you will never be a grown up,' replied Dev simply and in so doing, caught Bat at that exact right moment.

Bat sat slack-jawed and wordless, the rest of the class, returning their attention to Dev Menton, earning what he was giving them by their behaviour simply deserving it, giving Bat a glimpse of himself and how he would have appeared to them.

Bat will tell you that his peers that day learnt about sonic treatment but that he learnt everything else. He learnt that he would always be learning, he learnt to respect everything that he could, always, and he learnt that if you throw an unnecessary punch, you deserve to get caught on the counter.

Dev's simple words played a significant role in forming the man that now sat next to Kick – proud, humble, flawed, receptive, improving; a man aware that only when you have passed all the tests in a subject can you then test the subject itself.

Powdermouth, along with the crew, having gone ahead as usual, would be through The Gorges by now and Bat resolved to take him aside and point out the unnerving delirious funk that his friend seemed to be in. To most – even Zip and Riot – Kick would appear to be simply snoozing but there was something about it that Bat didn't like and he would tap into Powdermouth's wisdom.

Next to him Kick drifted in and out of a shallow delirium, coming round occasionally to find that the day still bore him a grudge, retreating into a dream-state fragile enough to surrender an outright claim on his consciousness, committed enough to keep pulling him back from his struggling attempts to awaken fully.

He dreamt of threat, the sounds and visions of his environment slipping in and out and over each other, each sound an intrusive image, the occasional soft whistle of the vehicle's brakes becoming the relentless whine of someone else's spoilt child, always out of sight, in a diabolical disobedience.

He was the captain of a ship, a great sea everywhere, a crew that was his to protect.

In brief moments of clarity, he would be awake, of sorts, aware of Bat's reassuring presence next to him, Riot absently tapping his drumsticks against a hard surface, before freewheeling away again, forlornly staring back at his ship from a life-boat, the only comfort being that his crew was safely on board with him.

He turned to them to find only their clothes and a few personal items keeping him company and the surprise woke him again, his eyes open and focussed just enough to recognise the narrow channels avenued between tall rocky terrain ahead. And still with the gentle drumming tap of Riot's sticks.

The boat had gone and he found himself alongside the vehicle, dreamily removed from his own fitful slumber, weight-free and boundless, the only connection left being his desire to reassure Bat that everything was okay.

He sensed the approaching Gorges ahead, their shadows spilling into his awareness, smoothing around him with a thorough attention, Riot's now regular steady tap a distant countdown to some imminent gentle touchdown.

As Kick focussed absently on the sound, he became aware of the shadows moving, sliding like currents, lifting him, dropping him far from where he thought he was and then appearing elsewhere, the tapping of Riot's beat now filling the space where they once were, increasing its intensity and building a now humourless stalking tempo.

Stranded, annexed and slipping away, Kick watched as the shadows writhed over and around the tour vehicle, his attempts at shouted warnings smothered by the depth of his separation, lost in the punishing crack of a beat that was now everywhere, as urgent and as loaded with intent as the sound of an angry woman's walk.

And just as the racket became everything, the attack began.

Kick found himself back in the vehicle, Bat on top of him, covering his own ears from the din.

Back in reality but several steps behind the narrative, Kick still felt the need to warn Bat about an impending attack but the words wintered in his mouth, each frozen syllable ice-hard and intent on bringing him up to speed with cold, impatient urgency.

A white-hot projectile fizzed through the air, breaking in over his head, breaking out over Zip's, trailing sparks in a ferocious display, spitefully followed by others at irregular, rapid intervals, each describing cruel courses of differing directions, daylight darkening in deference.

There was a metallic, grinding wheeze as something heavy pushed down on the roof and the vehicle, having inevitably stopped, now began to tilt, its creaking complaints an unlikely rhythmic accompaniment to the syncopated clatters still beating on and through its surfaces.

For a brief moment it stayed like that, tilted to its tipping point, its centre of gravity up for grabs, before being released to fall back upright with a grating shriek, the last sound before a silence so total that when the clip-locks on all the windows started twisting with a squeaking reluctance, they mistook it for the echoes of their attackers escaping through The Gorges.

Kick knew better, watching as the locks coiled and buckled, the words 'Join us' being his to hear alone as the telekinetics, their point made, faded away along with their static crackle to become part of a blameless background once more.

♪

'Thugs,' said Iodine surveying the vehicle, hands on hips.

'Beautiful though, wasn't it?' responded Zip.

Riot grunted a grudging agreement, inspecting a mangled lock which now functioned better as a noun than a verb.

Everyone was rattled, more so than the vehicle, which ultimately suffered only cosmetic damage.

Iodine and Entenne felt it more than most, being security. They were helpless against this kind of breach yet they attempted to make amends for what they felt might have been their failings by recruiting Riot to help them force the roof back up into an acceptable shape.

A group effort of patching up broken windows and smoothing sharp edges later and they all sat gathered with the dusk, the shock easing into the space now vacated by industry and action. Patient as it is, shock is happy to wait if need be.

It was Kick who felt the responsibility most; he was an empath and should have seen that one coming, as overt as it was.

He knew he had been deliberately, strategically incapacitated, that Dessel's designs intended many things including some kind of sprinkled layout of disjointed travellers sitting outside their own vehicle, uncertain looks on their faces.

Kick had Malt's warning so considered himself a touch more informed than those around him who had, by now, become used to U.S. and their attempts to recruit The Fifth Season. Despite this, his question would essentially be the same as theirs in the face of such significantly raised stakes…why?

He was still groggy, his sense of failing to protect his charges an intrusion on his ability to focus. Were they looking at him now to apportion blame? Or to find a solution, a what now?

He glanced up through The Gorges, the fading light casting their stony walls as ideal theatres for further villainous productions. That didn't feel credible; he knew they were safe from harm for now – and was sure that there had never been any intention to harm anyway.

A faint orange glow beyond the first curving sweep reassured him further and fifteen minutes later, the vehicle secured and safe until daylight, Kick led his ragged band of bleary, blinking cohorts into the warmth of The Out-Of-Towners's camp.

♪

The Out-Of-Towners had their own language, developed over time as a means of protecting themselves, recognising each other and excluding others.

Entenne, as a newcomer to The Fifth Season's tours, was unaware that travelling bands were accorded Out-Of-Towner status by virtue of their lifestyle and despite taking her cues from Iodine, took a while to relax into the realisation that here was where her skills would be needed least.

Kick casually slipping into this language came as more of a surprise to her but would have been even more of a surprise to Kick had he even been aware he was doing it, had ever done it.

Kick, his band, his crew, were Out-Of-Towners in their own way. They spoke the language.

Slopehound tended to stick with his beans.

The bedraggled group were all so fatigued that they didn't notice the glances between the Out-Of-Towners and the eyes turned briefly to the floor as Kick introduced himself and his situation.

Certainly, Kick didn't notice.

His own fatigue was scrambling his reception to the extent that he was unaware that, beyond the brightest wash of the firelight, in the secrecy of the flickering shadows, a little boy with a red cap was being consoled by his parents, a sadness overwhelming him the moment he saw Kick.

In other circumstances this sadness would have encroached on Kick, even – or perhaps especially – when he was tired and a little exposed but as the boy was led away deeper into the dark and a night of troubled sleep, Kick felt only a lingering sensation that he had not protected his people enough, that he was losing them on some level.

A feeling that was complicated by the looks on their faces, the expressions of hunger, weariness and a little fear appearing to him like distrust and accusation in his current state of mind.

He was unaware that they all felt the same, Entenne and Iodine even more so, or that Bat was labouring under a guilty feeling that he had not protected his unwell friend enough.

Kick Vivid, empath, was unaware of this.

Powdermouth knew that they were running late, had allowed for it, so as they all sat and enjoyed the hospitality of the Out-Of-Towners, one by one succumbing to a full-bellied sleep on makeshift beds, they were not missing from any expectant gig venue.

It didn't prevent Kick from feeling like he was meant to be doing something and after a period of trying to reach sleep through his jangling thoughts and the rat-a-tat-boom of the attack on the vehicle looping in his ears, he opted to walk it off through The Gorges.

In the silence around the last crackles of the dying fire it was easy to hear the stream in the dark and Kick followed the sound until he came across it.

Flowing in from his left and falling a hypnotic wash over a rocky sill, the water steadied in front of him, its momentum checked by the depth of the expansive pool and the current of another small stream muscling in on the far bank.

Kick sat on a rock, removed his shoes, placed his bare feet on the cool, giving soil at the edge of the river and in doing so experienced his first moment of anything like peaceful that day.

He closed his eyes, connecting with the sounds around him as directly as he connected to the land beneath his feet.

Deep in the tumble of the water was a rhythm, a tinkle, wash and burble on a complicated repeated cycle and the musician in Kick sought to find it.

He always did this next to running water but tonight it served another function, the water washing away the other noises in his head, seeking out the corners that needed cleansing.

His breathing deepening, his body relaxing in stages through a series of softly sinking slumps, he finally became still.

'You look like shit.'

Without opening his eyes, he replied, 'Well, I'd hate to have to go through a day like today just to look good.'

He flattered himself that Tempra Kay was smiling in the dark.

'What's with you and water anyway?' he asked to the shadows where he thought she was sitting, the sound of the water making the exact position difficult to fix.

'I turn up in the middle of nowhere in the middle of the night and it's just the water thing that you're curious about?' responded Tempra, giving Kick something to think about. But not now. Tomorrow maybe. Maybe the next day.

For now, he was enjoying the stillness that meant he was more able to approach the subject he knew she was here to talk about without it troubling him too much. Still, he waited a few minutes.

'Today was a little bit a lot messed up,' he opened and when there was no response he continued, 'I mean maybe I deserved it but the others weren't THAT bad in a previous life right?'

Thinking that his humour had an airy carefree to it, he was a little crestfallen when, through the gloom, Tempra Kay told him he was the funniest man she had ever known, in a tone of voice clearly suggesting otherwise.

Not allowing him to wander off-subject was one of the many reasons Kick had a profound trust in her, however she managed to achieve it, and it was him that smiled now – a smile that slowly faded, taken downstream perhaps by the gliding water and he took a deep, lazy breath before putting his thoughts into words.

'If this is how it starts.'

Tempra Kay's silence offered no help in arranging his words.

'If...how...what does the thick end of that wedge look like?' he finished unsatisfactorily, the words falling in a clumsy disarray.

Tempra deftly prevented them from landing too hard.

'They'll continue shaking you up like that to test your commitment, increase the intensity and frequency no doubt,' she said almost matter-of-factly.

'My commitment to what?' Kick asked, aware of the deliberate denial in his positioning, aware that Tempra Kay's subsequent silence was a means of letting him see it for himself. She paused long enough for his words to become forgotten before pressing her point.

'Don't you have something you should be paying attention to?'

'I don't owe him that,' reacted Kick testily.

'Maybe you don't but you made a promise to Kelly and, Kick,' Tempra Kay punctuated her words with a moment of silence before finishing, 'if you don't have your word, what do you have?'

Kick, a little startled by Bubon's words echoed in Tempra's mouth, wanted to react again but felt much of the fight go out of him, only the last friction of resistance remaining.

'I'm not sure I can trust myself to do anything much after the last few days.'

'Never has your genius been more brilliantly disguised.'

Knowing that he was being mocked, Kick burst into a smile without inhibition, sweet and liberating, bounced out of his self-pity not for the first time by Tempra Kay.

He struggled to contain a grin that stubbornly compromised only into writhing contortions as she went on.

'Kick Vivid I do believe you're falling for their attempts to plant self-doubt in your mind. You of all people...'

'Yeah, yeah I know. I know what they're doing. Wearing me down, making me afraid and vulnerable. Creating a problem for which only they have the solution...'

'The classic strategy of politicians, religions and advertisers...' Tempra finished for him.

Kick sighed before continuing.

'They have such means, so many resources...'

'You have all you need,' said Tempra Kay but Kick had already started his next wriggling comment, over-shooting the opportunity to ask her to clarify what she meant.

'Besides, I'm on tour. A little busy you know.'

'You're a tight, experienced outfit Kick, you could do the tour in your sleep.'

'The way things are going,' said Kick reflecting on his state earlier in the day, 'I'm very likely to.'

They sat in silence for a while, Kick now willing to let the last of his defensiveness drift off into the night sky. A black shadow skimmed across the surface of the languid pool in front of them.

'Bat,' said Kick.

'Fantastic,' added Tempra and, responding positively to the humour, Kick finally spoke to her.

'I'm worried that I'm losing the band and crew. After today I think they trust me a little less. I should have seen that coming.'

'You wouldn't have security, crew or anyone else for that matter if you were responsible for everything Kick

– there's only so much you can do. Besides, I think you should credit them with more than that – I suspect what they're feeling most is concern for you.'

'It troubles me that I can't tell the difference…given who I am.'

'Which is how they want you to feel…'

Kick knew this to be true and by way of agreement, said nothing.

'They work on trust, dig away at it, create definitive reasons why you should do this or that based entirely on contrived breaches of it.'

'You're talking politics, advertising and religion again, right?'

'You're so hell bent on being one of the good guys that you completely forget that others aren't…and stop avoiding the obvious Vivid.'

'Yes Ma'am.'

'What is it about humans that means they focus on the tiny cracks in a system rather than marvel at the whole?'

'They?' said Kick.

Tempra Kay paused. A little too long.

'My point is every day, all day, trust is fundamental, profound…almost total. Someone prepares you some food, you eat it. You simply trust that they are not poisoning you. You take a walk next to a road, no-one is going to whimsically run you over and you know that. You stand on the third storey of a building, trusting the people who designed and built it – people you have never met – to have made it safe enough for you to do so.'

Kick listened.

'It's why, when there are breakdowns in trust, it is so shocking. It's why there are laws that represent the value societies – all societies – place on trust that, when broken, involve custodial sentences. When trust goes, society goes… if they weaken the trust between you and the band…'

'Yeah…I know…'

Kick did know this. Tempra Kay was giving him the talk he would have given himself had he not been so frazzled from the last few days. He knew also that they were only trying to make him uncomfortable enough to succumb – he was no use to them without the band so the intention would not be to destroy.

Tempra Kay had more to say though.

'There's an intelligence to co-operation Kick, it makes you all safer. If you are looking each other in the eye, it's harder to stab each other in the back.'

'You…?'

Tempra Kay adjusted her position slightly but made no other sound.

'Are you suggesting I break bread with Dessel?'

'That's not really what I meant, although I do think you should do whatever *you* feel you should do. No, I meant,' and she paused a moment, wanting her point to be heard this time 'you have all the resources you need.'

'Are you giving me a riddle this late at night?'

Tempra Kay laughed and the softest of breezes drifted over the scene, through the trees, across the surface of the water.

'No, you're just being real slow Kick. Why be so careful and spend so long assembling those around you and then not rely on them when you need them?'

Keen to demonstrate he wasn't all that slow, Kick clutched at a flaw in her argument.

'Entenne is really new.'

Tempra Kay raised her eyebrow, unseen in the dark, the universal expression of the unimpressed.

'I could say that Powdermouth found her and you trust him with your life. I could say that maybe you haven't needed her before which is why she's new. Or I could say, grow up Vivid.'

Kick looked skyward, chastised.

'Have faith in them Kick.'

'Zip would tell you that faith is just an opinion.'

'Yes, I know but that would be to do with the Great Religions and maybe he would be right but isn't it essential to the human condition? If you don't have faith in something, why are you getting out of bed in the morning?'

'Faith in the Great Religions was fatally undermined.'

'You're jumping to conclusions Kick. Faith just migrated to U.S.'s more appealing replacement. Nothing got disproved.'

'Maybe.'

'Besides don't you think it's more prudent to allow for the possibility than to fully dismiss it before the evidence comes in?'

'Maybe.'

'There were sceptics about ghosts until you were able to fully explain what they were.'

'You?'

'You collectively,' she clarified but Kick wasn't sure that this was the thread he had been trying to pull.

It evaded him and they sat a while in silence, the first stage of the encounter being reflected upon.

Kick broke the reverie.

'The Great Religions failed not just because of U.S. – they were offering a pay-now-have-later model in a have-now-pay-later world.'

'That's true but it doesn't mean they were wrong. Religion gave order, reason, a sense of belonging. And why not reassure those that are anxious? Solid and for the most part, positive motivating influences.'

After so long in the darkness, Kick could make out the hazy outline of Tempra Kay – he turned her way.

'Or,' countered Kick, 'scare the hell out of people with the threat of hell and damnation…unless they do as they're told.'

'Hell is just where you don't want to be and The Devil is just the one who takes you there,' said Tempra by way of initial reaction before going on in a more considered way.

'Though that is a fair point. But avoiding darkness is not a surprising motivation either – it's part of the natural world to move towards the light…isn't it an extension of that?'

'The flame makes no such promises to the moth,' Kick responded and, realising he sounded more cynical than he felt, then asked, 'How did we get on to this?'

'We're always on this don't you think?'

Tempra broke the next reverie.

'You don't believe at all Kick?'

Kick believed many things and whilst he wanted to be open with Tempra Kay, he felt there would be other times to expand upon the précised theme he presented to her now.

'I believe there's something bigger than me but that I'm also part of it. I'm no more afraid or aware of it than one part of a river is of another.'

Sensing that Kick had more to say on the subject but was beginning to tire, Tempra Kay said, 'Shall we change the subject?'

'Yes,' replied Kick with an appreciative tone of relief, 'I don't think this one fits in my head anymore.'

He turned again to Tempra Kay.

'Any last thoughts before I go and pull myself a very long bed?'

Tempra's thoughtful silence broke with:

'It's not about what you expect, it's about what you accept. Take control Kick. If you're not committed to something then they can work on the doubts found in the gaps. If you chase something, intend to catch it, otherwise you are just being led by it.'

Kick smiled, not only as a reaction to the soothing tones of Tempra Kay's voice but because for the first time ever, just as he reached for his shoes, the river gave up its secret. He found the first beat of the cycle, the pulse of the water, the unmistakable breath.

He stood.

'Besides, you don't need the solution right now Kick, you just need the next step.'

And as he walked back to the camp, shoes in hand, he replied, 'Thank you Tempra.'

'Today needs to be something that happened yesterday,' he added and knew that he would now be able to sleep.

And then the rain came.

Chapter Eleven

The light of the overhead sun glinted irregular and elusive on the swirling surface of the river washing silently by, the far bank an irregular weave of rushes, hedges and low trees, no sense of what lay beyond.

Slowly, he engaged with his environment, his consciousness feeling its way into the meadow, instinctively aware that this place was all – yet this place was finite; he knew it was bordered but couldn't grasp quite how or where.

He sat upright in this place of stillness, glared at by a sun that should have been crueller but instead warmed without burning, the flat green expanse of the meadow before him and the river off to the right playing host to the variety of summer's play.

Butterflies and bees, their tenuous mastery of gravity manifest in their drop-lift flight, cheerfully bounced between temporary stops of dandelion and buttercup. Along with the other flighted insects, they provided a visual buzz and hum to the scene – and meals on the go for swooping larks and surface-feeding fish.

A hawk waited in the shade on a branch on a silver birch in a soft wood line at the far end of the meadow directly in front of him and whilst he knew the meadow was bordered to his left and behind, the details were vague and of no particular interest to him.

The view was enough without turning, the colours a splashing display accentuated by the stillness, yet fluctuating in a heat haze that swelled benevolent.

An ant crawled across his toes, busy with nothing other than the necessary business of staying alive.

He knew he should have been thirsty but he wasn't.

Yet he wasn't entirely comfortable, something was concerning him. Perhaps a predator or maybe an unresolved thought that still needed his attention. He felt no threat, more a kind of discomfort – because the one thing he did know was that he would have to leave here soon, this beautiful place.

He didn't know how, although there seemed to be a clue in the only real sound; tumbling water, its presence seeming to be everywhere.

But the meadow was flat and the water had nowhere to fall.

With the sun directly overhead casting no shadow, providing no compass, the sensation of not knowing where he was began to mix with not knowing how he got here, becoming – like the river – a soft ongoing unease, passing by just as more arrived.

Chapter Twelve

Kick, a cultured man, stood at the wall-mounted trough serving as a toilet watching another man's urine glide blamelessly by and wondered how this had ever got to be centuries' worth of civilised.

When Honeytongue had suggested he be more grateful as to how convenient that was, a part of him agreed but he felt compelled to ask her what her reaction might be if she was in a space the size of a lift and the man standing next to her simply took out his genitals.

As he rejoined the band, he remembered her face, scrunched-up in amused horror, scrunching up even more as he had invited her to add urine to that image. He smiled at the memory and missed her intensely.

The band were in a bar in one of a network of suburban regions that comprised what they referred to as The Nowhere People, a term either used as a taunt or a tease depending on the individual, the mood or both.

A place, standardised and safe, homogeneous, almost a town, almost rural but in actuality, neither.

Polite, tidy, genteel to the point of hostility, an environment tightly under the control of its inhabitants who, in aspiring to as little going wrong as possible, achieved no more than as little going *on* as possible.

Of the over-indulgent parents who treat their children as the only ones that ever lived, the highest proportion resided in these areas, fielding their kids as unwitting school-age soldiers in rivalries with other like-mindeds whilst simultaneously shielding them from anything unpleasant that might actually happen to them.

They had experimented on their children across these regions, famously attempting the elimination of swearing, forward-thinking that at least future generations would not associate such words with thuggery if the Early Years class mouse was called, on this occasion, Cock Fuck.

Their benign delusion that their world was not connected in any way to a global information network was dented only slightly when the inaugural year group grew up enough to engage with that network and displayed their new-found awareness by calling each other a 'fucking class mouse' in the rare moments of childhood vitriol that slipped through their upbringing.

The idea was shelved and – as is often the case in such societies – never mentioned again even at delicate barbecues where poised summer-dressed mums, expertly avoiding eye contact, continued effete conversations as sprinkles of children launched 'Cock Fuck Cock Fuck!' at each other in percussive accompaniment to their burger-fuelled play.

In the absence of anything that might cause actual anxiety this society embraced self-obsession and called it the same; a group of people less concerned with talking about important things as they were in simply appearing to do so.

Zip had many names for them, The Chatterati, The Pseudo-Nobility and the Non-Thinking Intellectuals being but a small sample.

They were either profoundly satisfied with their world or uniquely subdued and defeated, a world of women who had long ago stopped looking to the horizon and of men for whom the closest they got to happiness was the pause button.

They had forgotten, or had maybe never known, that the future is an adventure, always.

Even the next generation, whose eternal role is to accept the things given to them by their parents and then mock them for not having had them in their own youth, seemed indifferent to the task.

You might then expect The Nowhere People to be a source of great teen angst, a hotbed of creative expression but the conditioning was so complete that the closest the youth ever came to rebellion was to reinforce their diffidence by sucking smoke-tendril apathy from a spliff.

Only one band had ever come out of the entire region, contemptuously referred to by Zip as Bland Jivy, the kit car of rock and roll…looks like rock and roll, sounds like rock and roll, isn't rock and roll.

When The Fifth Season last toured here, one of their support acts, The Original Fuck Ups, had had to change their name to TOFU which had struck Kick as both appropriate and not entirely unreasonable but had sent Zip into an impassioned verbal assault, ironically framing the sensibilities of the locals by wondering, with an open-ended question, as to whether their fellow musicians would have been wiser to claim that they were not, in fact, a rock band, but the new school rabbit.

The upshot of this particular event was that less controversial support bands were politely insisted upon for this tour.

HappyGoingNowhere, for example, were deeply unassuming, a band so dazzled onstage by the attention they were getting that each successive gig might well have been the next exercise in a self-help book about facing your fears.

If the tour was a movie, you could fast-forward through The Nowhere People and miss nothing of importance. Usually.

Zip was not in the mood to criticise their hosts on this tour it seemed, perhaps considering it a place too bland to waste any further superlatives on but, as he sat in the pub, his eyes widening as he scanned a local catalogue left on the table and marvelling at the insight the 'items for sale' gave into the problems that apparently needed solving in these people's lives, Kick felt something was brewing.

There rarely wasn't, in truth, but Zip wasn't coming to the boil quite yet.

This series of gigs through The Nowhere People was the workload of the tour, the novelty of the new now no longer fuelling the enterprise. This was where they earned their money, figuratively and literally and they knew from experience that it was a case of putting their shoulders into it and working at it.

This ideal, unruffled environ provided a stability that not only allowed but supported those willing to seek reward with the application of such an ethic.

The band earned here, not least as a protection for things going wrong in the later stages of the tour.

So here they were, pre-gig in another nondescript bar, sitting beneath a poster headed 'Events' which appeared to have been on the wall for years but – Kick was sure – was entirely up-to-date, even if the 'When there's nothing left to believe in, what do you believe in?' tour poster was the only thing that suggested so.

He scanned the room. Visually. It could have been any place from the last two or three weeks, the cast of characters interchangeable.

Essentially a group of people, scattered into small clumps around the bar, who seemed to want sitting around in a bar at 30 to be the memories they took to the bar at 60. This was their world, contained, defined, comfortable, the occasional suspicious glance over at the band testament to their presence being a bump in the regular contour of their daily routine.

They weren't bad people – Kick had some skills in his locker that would have found that out pretty quickly – but, as Zip put it earlier in the band's career, 'I'm not saying it's boring, it's just that there's a lot of room for something interesting to happen.'

At the bar, a conceited young man entertained three friends, the look on his face suggesting that he had had to give them some of his own personality just so he could stay interested in them. Being the one-eyed man amongst his blind followers buffed his ego but his sense of superiority would never extend to actually leaving this place and the possessive grip with which he held his girlfriend likewise suggested that the only limb she would ever be going out on was his arm. And probably only to this pub.

An older couple, small drinks half-finished, sat wordlessly at what Kick assumed was their regular table. So withdrawn as to possibly be experiencing themselves in the third person, they stared at the big screen above the bar, their faces set in defeated compliance as though polishing resentments instead of the trophies that, perhaps, they felt they might have, at one time, looked forward to winning.

The sugar-stream of gossip, oh-my-Gods! and non-news on the screen washed over their glazed gaze, the subject matter leaving them unmoved but representing what Kick thought of as the endless stream of ankle-deep celebrity litter through which everyone had to wade to get anything or anywhere; the triumph of the trivia.

The prodding positivity of the adverts in the breaks suggested that, whilst Hell might be different for everyone, a good time for all could be easily defined. And purchased.

On another screen was an awards ceremony attended by fantastically successful actors who, after surveying all that they had, measured in more money than they could spend and multitudes of adoring fans, still found the space within the perimeter of their ego to find a hole where they felt an award should be.

The barmaid had a look on her face that was so far into couldn't-care-less as to be comfortably into couldn't-give-a-shit and a young man at the end of the bar, mirroring her ambivalence, weighed the level of his attraction to her as though his first thought might have been 'If I was drunk...' but his second thought might then have been to get drunk.

Kick thought the outcome might be more Friday Night Failure than Saturday Morning Smug.

Zip's boredom refused to be contained any longer – his subject matter, a piece of solo guitar from The Past that was universally highly-regarded, got raised and delivered suddenly as though the band were expecting it – which, of course, in many ways they were.

'Are you really telling me that's a wonderful piece of playing, a soulful, heartfelt delivery? The whole thing is drenched in melodrama from the giant pretentious reverbs and delays to the bends that are meant to be oh-so-expressive in their emotional use of quarter-tones and deliberate off-key sharpening but which really only sound like he has no control. If you're going to use quarter-tones, they have to be the right quarter-tones.

The left-hand/right-hand co-ordination is lamentable but, no, that's soulful right? And we are all just meant to agree. Especially since – so the story goes – he was told to simply go and play like his mother just died. Well, I don't know about that but maybe it would have been better if she had died before she gave birth to him or even killed after he'd recorded it as a fit and proper punishment…'

'Zip…' cautioned Bat, a warning that the engine was over-heating into un-Zip-like territory.

Zip used the pause only to draw breath before continuing, 'It is a hysterical piece of playing, it's overwrought, awash with its own self-importance and clichéd in its delivery. It is not the expression of an adult's existential agony, it is the sound of a teenager slamming the door of their bedroom and screaming "I hate you!" before throwing themselves on the bed in floods of tears. Again.

For people to gather around in collective mutual self-regard and cluck to each other that they are sooo deep for feeling it the way they do…man!

It's a solo for people who don't know any better and frankly, the only good thing I can say about it is that it is not as much of an arsehole as the person who was careless enough to introduce it to me in the first place.'

In the calm after the storm, Zip took a deep breath, nodded his head in curt confirmation of his position on the matter, glanced at Bat as if to acknowledge he had veered over the edge of taste, placed his palms on the table in front of him, looked up at the entrance of the pub and started booing.

The band, rarely up to speed with Zip anyway, belatedly followed his gaze…to find Dessel standing looking at them, smiling at Zip's reaction.

His arrival, especially in this environment, came as a surreal surprise, a weird situation made weirder, as though out of nowhere the vowels had turned up at a meeting of consonants to complain that they were working too hard.

And – again – Kick had not felt him anywhere near.

Dessel looked from one band member to another and, adopting a look of feigned disappointment, partnered it with a gentle shake of the head and offered, 'Groupies must be having a lean time,' before breaking into a smile.

The truth was, Dessel's presence, in good humour or not, fouled up the room like an insincere apology, prompting Riot to respond, 'If you were a dog, I'd rub your face in that comment.'

Entenne and Iodine watched closely from their position nearer the bar.

'Please,' said Dessel, beginning to grind his teeth to control the urge to hurt something, 'don't be an arsehole.' His resistance was limited it would appear.

Riot came back at him.

'I'd rather be an arsehole than what you want me to be.'

Dessel sighed, the fight apparently gone from him suddenly. He said gently,

'That's not a good start.'

Riot, not yet ready to cease reminding Dessel what they thought of his presence, responded, 'No, but it makes a great ending,' and glanced at the exit and then back at Dessel, the message clear.

Dessel took another deep breath, held his hands up and said, 'I'll back down first, anyone care to join me?'

Four disinterested faces. Silence.

Dessel cautiously pulled up a chair next to Kick who gestured to the band that there was no need to hang around. He preferred to deal with Dessel alone and often found the other band members' instinctive loyalty misguided to the point of disruption, distracting him from handling this very powerful superimposer as carefully as he would like.

Dessel often preferred them to be there, perhaps to give Kick more to be concerned about, so as the band got up to join Entenne and Iodine he said, 'Wait…please…'

Zip, for whom the biggest problem with waiting had always been that it took too long, stopped and held Dessel's gaze long enough for his turning away to be dismissive. He followed the other band members, muttering something about there always being lice trying to live on something healthy.

Dessel and Kick sat alone.

'You know I wouldn't mind his behaviour…if it wasn't so totally unacceptable to me,' he said pleasantly, one leg over the other, hands clasped around the raised knee.

'He's not as good as you think he is, just not as bad as you want,' replied Kick, his voice conveying a weary get-to-the-point through the laboured humour, but he knew that Dessel would get to the point when he was good and ready.

He also knew that, on this occasion at least, Dessel was not inclined to confrontation. The setting, the tone and then a mere beat of silence before he spoke again implied a theme of negotiation not confrontation, perhaps because their last encounter had been so fractious.

'Kick, look, you need to know that I have thought about what I do, who I represent. This is not just a job to me; I believe in what I am offering.'

Kick thought about Bubon's endorsement of Dessel's critical approach to his work and in fairness, could find no level of insincerity in what was being said to him as Dessel continued.

'The thinking is sound, based on the best for all. War, famine, disease. We are looking at all of these things and we are confident that we can eradicate them all in time if everyone is pulling in the same direction. What do you think my bosses want? Everyone dying? Everyone poor? Everyone…afraid.? It doesn't take much thinking to realise that is…counter-intuitive.'

Kick wanted to interrupt, to point out that no-one had ever seen Dessel's bosses, just suited representatives, but it was reflex and he considered it more appropriate to let Dessel continue.

'My bosses…me…I recognise that we are all just trying to get through each and every day, each with our own worries and fears. We are just trying to alleviate that, offer day-to-day solutions and, of course, an end to the fear of dying. Such a disruptive motivator I think that one.'

'And,' referring to the Great Religions he went on, 'we don't insist on a joyless existence while you're alive either.'

Kick gazed ahead, aware that Dessel was watching him to gauge the effect of his words, assessing the need for more before getting to the point they both knew was coming. Dessel assessed that a few more would not harm.

'We're no threat to you Kick. We're no threat to anyone; I can't speak for everyone in our employ but our motives are generally speaking well-intentioned.'

Dessel looked away from Kick, apparently distracted by the big screen and allowed his words to ripen in Kick's mind.

Eventually, casually, he said, 'We don't have to be up against each other. Really. Kick we could use you. Come on board.'

Kick smiled, turned to Dessel and said, 'It's number two on my list of things to do with absolutely everything else being number one.'

For a moment Dessel didn't react before breaking out into a smile of his own and any observer in the bar might have thought that two old friends were sharing a joke.

'Yeah, yeah, okay.'

The smiles slowly faded from each of their faces leaving them both a little sheepish at their odd moment of bonding and Dessel filled that space before it developed into an embarrassment that would work against him.

'Look, I'll be honest. We could use your influence, we are having real trouble reaching a certain kind of… customer. You could be a key element in our future. In return, we can provide all manner of support, reduce your workload, your financial exposure, increase your reach. I know you have heard this all before but it all boils down to one thing. Kick…we are not bad.'

Dessel let that notion breathe before suggesting quietly, 'Come in and meet us. Properly.'

And at that he turned back to the screen, engaging with it for a few moments before giggling and letting, 'Idiots,' fall out of his mouth as a summary of the bickering characters on view at that point, normalising their shame by shouting it loud. He found something fascinating to look at on the tips of the fingers on his left hand and presented, 'Kick, name your price.'

'Money doesn't matter to me,' came Kick's stock response and without missing a beat, Dessel leaned in, winked at Kick and said, 'How much do I have to offer before the money does start mattering?'

And, smiling with Dessel again, the oddest of things happening in the most normal of places, Kick actually thought about this.

About Honeytongue and spending more time with her, about how tired they got at this point in the tour, about how long he would be able to keep this up, how long he would be artistically and physically vital, about how the money might not matter now but what about as he got older, less firm, less able to earn?

He didn't have to like U.S. any more than it was likeable right?

Maybe it wouldn't stop being his and start being theirs?

He thought about greater reach, extending to new audiences, the things he could say to them.

Sensing this, Dessel eased back into Kick's attention.

'You needn't lose your identity. Rock and roll will always be about rebellion. We wouldn't change you at all, just make the same thing...bigger. As for your credibility,' Dessel was cute enough to know what mattered to most musicians, 'no-one will judge you by what you have but how you behave when you have it.'

Later Dessel would reflect that he had made small in-roads with Kick, that on balance it was a successful meeting, perhaps the first, but at the time Kick took a sip from his drink and replied, 'I understand what you are saying Dessel...but...I am not comfortable being a representative of any ideological or corporate narrative other than my own, either directly or by association.'

And Kick felt good saying it, the flash of anger in Dessel's eyes nothing less than he expected and gone the moment it had arrived.

'Well, that's pretty definitive,' said Dessel, aware of when to push and when to back off, the humour back in his tone.

'I find myself refreshingly candid,' responded Kick in kind, pinching from Bubon.

Dessel regarded Kick for a moment longer as though he too recognised the description, before standing, bowing slightly and gently, almost tenderly saying, 'Be sure that you can claim to be who you think you are.'

He moved to the door (Zip cheering from the bar) and just as he was about to pull it open, Kick called after him.

'Dessel.'

Dessel turned, his face curious, open, perhaps a little hopeful.

'Rock and roll isn't about rebellion. Rebellion can be

co-opted by people trying to sell you things. Rock and roll is about thinking for yourself…and that can't be.'

A smile snaked a creeping presence across Dessel's face.

The two people at the table closest to the door began to hold their heads, burying them in their chests as though better to contain the pain that they were suddenly experiencing. The nose of the one nearest to Dessel started to bleed.

'Well,' said Dessel pleasantly, 'I learnt something today.'

He turned to leave, the two people at the table instantly relieved the moment he left, taking deep breaths of recovery, alarm and confusion and relief jostling for priority on their faces.

Tick ♪

                                        tick

            tick

                                                      tick

Chapter Thirteen

Not for the first time, the boy came to the attention of some Out-Of-Towners.

The network had spread the news that he was traveling alone to some unknown destination, perhaps internal, and they ghosted him whenever they were nearby, checking on his well-being, not wanting to intrude or intervene. Not feeling the need but watching for it.

The boy was doing fine, the gaps in his knowledge occasionally making him vulnerable but acting more often as receptacles for new knowledge, easily absorbed to make a more solid whole.

Llo Spuntinoh, the elder of this particular group, had good instincts to go with his sense of the bigger picture and an eye for the details that, however small, were essential to the entire.

In his time, he had seen so much across so many zones, so many cultures and so many generations that he thought of nothing as out of the ordinary.

He'd considered, among other things, child-birth, tsunamis, people who loved each other but hurt each other, camouflaged animals, sprites, disappearing sea vessels, dogs barking at a point on a wall, sentience and being all with the same unsated, curious eye and had concluded that nothing could be a freak of nature when nature itself could be so freaky.

Over years of listening to stories of those traveling from zone to zone, of watching his own people, of being an observer, even, of himself and his own reactions, he had concluded that joy was earthbound. What was here and now mattered the most, despite so many seeking a satisfaction somewhere beyond both.

He also thought the time was right to say hello to the boy, although how to do so without alarming him was currently beyond even the wisdom of Llo Spuntinoh.

The boy had been avoiding people on his travels, he knew, but the stoicism with which he had accepted the occasional anonymous helping hand from passing Out-Of-Towners suggested the boy was not as troubled as he might have been by them being near.

He decided to wait until the boy was dozing in the sun, a habit he had after a swim he took each morning – ironically it seemed to wake him up.

Slipping gently into the water from the opposite bank, he began a casual breast stroke around the pool, pointedly not looking in the direction of the boy who, upon hearing the noise, sat up, startled.

He relaxed a little seeing that it was an elderly man swimming away from him and was just about to seep back into the bushes when, timing it exactly right, Llo Spuntinoh turned and feigned shock at seeing him.

Reflexively the boy sought to reassure him that he was not a threat and so it was that twenty minutes later, the old man and the boy with sun-lightened hair walked into the camp discussing fish traps and lichen growth as the other Out-Of-Towners prepared breakfast, now for one extra.

Some eyed him with curiosity, others – more traveled – with a kind of sadness but all with a welcoming familial kindness. They all knew the boy or knew of him from others and likewise he fell effortlessly into the rhythm and flow of their existence.

Over two days and nights he learned much from his hosts; the examples they set, their interaction with each other, the sense in their co-operation. More directly, they showed him their ways of hunting and fishing, listening to the land, accepting what it offered and how to be its respectful guest.

They showed him how fear could be his friend.

'You need to be a little afraid in case you forget that things can be dangerous,' was how Llo Doval had said it with a smile on her face, going on to explain that fear need not be just a reaction to events, that, used properly, it can allow you control over them instead.

They prepared him for the time they knew he would leave, Llo Spuntinoh overseeing his people's co-ordinated efforts to instill what they knew the boy would need for the weeks to come in what amounted to a few short hours.

Being at that age where new knowledge fitted into his mind without him needing to reshuffle old information to make room, the boy absorbed it all – especially when in the form 'how to…' – and his guileless curiosity facilitated the process and informed direct questions, often of the type that made Llo Spuntinoh smile with delight.

'How old are you?' asked the boy on his last morning, staring at the wrinkles around Llo Spuntinoh's eyes, each an expressive line in a story of a life well-lived, now crinkling with pleasure while the eyes themselves lost a little focus in reflection.

From his earliest memory of running towards a river in spate and the panic it raised in his parents, despite his own sense of extraordinary liberation, to the (first) girl who broke his heart, the second, through to a bad leg break while showing off to the third, his own children and the laughs and alarms they brought into his life, the good times, the bad.

He thought of the fights that lingered beyond their duration and the joys that did the same.

He thought of the time wasted thinking about the wrong things but that – if you were lucky – experience meant you wouldn't change a thing apart from the way you did things next time.

He thought of the tree and how the bark protected the young and growing core.

Llo Spuntinoh was at the age that, if you guessed it right, he would not hold it against you.

The boy saw a wry smile play across the older man's face as he reflected that the older you get, the more comfortable you are in your skin but that the trade-off was that your skin had to become a touch looser to allow it.

'I am all of my ages all at the same time,' he replied eventually and the boy remained silent, perhaps understanding, perhaps filing it away for later.

Llo Spuntinoh needed something from the boy before he left so, once the boy had said his goodbyes, he said, 'Let me show you something.'

They walked together back towards the river where they had met and Llo Spuntinoh led them to a rocky beach, a garden of varied boulders, having been worked on and deposited by the waters, breaking up the flatness of the shore. Over time the land plants had claimed them as their own, wrapping them in green tendrils of different shades and widths, as though possessive of their attention and afraid of them leaving.

Llo Spuntinoh called softly as the two of them stood there – a name, Llo Klinny Pipp – and a clutch of the criss-cross greenery moved as though someone had disturbed it.

It took the boy a while to realise that the movement he had seen was a someone. The foliage had been tattooed onto a man, naked and crouching, facing away from them into a hollow in one of the larger boulders.

As he stood, still facing away, it was instantly clear that he had been present all along, that the configuration of tattoos, now scattered randomly and incoherently at various points of his body, locked into place as perfect camouflage only once he was hugging his own body, on his knees, head down and facing away.

He turned his head, eyes still fixed on the ground and the boy said, 'Hello.'

Llo Spuntinoh squeezed the boy's shoulder, whispered goodbye and disappeared into the scenery in his own way, leaving the fascinated boy before he could reply.

Llo Klinny Pipp, his voice faint from lack of use, responded with a dry, whispering, 'Yes.'

The boy knew then. He knew that Llo Klinny Pipp had loved someone, had loved someone so deeply that his own well-being amounted to nothing, that his only role, his only reason to be, was to make them safe. He knew that Llo Klinny Pipp had never forgiven himself for this person dying in an accident despite it being no-one's fault and despite not being there when it happened. He knew that Llo Klinny Pipp blamed himself.

He knew that he wanted to hide, that the tattoos suited him, that he could disappear and blend in but only when crouched into this broken, submissive pose, that this completed him and that his tattoos only made sense, he only made sense, when in this position.

Guilt, like anger, might manifest as a prison but the boy did not know this – he was not profound, despite being, to many, of a certain significance. He was young and instinctive and reacted as such.

He knew why, so the question quickest to his lips was how long and he said so to a croaky response of, 'Ever since.'

He marvelled at the discipline of this and in saying so took Llo Klinny Pipp – who had never considered his dead life from such a position – by surprise. He turned a fraction more towards the boy who was still trying to collate comments and questions to express his curiosity and concern.

He said it seemed a terrible event to have happened to a loved one but also a terrible event to continue to happen to Llo Klinny Pipp and that, young as he was, he hoped nothing like this would happen to him in the future.

As he said this, he remembered Llo Doval's good-natured comment about fear, the mixture of warning and good-humour and this was almost certainly conveyed in his voice. He thought of Llo Spuntinoh's words earlier in his stay (or did he dream it?) about how, with destiny, things happen for a reason but that in real life there was usually no reason at all and he thought of the helplessness he had briefly felt before the sense of liberation that followed and this, too, was almost certainly conveyed in his voice.

He thought the tattoo was amazing and said so but, showing that directness again, after a short pause and tilted-head assessment, offered suggestions as to how the separate elements could be developed into individual tattoos, each in their own right.

The boy took Llo Klinny Pipp's silence as an indicator that perhaps he should be on his way but also recognised that this man, who lived alone and naked, yet safe in this environment, could teach him so much about how to do so.

The boy asked the man for help and they spoke for some time before the boy left, asking the man to say thank you to Llo Spuntinoh, because he had been distracted when he had left. The man said that he would.

The boy knew this to be true and that the man would mean it when he did.

Chapter Fourteen

Kick sat on the flat mountain top that formed a giant horseshoe above The Religious Zone, an immense natural feature that served to contain and define a population densely-packed into a semi-circular plateau at the base of the slopes that plunged off each ridge and evened out softly before greeting the sea's lapping kisses beyond.

He was struck, as he was each time the tour reached this point, by how vast this space was, the mountain offering a false perspective suggesting a quick trip down to its base but in fact it would take between two and three hours from this point before they encountered the first of the level land and an hour beyond that to reach the first of the outskirts of the city.

Along the way – and even high up at this point – they would encounter the usual hired-hand hatchetry of U.S.'s lowest-level loyalists, this time encouraging travellers away from the population centre.

It was not in U.S.'s interests for potential customers to have options beyond the grave.

Many of these musclers – here and across all of the regions – had originally been inhabitants of the Religious Zone, often fiercely committed to their beliefs and it was this inclination, this mentality, that U.S. preyed upon in recruiting them. Any environment where individuals were primed to act to extremity for their beliefs was a natural place to plunder for U.S.

The Religious Zone had a high proportion and all U.S. had to do was give them something better to believe in and then leave them to it.

The Religious Zone was an anomaly in a post-religious world it was said. But Kick had, with time, come to accept that assuming so was in fact the anomaly, instead recognising the need for – and the motivation of – belief. After all, as Tempra was prone to put it, some form of it kept him alive, gave him a reason to get up, do things, care for others, made him accountable.

In his thinking, he considered the most important part of the world as that which you came into contact with and endeavoured to treat that constituency as well as he could.

Regardless of his position as some kind of public figure, he had always considered himself – an adult – as having a responsibility to behave like a role model to everyone he met in whatever context he met them.

This thinking expanded into caring less about what others believed and more about how this might manifest in their behaviour since this affected society as a whole.

His belief was less about systems and ideologies as it was about ultimate outcomes.

U.S. – so they said – had the answers beyond death, with science the deity that could essentially eliminate it, yet still no-one, not one, in The Religious Zone believed in them.

For them, science explained everything...except everything.

For many of a theological conviction, empirical evidence had steadfastly remained quaintly beyond the persuasive for centuries and, in claiming to be the answer to all prayers, U.S. had merely established itself as the earth-bound Devil in the beliefs of those in The Religious Zone. At the very least, a belief in U.S. was not as reassuring to them as their own beliefs were.

For this reason, there were more older people in the general population and it was the better for it.

Whilst Kick was as interested in religion as a salesman might be in a room full of bankrupts, he appreciated the mentality, the construction of systems to reflect concerns, priorities, fears and loves – in The Religious Zone you could find something to suit and soothe any version of this that you carried with you.

Potentially a difficult place to gig due to the variety of factions, actually, like most places, people simply got along.

After all, no harmony and no solutions had ever been found by those fixed in polar positions of separate perfection and instinctively Kick distrusted the arrogance of any system that claimed to have all the answers, be it religious or political. He tended to like the representatives of each that he was best able to ignore.

As with politics, the extremes tended to argue their position with an aggressive righteousness that belied the responsibility they had to keep those ideas alive – from almost any perspective, at least 95% of other people are plain wrong and accepting that you were in that percentage for many others was the only way to get along and get by, he thought.

Those that didn't, who did take it that stage further by bombing a rival place of worship for example, were in a stark minority and whilst the weapons required were always provided for profit by U.S., they were also occasionally detonated by them, perhaps when bored but most usually to prevent peace settling in too surely, inhibiting further sales of weapons for profit.

Peace did not suit U.S. in The Religious Zone and most terrorism of any kind bore their hallmark or their calculation.

Once they had made their way down onto the populated plateau and begun to encounter this gestural city of monuments and statues to archaic deities that reminded Kick so much of those erected in honour of athletes and singers in other regions, they would mostly be surrounded by good people, living by a religious code, and by good non-religious people who simply liked to live amongst this population. These would wake every day to the sea on one side and a soaring mountain surround to look up to in awe, rather than some entity of a more ethereal and less implacably tangible quality.

Zip joked that he had been to some koshe places, some kosher places but this was by far the koshest and Kick knew that, as usual, Zip would struggle to keep the mischief from playing tunes for his tongue to dance to for the duration of their stay.

Loyal, smart and ultimately very decent, Zip's thought processes in this place always had the same potential for chaos as a drunk elephant in high heels at a plate-spinning party and Kick would have a hard time curbing him; Bat would perhaps be of some help but Riot would be a whole bunch of useless kept in a bag with a hole.

Riot had noticeably become a little distant from Kick and the moment it began could be isolated to the last night at The Indulgence Junkies. There was no animosity, no bad feelings, Kick just felt there was space between them that hadn't been there before.

He knew what others didn't about Riot and had never shared it, their friendship tested over years on this and on many other levels. Towards the back end of any tour each band member tended to drift into a different head space from fatigue and over-exposure to each other but this was a little different – Kick felt that he was losing Riot somehow. Passively. Slowly, maybe, and without rancour, but irretrievably.

For now, as he sat alone on the crest of the mountain, this was all for later. He removed an intoxicatingly fresh lungful of air from this elevated altitude and looked over to Crunch, Mangler and Slopehound, all of whom were struggling to focus on Zip's monologue, their faces forming an unsettled spread of nausea, their expressions suggesting they may never trust that air could be fresh ever again.

The three amigos were no doubt re-considering (i.e. not for the first time) the wisdom of spending any time in the sealed room of a Gusty Pedant show.

Kick knew – no, everyone knew – that you only do this for a bet and then you make sure that you lose the bet but the three of them had obviously talked themselves up into this and not one had been prepared to back down, a folly which Zip felt deserved a lot of his attention.

He was particularly intrigued by Slopehound's current position given that 'Cool Beans' gave him plausible deniability when it came to appearing (or not) to have agreed to anything. Yet still he had found himself unable to have backed out.

Slopehound's beans were anything but cool right now.

Gusty hadn't always been Gusty although becoming so had proved to be the making of him – a double-edged sword of a most unlikely kind.

He had started his stand-up career as the less-memorably monikered Bicker Helm, a comedian who understood comedy on both an instinctive and cerebral level.

Whilst his application of the daft rarely failed to hit the target, he also understood laughter as that moment of freedom when you are released from the gravitational pull of doing, or thinking, the right thing; the carefree weightlessness of being liberated from that which might trouble you and your usual response to it.

His comedy contained an inherent, perhaps irreverent, invitation to uncouple from the pull of your conscience, if only for a moment.

Some might say, subjectively and therefore accurately, that this was in poor taste but Bicker's audience always felt they were in safe hands – they never lost touch with their conscience so much that it instead drew attention to their concerns and slapped them back hard against them. And they were never so far removed from its gravitational pull that they spun off into a heartless void – Bicker knew the difference between release and insensitivity.

His sensibilities had a comedic maturity that made you think without ever presuming to do your thinking for you.

In a very early show he had made what had proved to be a career-changing decision to stop and take issue with an audience member for passing wind both noisily and – as it transpired painfully slowly – with a creeping insidious stage-ward reach.

The irritation that showed on the then Bicker's face at the noise, which became a grimace of discomfort as he challenged his leaking assailant, followed by the wave of panic, almost fear, as he realised that the full extent of the assault was now by both smell and bridling taste, was all captured in a hypnotic video that went on to become one of the highest viewed on social media and earned him the nickname Gusty Pedant.

Had he chosen not to confront the audience member it is very possible that he would have gone on to have a successful career as Bicker Helm with his ground-breaking fare but changing his stage name to Gusty Pedant, and taking advantage of the thrust of exposure he would now get under this title, was too good a career opportunity to miss.

Which is where the trouble began.

Gusty found that his audience began to contain a greater number of individuals for whom flatulence was the norm. At first, this was greeted by his established audience with impatience and disdain, a contempt for the crass, self-entertaining opportunism of this new breed of attendee.

This deterred the fly-by-nights and part-timers but seemed only to encourage the dedicated – a small group, granted, but one that vociferously booed throughout entire shows when Gusty attempted to counter the increasing fumes with dozens of lit candles onstage during his 'Open Flame' tour.

At this point, Gusty took up the challenge, refusing to be bowed and from then on worked exclusively in venues with low ceilings and doors that could be tightly sealed, his thinking being that if he was to be locked in with noxious air then so, too, would the audience.

What began as a little provocation on the part of a teasing audience had now developed into the oddest of confrontations with absolutely no-one at a Gusty gig interested in his material, his skill as a comedian somehow made more starkly obvious by his playing of immaculate sets to mostly silent rooms.

Instead, as soon as Gusty announced a new tour, a team of olfactory terrorists mobilised, including chefs ('cookers') and gig-attendees ('delivery men') who had a skill-set of a very particular kind. The science of food recipe as weapon was born and ingredients were tried, tested and discussed amongst a community for whom making Gusty stop a gig was the target and the ultimate measure of their abilities.

Rumour had it that a large food supplier had secretly offered a reward to anyone who could do so using one of their products but it was also rumoured that this was a rumour spread by the large food supplier, these things being hard to prove all round.

No-one had stopped Gusty in his tracks, something that was of great professional pride to him but it was also true that when he saw certain people in his audience, tilted in a certain position ('the clean releaser') he knew he would be in for a difficult night.

He would (almost respectfully) acknowledge his more established foes by deliberately standing in their most recent releases, delivering his intellectual, high-brow material which, when seen on digital release later, would only occasionally expose the briefest of expressions that betrayed either an involuntary gritting of teeth, or a look that was either gulping or a concerted effort not to.

The silence would occasionally get broken by an outbreak of applause which would have nothing to do with what he was saying but all to do with an appreciative audience acknowledging the time he had spent in a particularly venomous cloud – Gusty's audience knew their stuff and for his part, he stuck diligently to his delivery, never getting distracted into even so much as a nod of the head by way of thanks.

Over time, the recipes had targeted other senses in a focussed barrage of designer vapour and Gusty had watched as many an audience member, who had thought that a blocked nose would protect them, bolt from the venue spitting, or with eyes watering.

Some played the long game with him, the chefs working creatively to construct a meal that would allow a continuous release, in an attempt at slowly wearing Gusty down over the length of the show. Times of ingestion, a schedule of releases and so on were practised and perfected diligently by the delivery men and tactics were discussed, often the biggest decision being whether to save a knockout blow, as it were, for the encore or to go all out to prevent Gusty returning for one which would be a credible result in this most relentless of unnecessary wars.

Whichever strategy was adopted, the chefs set about the science.

Almost exclusively men, the arrival of the first woman at a Gusty gig created an inhibition amongst the established, familiar fraternity; a kind of moral and ethical dilemma, the unsure shuffling of feet an expression of a rather touching chivalry.

The room did not know how to react until, that is, she proved her worth; the faintest movement-on-leather sound meaning that, as straight-faced as she was, she had a little to learn on delivery but the substance of her work suggested a significant new player in town.

Instead of holding their breath, cautiously her new-found peer group inhaled, welcoming her in, then held their breath, impressed and visibly relaxing as they did so.

Gusty's crowd kept him afloat but fans of his core skills watched from a safe distance.

Kick had met him once, and had quite liked him, but felt he had a vague air of distrust and disappointment, and had seemed to be keeping a kind of distance of his own.

Kick did not find this surprising in a man who could only secure a gig in a limited number of willing venues, had learned to accept solid income from air-freshener sponsorships, and for whom increased ticket sales could only ever be a mixed blessing.

It was into this sticky miasma populated by the hard at work that Slopehound, Crunch and Mangler had gone holidaying and it would take until the end of the day before Slopehound's beans would be back or even mentionable.

And, hopping off the rock he was perched on, Kick smiled at their foolhardiness, breezily stating, 'Come on, back on board.'

Mangler's T-Shirt stated 'My Brother Went to an Out-of-Body Convention and All I Got Was a Lousy Piece of Saturn' and the look on his face suggested an inhospitable gas giant millions of miles away was preferable to the local kinds he had experienced last night.

Zip was delighting in this and considered their evening's outing as both a learning experience for them, and something to pick at with the casual inclusion in his vocabulary of references to public latrines and canned dog food.

All of this was done with a gleeful faux innocence that had Bat struggling to keep a straight face.

Blanching at the thought of getting back into another closed environment, Mangler suggested the three of them travel down the slopes in the fresh air of the old-style opened-topped train providing rides into the city for visitors.

Kick said he could see no reason why not and had an image of them all huddled over, with the rhythmic sound of the ancient steel wheels resembling the repeated taunting question 'what-did-you-do-what-did-you-do?' providing much less comfort than they might have hoped for as they sparked occasionally over their tracks.

♩

A week later Kick sat at almost the same spot as the band made their leave of The Religious Zone; he liked to bookend their visit with the immense view afforded from this vantage point. The other band members and crew left him to this, a kind of meditative debrief, each of them busying themselves with their own coming-to-terms.

Unusually, throughout their stay, he had felt like he was the one who had needed stabilising, not Zip, his casual, benign detachment had made way incrementally throughout the trip to a sly anxiety that stalked him patiently at decreasing distances, always just out of sight but tangibly real.

He had stuck close to Zip, trusting his brisk, inquisitive mind to shape the questions that jingled like beads over uneven rocks. Zip questioned everything in the end and Kick had come to hope throughout the week, that eventually one of his questions would resonate and alert him to listen closely for the answer.

Zip, too, was uncomfortable in this giant city, amongst this thinking but whereas he made light of it by declaring he was as lost as a colour-blind greenfly feeling blue (artfully expressed with his own impromptu blues riffing accompaniment), Kick felt it more keenly.

He felt like a jigsaw piece, the right shape, the right size, sitting on top of an otherwise finished puzzle. He was at the wrong angle and if he could just rotate a fraction, he was sure he could fit, falling off the lips he lay on into a snugly-fitting space. Yet, being a jigsaw piece, he had no say in it, no independent movement. And so he lay on top of the puzzle at the wrong angle for the right space. So close. Almost.

As this sensation had heightened across the week, he had struggled to keep this from manifesting as irritation and moodiness and have Mangler ironically hand him his 'Queen Bitch of Hissy-Fit Castle' T-shirt as he had done on a few occasions when he was a younger man, tired and much, much less able to screen out all the noise.

It never affected his performances; the stage time was what he lived for, was his. Besides, he could rely on his dedicated professionalism should this fail to be enough. Yet here, of all places, he felt that unseen presence crowding, watching and judging – an intrusion he found particularly uncomfortable with the nagging questions he had of his own.

The feeling abated briefly during an incident late in the week.

Zip, in a rare moment of presumption, decided to raise a few issues with a kindly-looking older man who he assumed was a priest. Kick felt that the man could be a priest, a rabbi, or merely some guy sitting on a bench in a square but the fact that he was staring serenely at a statue of a woman with a child was enough for Zip to reach a conclusion.

Thinking about it later, Kick realised that he had perhaps been the one to make an assumption about Zip's reasoning – aside from his own unique skill-set there was no evidence Zip had thought this man was a priest and recently Kick was not sure he could trust what his own readings were telling him anyway. Besides it made little difference what Kick thought – in the end, Zip had decided that he wanted to talk to 'this guy' about what was on his mind.

As benign as the man's comportment might have seemed, sometimes Zip's piercing focus could be as welcome as a winter diet – especially if it disturbed you from a quiet reverie – but the man accepted Zip's presence like a safety net might a falling trapeze artist, absorbing the initial impact before settling into a kind of uncertain stability, with the potential for an unpredictable dismount always a possibility.

'Beserkers,' said Zip.

'Uh-huh,' said the man, keeping all options open.

'See, right there,' continued Zip, 'right there is the flaw in faith.'

'Uh-huh,' said the man, now only keeping most options open having rejected several by turning slightly towards Zip, a reaction Kick had seen many times, strangers somehow unable to resist being drawn in by Zip's colossal conversational gravity.

'Not the only ones but a good example of warriors unafraid of dying – in fact, welcoming it.'

'Beserkers? I don't believe I've heard of them,' said the man, the curiosity now more apparent in his eyes.

'Not surprised,' responded Zip as he turned towards the man, the two of them now obviously in conversation. 'They were Ancient Past northern warriors who worked themselves up into a trance-like state of aggression, chemically-assisted, before battle. Their opponents would encounter drooling, shouting, singing packs of sword-wielding beasts who had no fear of dying and I would imagine were mostly beaten as a consequence before the first swords were even crossed.'

'And this is the flaw in faith...?' encouraged the man.

'Yes. You see they were unafraid of dying because they believed that dying on the battlefield would take them straight to their heaven, that it was an honourable death. In fact, the most desirable.'

Zip, his thought processes ahead of his tongue, considered his case made and lapsed into a silence.

'And this is the flaw in faith…?' nudged the man again, a playfulness in his eyes that Kick appreciated.

Zip put into words the logic that was obvious to him.

'Imagine, you are the most committed and skilled warrior, the leader of all others, the example set in the destruction of your opponent. In other words, the one most deserving of your place in heaven. But your skill and dedication in honouring your God on the battlefield means that no-one can beat you so there you are, sitting at home, an old man, never beaten in battle, denied heaven and wondering how you have displeased your God so that your death will not honour him. And you can't induce death since that would be dishonourable too.'

The two unlikely participants in the conversation sat in companionable silence for a while, Kick annexed and attentive nearby.

'It seems unlikely that a warrior would be sitting at home as an old man,' suggested the man eventually.

'I can't see him shopping for slippers, granted,' conceded Zip.

'I take your point though,' continued the man, 'although it is focussing on a very narrow example of faith. Its reach, its depths extend beyond the thinking of those that are habitual killers.'

Zip nodded an agreement and offered, 'But it can also make killers of people.'

'No doubt,' allowed the man, 'but not of the majority. The use of weapons often becomes an option only when righteous zealots fear that their ideology might fail without it…or is out-numbered.'

'Or they're thugs,' said Zip and the man smiled in acknowledgement.

Again, the two men paused, the younger man breaking the silence first.

'If you base your beliefs on an unprovable premise then that premise might easily betray you right? I understand that it is personal, that it is a faith, I just don't know why?'

'Why…?'

'What is the virtue of us having faith? Why should heaven be the reward for faith? Why doesn't God just show us Heaven and then say, okay kids, see? Now, just behave.'

'Why should you have to be shown Heaven before you behave?'

Zip recognised the logic of this point but stuck to his central point, 'Why would you need religion to make you behave? I don't trust anyone who knows for sure…the institutions here for example. Plus, they don't seem to have any connection to the world I know.'

'Society is always more advanced than its institutions,' said the man and then almost immediately corrected himself, 'Well, I say that but look how long it took for society to catch up and finally produce equality, despite everyone recognising the need as far back as The Past.'

Zip nodded, 'What a horrible world that must have been,' and the older man's body language agreed.

Zip continued, 'It seems that change is a big wheel turning sometimes and the best intentions don't make it turn faster than it wants to. You can't let that stop you pushing though.'

'Such as it is, such as it was, such as it has always been,' said the man and, regarding Zip thoughtfully, asked, 'Do you have belief at all?'

Zip looked surprised, almost taken aback, at the question and for the first time a mild alarm showed on the old man's face as Zip lifted his shirt and turned away from him, displaying the permanent tattoos across his back.

Zip spoke over his shoulder to the man, now engrossed by the artwork on his back.

'I am constructing my God, building my God as I grow and learn, assembling my God with things that I consider worthy of my faith, whether that is what I think we should give or what I think we need.'

On Zip's back, carefully arranged from the base of his spine and spreading upwards, not (yet) fully covering his back, were artistic representations of things he considered worth believing in, each a constituent part of an evolving whole.

'I know that it may look like a series of random characters and symbols to you but there you will find trust, understanding, love, truth, loyalty, integrity, compassion, honesty, loss...'

Kick watched as the man took in what was, actually, a very beautiful piece of art, Zip's philosophy on skin.

'I wear them as temporaries and only if they resonate with me, only if I find them to have an essential truth, do they go on my back. I sometimes joke that it's a sin to be God-less but I don't want to be told what that God is. There is nothing else in life we accept on those terms. My God is being built, tested for strength, learnt.'

Zip put his shirt back into place and turned back to the older man, adding, 'With luck, I will feel like I have fully formed my God before I die.'

'With luck or with faith?' teased the man.

'Very good,' Zip said, smiling.

Another pause, moments of thought.

The man asked Zip how he would know if his God is fully formed.

Zip's answer, as clear as it was, left the man with nothing to say.

And Kick took a huge step towards an answer.

♪

It was as he was reflecting on this that Tempra Kay called to him, an unusual twist on her surprise arrival routine given that, ordinarily, she would be in close enough proximity before alerting him to her presence. He moved to be nearer to her.

It dawned on him that she was drawing him away from the direct eye line of the band and crew and he again had a moment of wondering whether his subconscious was aware that she was an imaginary friend and that she (he?) was simply protecting him (self?) from being seen talking to a rock.

'What are you smiling about?'

Kick shook his head and sat on a low flat stone that

afforded him a view of both Tempra Kay on a boulder above and opposite him and – with a small forward-lean – the tour vehicle.

The lightest of rains was falling.

'How come you always show up when I am in a bad mood?'

'Aw bless, Li'l Kick is in a bad mood.'

Kick broke into a grin, could barely help a laugh escaping from him with a momentum of its own.

'Bitch.'

'Don't you forget it either.'

Eventually the laughter petered out, Kick wrestling it into a suppressed smile before it finally settled – not unusually when he was with Tempra – into warmth beneath the surface.

♪

'What do you want?'

'You turned up on me, what do *you* want?'

♪

Kick glanced at the tour vehicle and the bustle orbiting around it erratically, breaking the silence with, 'I feel such a fraud here.'

'Go on.'

Kick wanted to. He tried to form the thoughts but found, in two or three abortive attempts, that he didn't have enough or he had too many or he couldn't find the right one. In the end he simply said something, in an attempt to break the seal.

'There is so much belief here.'

'Go on.'

Kick threw a you're-a-load-of-help look at Tempra Key who mouthed, 'Bitch,' at him spreading her arms, hands palm up, before folding them across her chest in a mock haughtiness.

'I'm not sitting here alone, it just feels that way,' Kick announced to the air, patted his thighs and sighed before returning to the original subject.

'Even Dessel has belief. It protects him. Zip too. And most of the people down there,' he continued, nodding to the immense mixed congregation below.

'I don't have what they have. I don't even have enough belief to feel safe from *their* beliefs.'

The subject matter Kick was choosing to express was now shaping in his mind, crystallising slowly.

'I feel vulnerable,' he said, both as a summary and as an introduction.

Tempra Kay listened. Kick spoke, the struggle he was having forming the words in his mind apparent in the changing expressions on his face.

'She's got the bit of me that's missing in me but I can mostly live without it is the thing.'

It was only when Tempra Kay said, 'Kick what are you talking about?' that he realised that his thought processes had not furnished her with a context.

'Honeytongue,' and he looked down to the ground in a kind of regret, 'she deserves more than I give her. I don't even seem to have enough belief in how I feel to commit to her.'

Tempra Kay intervened for the first time, 'Kick you're an empath – if you want to you could know everything about everything but you choose to know nothing about anything.'

Kick thought Tempra Kay would never make a lyricist – let alone a poet of his standard – with such wordy statements but, with the tone and content gently chiding, it was enough to make him turn to her, encouraging her to expand.

'She has choices Bozo,' was the extent of her expansion.

'Well, I feel better that I am only psychopathic enough to make my life difficult, not anyone else's. But that's not what I am saying...' Kick responded, running briefly aground again before going on.

'I can't figure out how to fit her *and* my life into my life. The time I spend with her…I'm content, comfortable. But there is also no motivation – I lose the ambition of my dissatisfaction, the thing that makes me who I am, the thing that gets me up in the morning, that makes me want to improve things by doing…this,' he ended, gesturing to the band.

'Relationships are really only orbits Kick, some close, some afar. Those that are too close for themselves are destructive, explosive by nature.'

It was Kick's turn to listen to Tempra Kay as she went on, 'It's not like she isn't busy – what makes you think that she would want you around any more than you are and getting in between her toes? Anyway, if you're feeling guilty, I am sure there are plenty of people down there who will accept your confessions and forgive you.'

Kick smiled, 'I don't believe any man can speak for any God in that way,' and surprised himself with the sharp tone of his comment.

'Hey,' said Tempra Kay, 'at least you *don't* believe something,' and they both smiled.

'I confess to feeling a pull from down there,' continued Kick, 'I can see the end of the tour now. It's close. I do at least understand the instinct to fill that hole with something, to be protected from the nothingness of that. I keep seeing things that don't go away when I close my eyes and maybe having a faith would see them off...having that anchor, that sense of home, of belonging.'

'Go on.'

Kick turned sharply to Tempra Kay, looking blameless, checking her nails.

'Oh, you're funny today.'

Tempra Kay waited.

'If there's one thing I could believe in it's The Maze but even that, a mystery in itself, is something I have to regulate, temper. Dessel, in contrast, seems increasingly able to understand it, use it, not quite control it but...ride it better. And I can't escape the feeling that it's because he believes in what he is doing. Like he is able to eliminate distractions better. I feel like I have increasingly less understanding of it, that it is encroaching, that I have less say in how it affects my life.'

'You think so much, no wonder they want you.'

Kick exhaled an ironic laugh before saying, 'It's a blessing and a curse but I'll live with it.'

'Maybe it's okay not to think Kick, maybe it's okay not to seek answers, maybe it's okay to succumb.'

'To some kind of faith?'

'Or some kind of lack of it. It might be much the same after all – martyrdom or suicide, either killing yourself for a belief or because you don't have any left…well, they start looking very similar.'

Kick turned to her again and she said, 'Sorry, got a bit morbid there, eh?'

She went on, 'The glimpses of insight The Maze gives you can be ignored if you don't find them any use Kick.'

'It's beautiful.'

'What orbit should you place it in Kick? How can you find the correct balance in your life?'

'It's tiring too…'

'Only if you choose it to be, Kick, others don't wear it like a cross. But then you never were one for peer pressure.'

There was a pause. Kick gazed down at The Religious Zone and Tempra Kay said the following before doing her usual disappearing act:

'Nor is the boy.'

Kick stood and turned away from The Religious Zone to rejoin his band and crew.

As he turned the corner around the rocks that had kept him concealed with Tempra Kay, there stood a man, aged, unshaven and toothless. He gripped a book that might have been a Bible, the Koran, or a novel and as he saw Kick, fire burst in his eyes and a rage flew from his mouth, spittle-flecked, as he screamed at Kick.

'So the engine ticks but what of the unknown silence beyond?!'

Rattled, Kick looked down and hastened his step as the man shouted at his back.

'Where will you go now? Where will you go now that you have rejected all that could save you? You better hope you see The Reaper because if you don't, then, as sure as day, The Devil has you.'

Chapter Fifteen

The meadow presented no apparent way out, each turn he made offering only a new perspective on a previous view.

He chose a direction, reasoning that, surely, the space would prove to be finite and he would eventually stumble upon an exit. Yet, as though for the shameless amusement of a callous child, he found that the borders – hazy and indistinct such as they were – remained steadfastly out of reach, forever the same distance away. In whatever direction he chose.

The sound of tumbling water was everywhere, infuriatingly nowhere in particular, intensifying in tiny increments, barely perceptible, more easily felt, such that, by now, he could be convinced that it was actually a waterfall. Somewhere.

His disorientation darkened into a deepening despair as he came across the blackberry bush he had seen ripe fruit on earlier, to find it withered and barren, momentary fear mixing with confusion. He was sure that the bush had been in the other direction to this one.

In this moment his mood tightened through impatience and frustration into anger – it *had* to be this way out, away from the silver birch tree but, as though just passing by, as quickly as it had flowed in, the anger dissolved, melting away and reconfiguring as panic as he realised that the birch had always been behind him, no matter the direction he had chosen to take.

And as the feeling established a hold on his demeanour, so the sound of water began to fade away, drifting off almost beyond range, taking with it the bulk of the daylight, the meadow now a dusky flutter of shadows, his situation one step further into isolation.

He stopped, the grass trampled down in the footsteps behind him staying flattened, having lost their earlier spring.

He took a deep breath. Everything stilled.

His anger was gone now and his bare feet became aware again of the prickly resistance of the mixed terrain beneath him. He accepted the sensation.

He turned to face the silver birch tree to the soundtrack of water once again.

Chapter Sixteen

Kick was happy to be in The Big Nowhere again, being in-between places suited him at the moment.

The tour had broken even at The Religious Zone, Powdermouth having planned, predicted and delivered it almost to the day and whilst no-one was strictly doing this for the money, there was always a lightening relief that the rest of the tour was bonus-time, a cultural left-over from the early days when the band leaked money whilst establishing itself.

This had the lightest touch on Riot, who, whilst remaining on good terms with everyone, was little more than peripheral at this point, present really only in performance. Kick, of course, knew why and also that there was nothing he could do but watch and wait.

Zip, likewise, was quieter; although actual quiet might be too far a stretch, he seemed reflective to an increasing extent since leaving The Religious Zone, his busy verbal flurries spasmodic and situational, any great debates in his world now almost all internal.

Even Bat, whose significant natural intelligence allowed him to pace the tour better than most, wore the air of patient deliberation, a dressing he took off only in the moments before going onstage.

In this context it was easy for Kick to follow his instinct and spend a night away from the touring party with a group of Out-Of-Towners, on the eve of their arrival at another population centre.

With night falling he walked into the camp and was greeted with typical warmth, offered food and a seat around the fire it was being cooked upon. Some knew him, others knew of him, or knew of those like him, and the conversation was instantly relaxed, unguarded. Feeling safe and welcome, Kick did not hide his air of concern.

Llo Shinoby, watching his flickering image through the flames as he spoke to the others finally asked, 'What's on your mind Kick?' and the group, knowing that the small-talk was done, settled into a supportive silence as Kick turned to her.

'The usual,' he replied, knowing that they would understand, 'but this time it's darker, more determined, more like an end game.'

And as if to consolidate this, the faintest of sounds in his left ear, or perhaps – hopefully – a misheard sound a long way in the distance, Mister Five's voice imploring him again.

If it had ever been there it was gone before Llo Shinoby spoke again, looking around the group before doing so to establish that she spoke for them all.

'It's easier for us Kick, we don't have as much that they want as you; trading with them is a pragmatism we adopt to feed our children. Mostly it's just the mouth-breathers that we encounter – no-one high up – but even they know that, though they could, it wouldn't be prudent for them to just take from us. We know how the land works here, buying food from us guarantees a fine meal…stealing that food…well, we also know what might cause someone to spend a day or two wondering if some rather unpleasant stuff will ever stop shooting out of their body.'

The group smiled, either at the idea or the memory; Kick thought the latter.

'The bottom line,' continued Llo Shinoby, 'is that, beyond that, we don't get involved. We can't change them, never will, but there's an intelligence in co-operation or, at least non-confrontation. It suits us. And in the end we make sure that our behaviour is affected by the good people in our lives, not the bad.'

'It's different for you Kick, we know that. They actively pursue you, want you involved and maybe they are right, maybe you can do good things with them from a position of higher profile, power and influence.'

They all laughed but Llo Shinoby continued through her own smile, 'Seriously, it is for you to decide how you want them in your life. Just be sure and there will be nothing to worry about.'

Kick felt certain there was something he should add, some thanks he should offer but another member of the group broke the stillness after Llo Shinoby had finished speaking by asking, 'So…off to Destination Beautiful tomorrow then…?'

'For my sins,' said Kick to the group, each of them pantomiming fearful body language, some cowering, others peeking through their fingers.

'I have an audience with you-know-who…' added Kick.

'Oh, that's got to hurt,' said Llo Shinoby, biting her lower lip.

'You might want to go to Maskelyne after that,' threw in one of the elders and the suggestion was so ridiculous that Kick laughed loud and hard before realising that he laughed alone, the faces around the fire kind – but not one of them even smiling.

♪

He camped with The Out-Of-Towners that night, laying his head down, half-dreading, half looking forward to Destination Beautiful, his head full of thoughts of equality and how it had finally stuck – or had managed to somehow more effectively muddle through – despite so many disparate views as to what it actually meant and just as many disparate degrees of giving a damn.

For some women, like a new pair of shoes, equality was something they really, really wanted then disinterestedly left neglected at the back of the cupboard, casual with the certainty of its acquisition; for others it was boldly taking the initiative and defining for themselves exactly what equality was.

Others had been happy with how things had always been; many had found themselves scorned and made to feel inferior or lacking in ambition – not by men but members of their own sex who belittled their position as something negative, their lack of appetite to 'have it all' as an unthinking retrograde compliance.

For others still, it was a simple matter of taking rather than hoping to be given.

Kick dreamt uncomfortable dreams of that unimaginable time in The Past, before equality, before it had dawned on women what it was that made them equal. Before they had realised that they had had it all along and that it had always been so.

♪

Kick sat in the reception of the offices of the City Leader in Destination Beautiful, sinking deeper into the softest of leather seats, discomforted only by knowing that its generous accommodation was not designed for his benefit.

Gradually easing towards the floor as his weight squeezed the air out of the main cushion, he found himself looking upwards to the receptionist at the desk in front of him, a deliberate indignity, knowingly compounded by what would be a struggling, graceless fight – ending with no obvious winner – as he extracted himself from the chair's cynical embrace once he was finally called through.

The calculated wait he was now being put through had given him time to absently gaze at the receptionist. Really pretty, typically. Long lashes and bee-stung lips that now formed the words, 'You can go through now Mr. Vivid.'

On unfavourable terms Kick negotiated a mangled release from his seating circumstance, gathered himself and strode through the heavy door into the office beyond.

Closing the door behind him, he said, 'Hot receptionist.'

'He's a cunt,' said Myelle from behind her desk, 'but he works well.'

Myelle had the kind of face that, if she was fat, people would say she would be really pretty if only she lost some weight. Except she wasn't fat and she wasn't pretty, her face a maelstrom of restless tension, the crisp impatience of her manner – so far tempered and relatively placid much to Kick's relief – was one of the many reasons that had Zip unapologetically asserting that she put the 'urgh' into 'girl'.

She played relentlessly with the curly black springs of her hair in a manner that suggested she thought it wasn't her obsession alone, that everyone else adored it too and whilst this narcissism didn't quite extend to Myelle believing she was God, she was damn sure that God would fancy her and Kick was just as sure that, should she deign to let the Divine deity deliver her a delicious denouement, then she would be damn sure not to let it show.

A living, breathing advocate of equality defined as women behaving as badly as the worst men, rather than men being expected to raise their game to that of the best women, she was furious if she didn't get wolf-whistled as she passed workmen. She had, in fact, sacked several mystified employees for just such a crime.

If thinking men had ever been waiting around for a general consensus amongst women as to what constituted equality before simply going along with it, then Myelle would have been the fly in all the ointments.

Yet, by definition, she was a profound product of a playing field she insisted on being level, never needing to weaken men to be strong herself.

'He fucks me off,' she said, finally looking up, 'but he also fucks me often.'

Not long after The Past ended, a consortium of dissatisfied women began the 'Damn, These Clothes Are

Comfortable' label, a reaction that, in retrospect, many considered overdue.

Inspired by, and contemptuous of, the fashion industry and its barely hidden disregard for real women, it first began as a movement on social media with women decrying a trade in which gay men and other women seemed coldly hell-bent on crushing the female form into ill-suited, cruelly-shaped, impractical clothes, before subliminally mocking them for being out of date and in need of the next collection of ill-suited, cruelly-fitting, impractical clothes.

This cycle had repeated not yearly but several times yearly, endorsed, supported and normalised by a coercive media for whom bone-thin, clearly unhealthy models were held up not even as reasonably-shaped but as ideals, albeit ones that looked as though vacuums had been inserted into their rear-ends to be sure that all possible moisture had been extracted, thereby achieving an apparent desiccation so total in the quest for the ultimate industry-compliant rejection of the female form that they looked as though they might crinkle should you touch them.

If it was true that these women were beautiful, it was only because they were gifted with faces that were beautiful when unnaturally lean and it was out of this insidious misogyny that a movement grew, one that loved women, didn't hold them in contempt, didn't try to shape them into little boys and from this concept, so came the clothing line of stylish, comfortable, generous and understanding garments championed by almost all women and worn by many.

Whilst having little empathy for the cause – or anything really – and considering fashion as being for those who never grew out of dressing up games, Myelle caught the wave just right, bought the company and with shrewd cunning and ruthless focus, turned it into a marauding monster, a commercial venture gorging on money to the point of throwing it back up in quantities seemingly always more than it had swallowed in the first place.

She wore power suits herself, though. Naturally.

Drowning in money offered no concern for Myelle, built as she was for it, believing, as she did, that she deserved not only its endless flow but the influence it bought and brought and – in an echelon still mostly inhabited by men – her consequent aggressive arrival at the level of City Leader genuinely put the cat amongst the pigeons or, as she once put it to Kick in a rare show of word-play wit, the pussy amongst the cocks.

She had invested some of her wealth and influence in the movie industry, making the move deliberately into so-called 'chick flicks' – oft-complained about as being an overlooked genre – but having sat through the Premiere screening of the inaugural production, had been so exasperated by comments like 'Oh my God did you see the main character's awful dress?' from the departing sisterhood that, her contempt refreshed, she refused to enter the market again.

It had only been a small proportion of the audience but for her it was enough.

It made her no money after all and if there was money to be made, she reasoned, some man would probably have done it ages ago.

Myelle scorned those women that wanted all the success of an aggressive competitive male without bringing the same qualities to the contest and, whilst many women felt that to do so might involve losing much of what was good about them, Myelle delighted in being blessed in abundance with the attributes required for a straight fight.

Including the motivation. And the ego.

She had once told Kick that, as a young girl, she had heard her class mates comment that if men had periods then period pain would have been fixed years ago and it was this innocent light-hearted banter, almost in isolation, that had fired both her ambition and her contempt.

That women could not solve their own problems, accepted that men could, and then used that as a stick to beat them with, appealed to her budding sense that everyone other than her was just plain stupid.

A few years later, crippled herself by period pains of an especially punishing kind, she resolved that she would be the one to eliminate this. And, beating many profit-chasing companies who had tried and failed to do so, she did – not for profit (and definitely not for womankind) but for herself. This was an obstacle in her way and an opportunity to make more money from those 'cunting bints who couldn't sort it out for themselves' was how she had put it to Kick when describing how she had used her wealth to finally fund the research to stamp all over – and benefit from – her erstwhile classmates' mentality.

Being canny enough to realise that including U.S. in a share of the proceeds and have access to their labs would be financially more beneficial than paying their taxes and taking all the risks was just one of the ways she had come to their attention and impressed them enough to be in the position she was in now.

But it was in staying ahead of the competition that Myelle spent most of her time. Not for her a satisfied complacency; enough was never enough – she would have a hard time defining it anyway – and she had a focussed, myopic eye for any young pretender to her crown.

She saw youth generally as having one aim and that was to kill her and take her place – most definitely not offer her a job.

Pioneers often don't reap the rewards of the efforts they expend, the long-term benefits being for an ungrateful later generation to take for granted and, being abhorrent to Myelle, this, coupled with a ferocious lack of patience, was what fuelled her urgent rise.

That and seeing everyone as competition. That needed beating.

Kick knew he would have to work to hold his own today.

It would be hard to say that he liked Myelle, just as hard to say he didn't. Her fiery unpredictability always made for compelling viewing and its impact was often so intense that Kick actually had a kind of soft spot for her, this cynical white female.

Almost as though she was part of him.

'You're looking good Vivid,' opined Myelle, peering closely at the well-camouflaged discomfort of Kick's face before adding, 'Are you one of those fuckwits who's had a little nip and tuck?'

Kick was happy to be interrupted as he instinctively opened his mouth to reply since he actually had no words to say.

'Arseholes. You'd think that by the time you're old enough to get wrinkles you'd have enough maturity to fucking realise that there's more to life than smooth fucking skin. Fuck that. Wrinkles are earned. Why give away so casually what you've earned the hard way?'

Myelle took Kick's continued silence as an invitation to keep talking. She would, in fact, have taken Kick having a heart attack on the floor in front of her as an invitation to keep talking.

'Yeah…you're one of the better examples of the species to reach land…why haven't I fucked you yet?'

Taken by surprise by the directness of the question, Kick scrambled for a response, a drowning man clutching at possible straws somewhere in the more appropriate catalogue of Riot's recent vocabulary.

'Just lucky I guess,' he said and sat very, very still as he realised how badly his panic had let him down.

Not unusually, Myelle wasn't listening and talked over his frozen body-language.

'I mean, you're a boy and I'm a girl but that doesn't have to get in the way…' a ghost of a smile played across her face, '…eh?'

Kick, relaxing, found this playfulness a little easier to deal with.

'I wouldn't trust you to treat me right, make me feel pretty,' he said with a smile.

Myelle barked an approving laugh, making Kick jump a little but the sense that his flippancy had put him on thin ice was hardly alleviated when the first words she then said were, 'Fuck you pal,' before continuing with, 'You know the expression the birds and the bees just means that when you get involved with a chick there's always a sting in the tail.'

She barked again at her own joke; Kick jumped a little once more.

'We should get a padded room and do it properly,' she said almost to herself.

'Anyway,' Myelle said, back in the room, 'I'm the bitch...*you* have to charm me.'

'Well, I'm the sensitive, artistic type...I'd probably write you a song.'

Myelle, playing with her hair some more, put one hand over her heart before asking in the least sincere way possible, 'Oh, how could I resist?'

'You're a girl, you'll find a way,' ventured Kick, appearing less concerned by the potential response than he actually felt.

Myelle let the room go quiet, used the silence, pressed it against Kick before lightly stating, 'I'll let you live for now,' before adding remotely, 'If I was evolution, I might not be quite so generous.'

Silence returned less threateningly but still Kick started a little when Myelle spoke again.

'For fuck's sake. Already they're dumb enough to not have The Insurance, right? Think about it, you're gonna do it when you're older, right? I mean, what happens if you forget you've had it, look in the mirror and haven't a fucking clue who the fuck that is staring back at you 'cos you don't look like *you* anymore?'

It took Kick a while to realise that Myelle was back on the subject of cosmetic surgery, this time with a dark reference to failing memory in older people.

'You're gonna be one frightened, freaked out cunt at that point, eh? Fucking *hell*! It's not like you ever look like yourself after having it anyway. Right? Twats!'

'Maybe celebrities only do it so they can have a lucrative sideline in being their own look-alike?' offered Kick.

The room went silent again, Myelle staring at Kick.

He didn't need any of his empathic skills to realise that only she cracked the funnies in this office, that he'd pushed his luck with several, that she resented not having thought of that one herself, that she admired the speed of his thought, his humour and his bold bravado in being in her space and genuinely occupying it in the way he did.

All these thoughts and more twirled around her head, much as her curls twirled around her right index finger as she regarded Kick.

'Cunt,' she said.

Kick, having waited long enough for an invitation, finally sat down in the seat opposite Myelle, a small presumption he seemed to get away with.

She regarded him with a steady gaze and said almost dreamily, 'Let musicians be musicians, they're no fucking good for anything else.'

Kick regarded his nails absently, waited. He didn't have to wait for long.

'Men,' said Myelle and Kick thought the word sounded demoralisingly like a ready steady for today's vitriol to come racing out of Myelle's mouth. He only hoped that it was something that he could observe, unlike many times in the past, where its gushing energy sucked him in as an unwilling participant with no finishing line in sight, the friction of Myelle's fury rubbing increasing heat into the situation, only the resistance of her own boredom providing the brake, its application birthing a spitting heat of decreasing sparks as she might quieten into edgy latency.

'They lack a certain intelligence…'

She almost added, 'Don't you think?' but didn't since she really didn't care what Kick thought.

'They need A, B, C not A, C, B rearrange. Dickheads.'

She leaned over the desk a fraction and skewered Kick with a stare.

'Don't misunderstand me. Women are arseholes too, let's be honest. Stupid fuckers.'

She leaned back before qualifying her statement with, 'All men are bastards 'cos women keep marrying arseholes and then spend their time complaining about it. Whining little cunts. Like it, ignore it or leave it, bitch.'

Her eyes widened, looked at nothing. She shook her head.

'They'll carp and moan about a man's fucking libido right up to and beyond the point they need to manipulate it for their own needs. Arseholes. You would have thought evolution would have weeded *that* out by now.'

She rolled her fists near her eyes in a mock crying gesture to demonstrate her contempt and Kick really didn't like the way this was going, could think of no way to stop it.

'Hysterical little bitches. Trust me, they can control their fucking feelings when they can control their man.'

And with that, she spun her chair and – facing away from Kick – looked out of the window and Kick appreciated the respite in whatever form it arrived; sadly, too brief on this occasion.

Revolving back to Kick, Myelle said, 'I don't think of myself as male or female. Why the fuck should I? That gets me nowhere. Fucking nowhere. Men have their uses of course, I'm not sexist Kick; if I hate something I don't notice the fucking sex now do I?'

Kick sat there returning her gaze, wondering if she actually wanted an answer to that, decided that, even if she did, he didn't know the right one. Stayed quiet. Wondered where this was going. Still.

Myelle spun away again, an oddly girly move, allowing the chair to keep spinning, bringing her round to face him as she pointedly said, 'Women? We *only* give life, right?' echoing Bubon from what seemed years ago now and then, as the chair turned away from him again added, mockingly, 'Gotta have a word with Mother Nature about this patriarchal society,' the chair settling to a stop, Myelle once again facing Kick.

Her tone suggested that it might only be Mother Nature with whom she was prepared to have anything like a reasonable discussion on the subject, although Kick wasn't even sure that what he was involved in was a discussion, this tour punctuated as it was, by invitations from City Leaders apparently committed to preaching to his static, seated self.

Myelle looked at him as though the same thought – 'Why are you here?' – was crossing her mind too, her body languid as she did so. She leaned forward, a lazy flex, and rested her elbows on the desk.

'It still – *still* – seems to be news to some women that some of us don't fit the fucking template expected of us.

Happy hookers? Oh golly, surely not; surely they're coerced and unhappy. Bullshit. Fucking remedial thinking. We're not violent either right?'

She fixed Kick with a stare that left no doubt in his mind that this really wasn't a question that needed answering.

'Men don't think like that…men don't think…generally!'

She barked that laugh again, sat back, continued, 'When they do, though, they are not cluttered by the personal. They want to get ahead of other men, sure, but really, it's about getting ahead of everyone. Women just want to bring other women down. Stupid cunts.'

'Some women,' offered Kick involuntarily, again this echo from his meeting with Bubon [how he would prefer to be there right now] – was this scripted or something?

'Shut the fuck up,' responded Myelle, confirming the assessment Kick had about the status of this interaction as a discussion.

'The whole world is distracted by fucking relationships, ones they used to have, ones they are in, ones they want. They make dumb fucking decisions based on emotional need. Fucking idiots might think long and hard about a fucking tattoo of a little daisy on their cute little dimpled butt cheek, ooh it's going to be there forever – but they'll happily commit the rest of their lives to another person on the bizarre basis that they make their body leak the right type of fluid or some such fucking bollocks.'

Myelle had talked herself up in volume and intensity and reached a crescendo of, 'Twats!'

A brief silence – the end of the first movement – before, 'Not successful people Vivid, not successful people.'

'That depends on how you define success,' attempted Kick.

'Cocksucker,' said Myelle.

Kick studied his nails again.

'No,' said Myelle, brightening, 'it's a good point. You're successful in your own way aren't you? Sitting here with me as you are.'

Kick was never sure if Myelle was joking and that remained the case now.

'You go about your business with a touch of class Kick, no doubt, never the star. You never let yourself become too big a personality – you know the art would get overlooked if you did and you would be little more than another talented attention seeker, another fucking fame whore. I get it. You see fame for what it is, a teenage fantasy that some people never fucking grow out of.'

Kick didn't allow himself the luxury of being complimented, braced himself instead for the point that Myelle was getting round to making.

'But fame – or your definition of success – is not power Kick. But that is within reach of you,' said Myelle, making it.

'Most people don't like powerful people Kick – at least when they meet them – and that's because powerful people genuinely don't give a shit about most people. We're arseholes in that way. But we're arseholes that employ people, get stuff fucking done. I know you've met many in your profession – those that want success just *so* they can look down on people.'

Kick recognised the narcissists she referred to, could picture the little gang of obliging sycophants they dragged around, and pontificated to, without resistance.

Myelle continued fleshing out the subject for her captive audience.

'We're driven. I've tried to switch off my ambition because it's fucking tiring but all I end up doing is sitting there getting impatient with growing older as each and every second ticks by pointlessly.'

When she went on to say, 'So, if I try and relax, I tend to just get angry,' Kick thought wryly that, in the time he had known her, she must have been relaxed quite a lot.

Despite the company, his thoughts drifted beyond the room, towards and about the gravity of anger, how it draws everything in around it, insists on the primacy of itself, an effortless transformer of things positive to things negative, yet the driver behind the opposite when on its best behaviour.

Little was as hungry as anger and only a few things motivated in the same way – he thought of Malt and his loneliness, of Bubon and the sadness he carried and how power, as it was with Myelle's anger, was the treatment of choice for each.

'So instead, I succumb to it,' Myelle went on as Kick regained his focus, 'accept my nature. And fuck me is that a feeling of liberation. You should try it sometime. I'm free to do whatever I fucking feel like and fuck anyone else and that separates me from just about everyone. Especially fucking women. Fucking whining little fucktwats. Yeah, I know it's fucking different Now but what was all that looking to men to hand over a little equality shit? What…the…fuck…*was…THAT*?'

And before Kick had debated whether this was,

perhaps, the first time Myelle had actually wanted an answer and had time to construct a response, she went on.

'It's the behaviour of losers is what it fucking well is. All this fucking bleating about male aggression and how the world would be better without it. You *think*? Macho gets things done. Macho wins. Macho is fucking evolution. Macho is "yes I can" and macho doesn't wimp out and go on the mush when I want a good seeing to. Rejecting macho is the indulgence of those comfortable enough to no longer need it. Macho puts food on the table. Male fucking aggression? We would be nowhere without it…and *why* do they have it?'

No way was Kick answering that one, wondering as he was, who the enemy was in Myelle's eyes at the moment.

'They have it because they have no fucking choice. They can't give birth. The lame arsewits are left with the dregs of creation, we should feel sorry for them. Bless.'

Kick concluded, not for the first time, that everyone was the enemy in Myelle's eyes, her rhetoric becoming increasingly vicious, her tone increasingly alarming as she gathered momentum.

'They have to work hard for their successes too. They've needed their aggression. Medicinal, mechanical, architectural, cultural, you fucking name it, it's been a struggle. Why the fuck did men give ground? It was the only ground they had, the poor fucking saps. Women? All they have to do is pour a beer down a man's neck and, hey presto. Nine months later, pop! Another genius piece of creation. Shove a dummy in its mouth and stick it with the others. We find it fucking *easy*! Men…equal to *us?!*'

Myelle had stood involuntarily as she spoke, arms straight, fists pressing into her desktop as she loomed towards her seated guest.

Slowly, she sank back into her seat, not once taking her eyes off Kick.

Holding his gaze, calmly, almost playfully she said, 'Pop! Here, have another one. Pop! Oh, and another,' without any expression on her face.

'It's not really male aggression that's of any use though is it Kick? That's not quite true, is it?'

As an empath, his guard could be up no higher and Kick trusted these measured tones less than the ferocity of her previous monologue, allowing as it did – as he knew it would – a greater room to expand into, the potential for a quickening run to an inevitable explosive leap.

'Powerful people aren't necessarily male, it's just that the male of the species is more likely to have the traits that seek and desire power…plus they can operate within the parameters of "it's not fair" better…'

A pause.

'Sexism,' she thrust at Kick, 'was a kind of inappropriate behaviour, almost always an abuse of power. Did those fucking girls think that men were never subject to similar things, every day? It just wasn't of a sexual or gender-based nature. Despite what those whinging little girls think, there was no meeting where all the men of the world got together and designed a plan to exclude women from positions of power.

Powerful men – if you want to see the powerful of the

world as men – want to exclude *everyone* from positions of power, not just poor little girlies.'

'Stupid, self-deluding cunts always looking to men to hand a little down to them from the top table, oh please can we join you, please. Did powerful *men* ask that? Did they fuck. They wanted power, they took it.

Took a long time for that penny to drop with the dumb fucks of my sex didn't it? And they *were* dumb fucks 'cos what kind of cock-snot-dripping pussy goes looking to *men* for any kind of answers? Eh?'

No, Kick still wasn't going to answer any questions.

It would be inaccurate to describe Myelle as angry, her demeanour so totally, universally aggressive and contemptuous as to be, in her own manner, some kind of normal but Kick sensed the meeting was coming to an end, either through Myelle reaching a frothing peak or by him simply not being prepared or able to take any more of this.

He was beginning to taste the hate in the room, its crowding spite finding a voice in the increasing volume of Myelle's words.

He prepared to stand, Myelle no doubt sensing it, the lightless coals of her eyes somehow resisting the fires deeper in her, remaining resolutely, coldly black.

'I have those traits Vivid. I want the power. I want the fear. I want the real-estate. I want men to fuck – at my fingertips – and I want to send them away with their tails between their legs but *only* when I have had exactly enough of them being between mine. Some little man giving *me* power? Fuck YOU! I *take* it.'

Standing again now, tight against her desk, the obstacle preventing her from reaching out and grabbing

Kick as she made her point and lost some of her control… willingly.

'I don't need anyone to give me a fucking thing. Food, space, resources…power is always taken. Such is power, such is the nature of power and such is the nature of those who seek it. And don't be some fucking stupid cunt who wants me to be reasonable about it. Wanting to win is unreasonable but don't *ever* forget that evolution likes winners. You think an invading army ever thinks it's wrong? You think founder members of anything designed to succeed are fucking nice guys? You think improvement is *fair*? Evolution is fucking *fair*?

You want my fucking power? You come and fucking take it from me bitch. 'Cos I tell you, I've had a few meetings of my own. I agreed with myself to suppress everyone, I want *no-one* to earn what I earn, I want *no-one* to have the power I have.

Whatever it is that you're given, someone else had to earn and you can tell those who have been given what they have – you take it away and they have nothing. Not me.

I am not interested in being given a fucking *thing*. I *earned* my power, it's *mine*. It cost me. So, if you're sure, come and get it, I'm ready for you. Fucking *arseholes*!

But even if you manage to take it, I am the same. I am Queen Cunt of Pussy Palace and that's how it fucking *stays*!'

Kick stood, enough of this.

Myelle's breezy reaction: 'Oh how nice, you're offering to fuck off.'

'Why am I here Myelle?'

She looked at him, an expression of unfeigned surprise on her furious face, innocence in a grotesque mask.

'Because you want to know you stupid fucking shit. Fucking musicians! Shit! Power is a spread-legged temptation for you too and don't fucking deny it…yeah, yeah, the humble sensitive artist. Tell it to the birds Vivid…you're big thing is that you don't want anyone to notice that you want to be noticed.

You're not so different. You're here for the close-up so do it…get a load of *me*.'

Kick was at the door of the office, moments from fresh air, any air that wasn't shared with Myelle.

He had barely taken his eyes off her at any point, the catastrophic potential of a black hole almost behind him now, not yet to be trusted as safely so, compelling all the same.

'What does Powdermouth know, Kick?' she asked as he turned the door handle.

She smiled, a smug, poisonous smile knowing that, despite Kick's best efforts to hide a reaction, the question had caught him by surprise.

He opened the door, turned away from her for the first time since he entered her office and as he stood in the doorway, she took him by surprise again.

'Who's supporting you tonight?'

After a moment of regaining his bearings he replied, 'Tits and Misses and Ma'am-a-Lady, I think.'

Saying the names reminded him, reassured him, that there was a world outside Myelle's office, it just happened to be Destination Beautiful and whilst these were all-female bands in her own spiky image, there were fewer women in Destination Beautiful than you might at first imagine.

'You're going on first bitch,' said Myelle and Kick realised that he had not, in fact, got away with sitting without invitation.

Sometimes it's a big thing to let the little things go and Myelle, clearly, would no more do that than a fish separated from its protective shoal would consider it a welcome opportunity for some time alone.

'Myelle,' he said, his relaxed tone hiding his irritation that tonight's stage times were now non-negotiable and had always been in Myelle's gift, 'I thought you said that nothing was personal.'

Myelle placed the fingers of each hand on her cheeks, batted her eyelids in the time-worn spoof of femininity and said, 'Oh golly, I guess I'm a girl after all.'

Kick turned to leave again and after a weighted beat of sly silence, Myelle spoke to his back, softly for the first time.

'You took on the promise Kick, it's why you're here. And you haven't got a moment to spare.'

Kick faced her again but the Myelle of just a moment before was gone.

She picked up the phone in her desk, punished some buttons and before giving her full attention to the call, looked up at Kick and said simply, 'Fuck off.'

Kick stood in the reception area with much on his mind, his numbed antenna finally relaxing and tuning into something coming from the receptionist.

It touched him that, despite the thick hide this pretty

boy clearly had to have to be able to work daily in Myelle's hell, somehow it was Kick that was his hero.

Kick smiled at him, thanked him and left, wondering, 'Well…what does your hero do now?'

Chapter Seventeen

Without being aware of having done so, the boy had fished The Great Waters and crossed The Big Nowhere, instinct his internal compass.

He had fed himself and kept safe with a mixture of this instinct and things he had learned from the land and those Out-Of-Towners that he had encountered along the way.

Periodically he had been struck by illness, usually from misjudging a food source and whilst it was certainly true that he had been lucky not to have a significant injury that may have become infected, the natural remedies and know-how taught to him by the Out-Of-Towners would have been the solution to all but the most serious.

Beyond that, the uncomplicated reality of his status as a member of the species firmly at the top of the food chain rendered him incomparably robust in most circumstances.

It was with a sense of his journey nearing an end that he came low over the brow of a hill and saw the cabin tucked into the side of the hill facing him. His natural response was to duck down, take his profile off the sky-line, despite it being months since his earlier naivety would have left him exposed in such a way.

A fixed abode was not necessarily a sign of a welcoming inhabitant and the positioning of the cabin, set back into the dense woods that covered the hill above and beyond it so that it could really only be seen from the position the boy was now in, suggested an occupant that valued privacy.

He had to retrace his steps before he found an appropriate pathway that would allow him to approach the cabin from another aspect and offer him the option of bypassing it altogether if he considered that wise.

With the stealth that had served him so well for months he watched the cabin for signs of life, feeding himself berries, his legs gently swinging from the sturdy head-high branch that served as a discreet vantage point, slightly above, slightly behind.

It was after about fifteen minutes that the tree disappeared, the boy falling upwards at the same time as the forest's carpet of mushrooms, bugs and weeds spun so that he had to look up to see the ground.

Only when things started falling out of his pockets did he realise that he was upside down and it was a short while after that before he realised he was being held there by whoever it was that had pulled him out of the tree by his leg.

The boy did not feel threatened, only totally helpless as his entire set of belongings fell past his ears and onto the ground.

With eerie silence, the man had approached the boy.

'What do you want kid?' he now asked in a voice with the rasp of a struck match, no obvious humour in its deep tones.

Not yet sure of his circumstances, the boy replied, 'I was just passing by. Sorry to disturb you. I'll just be moving on.'

'Are you going to The City then?' the man asked, lowering the boy gently to the ground, rolling him out and releasing his ankle only at the last stage so that the boy would not be hurt.

The boy stood, brushed leaves off his clothing and, having gathered his belongings, looked up at the man. He looked up a long way.

Hammer Flower was not a giant – although he was tall – but his presence was immense. His frame was blessed with a natural athleticism, each component in place, working properly, efficiently, an effortless postural precision that amounted to a potent whole.

Yet it was the eyes, the collected set of the facial features that displayed Hammer Flower's true strength because, in addition to the graceful flow of his body, there was the allied discipline of a mind that was even stronger.

In all athletes and performers of a physical nature, the body is secondary, a vehicle for the ambition of thought, a machine to be brought under control and trained to fulfil the mind's needs. Having a naturally athletic, flexible or strong physique was little more than a good start; the competitor was the cognitive and the first battle it ever needed to win was making its host perform to its will.

Hammer Flower looked like he had won that battle on a permanent basis.

Impressive even now, as a man clearly well into his retirement, a still rider on the well-trained beast of burden that was his body, its purring engine willingly and thrillingly held on – and needing only the lightest of touches from – his mind's leash. Ready.

Once the boy had stopped staring, he asked, 'What city?'

Hammer Flower gestured with his head in a direction over the boy's.

'Through the forest that way,' but he knew by then that the boy had not intended that journey, at least not knowingly.

'Come on,' he said, 'let's get you something to eat.'

♪

For the next week or so the boy stayed with Hammer Flower, setting up a bare but comfortable personal space in the small, cosy shed behind the cabin, even more snugly fitted into the woods than the cabin itself.

The man had a manner that, at first, had made the boy intend to stay just one night before moving on but, like a dog paralysed by some behind-the-ears scratching that was unpleasant, or maybe not, the brusque stimulation that made him want to leave also held him oddly hypnotised and reluctant to actually do so.

Clean water, relative comfort, safety and warmth completed the convincing.

In addition to what he already knew and had picked up from the Out-Of-Towners, he learnt much in that time from the older, more experienced man. New ways to hunt and fish, of spotting natural indicators of other things, be more humane.

'We eat so that we can be eaten,' described Hammer Flower, 'but along the way, we show no cruelty. Dying is a function of living but it should never be casual.'

The boy had always known this of course but it was an increasing reality to him the more he had travelled – as, too, had his awareness of others become. His learning curve had been steep in so many ways but his receptiveness to others' moods and needs (and often their intentions) had grown, developing naturally so that at no point did his increasing sensitivity to it surprise or alarm him.

His emotional vocabulary was limited so, on the tenth day of his stay, as Hammer Flower cut the lightened tips out of his hair, giving him a more mature look, he didn't know that it was shame, regret and guilt that was coming from the older man, just that there was a kind of sadness in his life.

He did now know, however, that it had been there for some time.

From Hammer he felt a sudden, brief flash of something that could have been irritation, fear, concern. It was gone as soon as it had appeared but the man requested that the boy go to the shed and allow him some time alone.

Brushing the hair from his neck, the boy said lightly that he would wash first. The man said no, now please, wash later and the boy did not argue.

Hammer Flower had seen Frankie Finesse coming over the brow of the same hill that the boy had appeared on somewhat more discreetly over a week ago. But then Frankie always did like to be noticed, even as the earthy terrain of the countryside wrestled with the urbane sophistication of his appearance in a jolting clash of styles.

Hammer Flower knew what this was about and after a glance to check the boy was out of sight, stepped out onto the veranda of the cabin to greet the approaching visitor.

Hammer knew someone would come and thinking about it now, as the elegantly-dressed figure narrowed the distance between them with each focussed stride, it was no surprise that it would be Frankie.

Dedicated and hard-working, Frankie was rising smoothly through the ranks at U.S., not least because he might just turn up on someone like Hammer Flower, alone and unannounced. He had a big future, one that would be rewarded by his employers who would be relaxed in the knowledge that it would be almost impossible to overpay him into complacency.

His commitment was only marginally less to his appearance, his long, tailored coat hugging his slim frame with a kind of love, the overall impression of finery barely dented by the slightly innocuous, muddied walking boots.

Yet somehow, like one of those girls who can wear white all day without picking up a single dark mark, the rest of his clothes and the small leather case he carried remained resolutely mud-free.

Frankie stopped at the foot of the steps leading up to where Hammer Flower stood on his veranda, calmly placed the suitcase on the upper step and sat alongside it, facing away. He removed his boots without a word, placing them on the grass before opening the case to reveal an immaculate pair of leather brogues which he put on, his beautiful face a study in considered attention, taking care that their soles at no point touched a muddy or grassy surface.

Finally, standing on the lower step as perhaps the only man to put shoes on before going indoors, he turned to face Hammer Flower who said, 'Don't you owe me money?'

Frankie's face stifled his sunburst of a smile and responded, 'I'll pay you a penny at a time on the rare occasions that I give a damn.'

'Come in Frankie,' said Hammer Flower and the cordial formalities over, they sat together on the veranda, two dangerous men.

Frankie sat poised, a neat, lean presence, thirty years younger than the other man and with a face that had drawn many a jealous response from threatened men bluntly intent on making it less attractive to their girlfriends, a challenge Frankie never failed to rise to.

He had convinced many of them to take time out to reflect on their behaviour from the luxury of a hospital bed.

He now sat in front of Hammer Flower, as dazzling as ever, almost totally still, except for occasionally removing a tiny piece of fluff from somewhere on his attire but Hammer knew that, beneath the surface, Frankie's ambition was as restless as a peacetime marine.

Not so long ago they had worked together, worked together a lot, and in a business that meant neither were likely to ever again expect the best of people instead of the worst.

In The Past, gambling was nothing, an embryonic idea, barely formed in comparison to Now.

Maybe it was the fact that immortality was on offer and with the yin of this utopian step forward came the yang of concern as to what the quality of that life might be without significant funds. Maybe it was the only thrill left. Maybe it was a way that the cynical made money from those with compulsions, addictive personalities or low resistance to seductive marketing strategies promising unimaginable wealth in the foreground with only the slightest hint of despair, bankruptcy or any other downside vaguely framed in an out-of-focus background.

Maybe it was all of the above but the hardest, coldest and most ruthless of all businesses neatly – and many would argue reasonably – kept their responsibilities where they wanted them to be in this particular dance with the twinkle-toed 'Please Gamble Responsibly' proviso on all of its literature.

Whether this was enough or not is, was and always will be a moot point given that this business never runs out of willing customers, whether it be the legitimate business or the black market version. U.S. had interests in both and paid attention with a personal touch wherever it could; the right personality, in possession of the right kind of bank account would be identified, isolated and encouraged to engage with the black market where the odds on offer were more attractive but where the interest rates on any debts or roll-overs left no doubt as to who was in charge.

The law always operates with a lighter touch when protecting the poor so U.S. was inclined to leave them struggling with legitimate bookies for whom the odds, the infrastructure and the system typically already worked in its favour.

Besides, the poor had been controlled for centuries by the selective prosecution of particular drug use – drugs no more or less addictive or dangerous but priced to suit the budget of those whose circumstances made them more prone to addiction. Disproportionate sentencing for the use of these drugs, as opposed to those used by the more affluent sectors in society, had made the poor little more than a plaything of a social experiment in the control of populations. Such as it had always been. They were certainly not considered a source of great revenue to U.S.

No, it was the targeted wealthy risk-takers who ended up with Frankie and Hammer at their door, usually after all manner of evasion and delay had failed them.

Hammer had always thought that for order and social cohesion, the law should be such that more money could be made by those who operate within it than by those who don't but if lucrative jobs came up related to illicit funds (that also allowed his essential self a free expression) then who was he to turn it down?

Frankie sat opposite him reflecting on the same shared history, mystified as to how Hammer Flower would end up here, in the middle of nowhere, away from everyone. This was not the Hammer Flower he knew, the one that he had never been able to control (and had never wanted to), the one that had an unparalleled sadistic streak and a catalogue of torture techniques, improvised so effectively that Frankie secretly suspected they had been coldly planned in quietly violent moments alone.

Frankie, who was afraid of almost no-one, except Dessel and a few twisted superimposers, was at least cautious of Hammer Flower, this brutal man who, if he was ever attacked by a shark, would surely come away with its teeth.

To be up here, hiding away from his real self, what he was, seemed as pointless and futile to Frankie as Bigfoot hoping to evade detection by donning a pair of shoes to camouflage his footprints.

He didn't say this to the dangerous man opposite him.

Instead he said, 'You turning into a weird loner or what?'

Hammer Flower replied, 'People will call you a weird loner when they realise that they don't interest you.'

Six feet and silence between the two men, both joking, both violent.

Hammer Flower, as host, moved the conversation on a little, 'I'm not mixing in any new circles, just breaking out from the ones I was going round and round in. Nothing more.'

Silence again. Not tense. They were familiar in each other's company, used to the silence of regularly waiting hours for a mark.

Hammer waited for Frankie to raise the subject he came here to raise, this compact, coiled-spring of a man in front of him who had always made him wary, being strong in different ways to him. As such they had worked well together; Hammer's crushing physicality and the nimble, violent brilliance of Frankie's mind, his cattle prod always out of sight right up until the moment it was needed, building their reputation through results.

Frankie's charm would often lull a shaking target into thinking that when he said, 'Now I'm going to trust that you'll have the money when we return tomorrow,' he really did trust them. Hammer knew better. He knew that Frankie trusted no-one and even if he did, well, you could be as trusting as you like when you're as vengeful as Frankie.

Despite this, Frankie was a professional, recognising that, in this most personal of businesses, little was meant personally; the application of the pressure he had access to was a business concern for him, and he considered that justice should be meted out sober. Revenge was a different thing altogether. Not always necessary – but justifiable if so.

He would often wait outside the house of a mark, business done, justice served, smiling at passers-by, while Hammer, whose definition of necessary was somewhat looser, applied an exacting revenge before feeling his job was fully completed.

Frankie loved his work and he had loved every minute of working with Hammer.

They exchanged a few words catching up but neither man had much time for small talk.

'We're looking for a boy,' said Frankie, 'travelling across The Nowhere. Actually, we are not sure where he is.'

He paused.

'Not even MessHead can see,' he added, a fleeting frown troubling his features for the briefest of moments.

He made a gesture with his right hand that suggested a frustration with this reality before saying, 'There's a reward.'

Hammer Flower replied, 'You know I hate owning money.'

'So take the money and give it to me.'

Two killers smiled before Frankie went on, 'I'm more concerned that, without knowing how important he is, you might have kept him for…your own…needs…'

Frankie knew Hammer very well.

'I cannot deny who I am Frankie but I am here because I don't always have to indulge it.'

Frankie didn't believe him for a moment, the image of Hammer somewhere in the woods behind the cabin with the neck of a wolf in his mouth resonating credibly in his mind.

They spoke a while longer before Frankie got up to leave, asking politely if he could use the bathroom and leaving Hammer on the veranda with his thoughts as he went inside to do so.

He came back out onto the veranda and patiently engaged in the reverse manoeuvre with his shoes, the brogues returning to their loving home after a close inspection for any new dirt or wear, the boots now hugging his feet as he turned back to Hammer Flower.

'They want the boy. He's important.'

'I'll let you know if I come across him,' said Hammer Flower and, without shaking hands, Frankie turned and paced away from the cabin and up the gradual incline of the hill he had come over.

Hammer watched him until he was over the brow, perhaps five minutes' walk away and, as is the way with such men, he watched until there was no more information available and Frankie, too, turned every fifty paces or so to be sure of Hammer's continued attention as he left.

Hammer pushed through the door into the cabin and immediately saw what Frankie would have seen on his bathroom trip; the boy's cut hair on the floor.

He stood there, a long, knowing exhale dropping from him as the picture came into focus. He had been out of the game too long. Missed this angle.

Frankie had shown no reaction, coolly giving no indication of the life-threatening information he possessed as he had returned from the bathroom. He would have known that Hammer would have had no choice but to dismantle him had he known that he had seen the hair and, old partners or not, Hammer would have had no hesitation, his only concession being perhaps to make it quick out of professional respect.

Hammer took a key from his front pocket, stepped towards the cupboard at the far end of the main room. Almost as tall as he was, its doors opened outwards to expose a display of cruel intent, perfect creations from the minds of twisted men who could only have been practising such things since they were boys.

Knives, saws and thumbscrews sat alongside conventional pistols and shotguns. Amongst these were razorblades, a variety of sprays, several customised drills.

Impressed again at the mental strength of his old colleague, Hammer knew he would be back and most definitely with decisive numbers.

Hammer also knew that Frankie would never get to see the boy.

He wondered how long he would have alone with him. Not long, surely, since Frankie would now know that he knew and would move fast.

Despite his urgency, it was with that eerie silence of his that he set off towards the shed at the back of the cabin.

♪

Tick

                                  Tick

    Tick

          Tick

                                                Tick

    Tick

Chapter Eighteen

The owner of the mansion had always proved to be a generous host although his perennial absence meant that the band, whilst benefiting from his largesse at this stage of every tour, knew only that he was a he. Little more.

They knew that he was an appreciative admirer of the band and many years before had approached Powdermouth through discreet channels to offer his house as a resource to save on tour costs.

Perhaps Powdermouth had known beforehand but the first time the band had taken advantage of the offer – and ever since in fact – they had been astonished by the facilities placed at their disposal.

In a vehicle laid on by their host, they had travelled, slow-eyed and weary, along the private track that led to the house, crowded on either side by a forest dense enough to be a jungle in a different climate.

The fatigue disappeared as the forest opened, as though clouds cleared by a sudden wind, swooning into an abrupt space where stood the mansion, a white, multi-mezzanine comfort zone.

As they stepped out of the vehicle and their footsteps on the elegant gravel driveway squeezed the silence out of existence, they were greeted by several smart but informally-dressed staff who, on each occasion that they had stayed, had attended to them with a touch light enough to be almost implied.

This suited the band and crew since not one of them was particularly comfortable with being waited on and the owner's staff made them feel like welcome, not paying, guests.

The owner was, for his part, Powdermouth hinted, cut from the same cloth and knew how to treat such guests. Despite the expansive setting, he was understood to be entirely self-made, his empire having been built with a dogged and focussed development of roadside cafes – starting with a humble mobile stall – which meant that, unlike him, at least his offspring would be born into a world of silver spoons, albeit greasy ones.

It was rumoured that at least some of his income was ill-gotten and when taking in the view of the giant estate for the first time from the rear terrace, the band spreading across it with the entropy of the curious, Kick had considered that at least some of their host's income might be of the kind that was legally tender.

On the last day of their stay on this tour, Kick and Bat – with Iodine dozing in the sun nearby – sat on the giant rear terrace, the house at their backs, the sprinklings of what was left of their considerable lunch tempting them into continued grazing, the conversation stop-starting around repeated, tasty mouthfuls that always seemed enough but actually only served as ongoing appetisers.

Before them, a grassy slope fell away on a comfortable gradient to the glassy surface of a small lake which, not unlike the house guests' continual ingestion, was made endlessly hungry for the river feeding it on its right side by the river leaving it on its left, rushing as it did, to the sea, just visible over the treetops beyond.

Before The Thinning, certain animals had their access to water increasingly limited, creating (somehow) unforeseen and perilously weak links in the food chain. This place, more noticeably than in any of the Population Centres, demonstrated the implacable determination of life and its ability to overcome.

Despite being deceptively far away, the sea threw its salty presence into the air and the combination of this, the dense surrounding forest, the thrusting river deep within it and what seemed to be endless sun, made for a lush natural environment that nurtured good health and well-being.

The band had nicknamed it The Sun Shrine.

Zip sat on the grass, halfway down the slope, out of earshot for Kick and Bat but his body language suggested that the conversation he was having with the journalist was as languid as the lake beyond him. This was the only press that Zip looked forward to – hence the journalist's presence in this of all places – a technical interview about his instruments, sounds and rig.

Today, it wasn't likely that Zip would be asked, as he often was, whether he has names for any of his guitars, to which his answer was only ever, 'No, but they all call *me* Sir.'

Despite working well together, when it came to rock and roll, Kick could appreciate (and value) Zip's intensely technical game but his own was more of a kick-about in the park and he was lost on the subjects he knew Zip was now discussing.

Some guitarists delight in the sounds they can make, others get frustrated that they can't reproduce what they hear in their heads – Zip was neither, somehow conjuring the soundscape inside his head out of his instrument, satisfied yet never impressed by having done so, simply seeing it as his role, one he dedicated himself to with a passion.

Kick could tell, however, that Zip was running low on involvement and – oddly – words. A brief, uninspired flare unworthy of him, questioning why Cinderella's shoe was the only thing that didn't change at midnight, half-heartedly lighting up a false dawn a few days ago, the old Zip not quite igniting.

Yo-Yo loitered discreetly around him. Her work was almost fully executed at this end of the tour and she would share the vehicle with the departing journalist as she herself left the touring party – despite this, her casual body language never fully hid her committed professionalism.

Beyond them, right on the lake edge, sat Riot and his ex-wife, cross-legged, staring out over the water, the easy manner with which they held hands evidence of an intimacy apparent even from a distance.

She had been waiting for them at The Sun Shrine, Powdermouth's instinct for arranging this proving to be well informed.

Riot had stepped off the vehicle to a hand-on-hip greeting of, 'So where are all these women I've been hearing about?'

To which he had replied, 'They're running around somewhere in all the clothes that don't fit you anymore,' but the petulance and defiance had dissolved instantly, or perhaps got crushed between them, as they rushed to hug each other, a gesture that inspired the band to both leave them alone and wonder if they would ever let go of each other again.

Kick had known this of course and the event had prompted Bat to remember what he had meant to tell Kick – that Riot had been so protective and careful with the waitress at The Inn. Kick had known this too, given that the waitress so strongly resembled the woman that Riot was now hugging as though she was his centre of gravity.

Kick had also known that Riot had never actually been what he had appeared to be; he had in fact left a trail of very frustrated women in his wake, the genteel manner with which they were taken home inadequate compensation for the lascivious night they had hoped for.

In Riot's own vernacular, amongst his array of beats, not once had he disturbed an adjacent room with the headboard polka or even a headboard slow shuffle with a dragging beat.

Kick almost laughed at how easily these daft phrases came to him.

Like they were his own.

Instead, he smiled, a little fondly.

And a little sadly – all those women standing open-mouthed, staring at Riot's departing back as he left them respectfully at their door. He had not even kissed the kind of girl who would have understood and not minded him accidentally calling her by his ex-wife's name.

Riot hadn't even been a standard guy, moving too fast for some girls, not fast enough for others – he had not wanted sex so much as wanted sex for the way it made him feel, something that only occurred with any value with the woman he sat with now.

Kick had effortlessly kept Riot's secret, his friend in pain. All these years in pain, across several tours.

Being estranged from his wife had not made Riot suicidal but it had detained his hope and – not unlike Malt, though for perhaps different reasons – he had fallen, without realising it, into simply waiting for his life to end.

Riot would have known that Kick knew the truth and was available to him at any time but he had never taken the opportunity and Kick had little choice but to respect his privacy.

From this distance it was hard to tell whether they were talking or not but easy to tell that they didn't need to and there was a little sorrow in Kick as he considered the time that they had lost, when time is that most precious of things that, when lost, can never be found again.

♪

For weeks prior to this Kick had been waking up and hoping beyond reason that he was looking at a portrait of some tired and distracted stranger whenever he looked in the mirror. He often thought that where you are in life is a balance between your knowledge and your denial and what he knew was that he could not deny that this tour was taking its toll.

The past few days at The Sun Shrine had ironed out a few of the wrinkles and stresses of the last few weeks and topped up his internal resources so that, sitting here in the sun, he felt rested, the image in the mirror each morning still clearly weary but less of a stranger each day.

He knocked around a favourite subject with Bat and in doing so, felt better still.

Refreshed from his own good night's sleep, Bat had bounced onto the terrace at breakfast, looked up at the stunning building and declared stridently that he would only need to have ten percent of the owner's money to be as perfect as him, a comedic bravado made more ridiculous by the fact that it was the most understated of the band members making such a declaration.

Needless to say, Bat was thrilled to be taken to task by each and every member of the band and crew, the comments ranging from 'You won't be earning that ten percent from your looks' through to the eloquent simplicity of a bread roll thwocking off his temple, the perpetrator of this yeasty assault, to everyone's surprise, being Yo-Yo.

It wasn't until Zip, looking all innocent, said, 'Who do you think you are, A 'n' R or something?' and everyone exclaimed a collection of noises confirming the extent to which Bat had just been insulted (with even Slopehound uttering an admonishing 'Cool *beans*') that the return-to theme of the day was established.

Kick opined that A 'n' R considered themselves to be so God-like that they would no doubt barrel out of Heaven complaining to the angels playing harps that they can't hear a single.

Bat agreed, adding that, if only they put all their creative know-how into a song of their own, it would surely be perfect but thought this unlikely since having any creative thoughts might leave less room for preconceptions.

Treading old paths now, Kick pondered upon how many truly amazing songs were lost to the world, locked up in A 'n' R filing cabinets for fear of anyone else hearing them and them losing their 'cool' as a result.

'In fairness,' said Bat, 'they *are* always right.'

'They *think* they are,' responded Kick, setting Bat up who duly provided the feed.

'What do A 'n' R think?'

Kick, 'Don't know, ask the other A 'n' R.'

They sat again in the sun, two successful men who, despite their in-jokes, appreciated the pressures A 'n' R were under.

But had little time for it.

It seemed to Kick that the U.S. labels, in particular, applied a science to music. Whilst the beauty of the Universe can be phrased in mathematical terms, they seemed to want to contain music – which is manifest as frequencies within a time-scale, both parameters that are mathematically measurable – under the same terms.

This might indeed make music, he thought, but music was not always art. The true worth of art was found when words and reason fail – it usually had the vocabulary to express the point.

The Fifth Season had been lucky to find their audience; many bands, brilliant bands, had simply missed that all-important ignition point. Kick was aware that hard-work, while essential, was rarely enough – but the band's contempt for the music business was rooted in their own experience of it.

Most of the A 'n' R they had met along the way had considered their own opinion of what was or wasn't good to be fact, that they *knew*.

This clashed with the band's own observations that even the most successful A 'n' Rs seemed to rely on a strategy of repeatedly throwing a lasso into an empty field until they were lucky enough to hook onto a passing mustang.

Granted, once they had one around the neck, the system and resources already in place and available to them meant that they could hold on better than anyone else.

However, when the biggest-selling albums, even in The Past, numbered in just tens of millions, even in a global population of around 12 billion as it was then, Kick did not consider this a particularly successful industry. Most trashy soft drinks would outstrip that on daily sales alone.

Add to this the follow-the-leader approach of the business, with one breakthrough act on one label immediately mimicked by the others, or the play-safe strategy of selling reliable old songs through photogenic performers and contemporary production, to an audience whose youth and enthusiasm was all that prevented them from knowing any better, and the conclusion that The Fifth Season collectively came to was that The Industry should just get over itself a little bit. A lot.

Whilst no-one in the band was naïve – each of them being aware of financial risk and of how staggeringly fortuitous their circumstances were – their contempt for art as defined by balance sheet, the criterion that most A 'n' R worked to, was alien, a job that none could relate to.

They had never wanted to be part of a project that involved accountants telling them what to do instead of the other way around. They recognised that it was an industry, that it needed to operate this way but it was an environment from which the artist instinctively withdrew and in which only the narcissists flourished, feeding on the attention of people who unwittingly adored them for the very qualities they, ironically, were most removed from, those being selflessness and a finger on a universal truth.

There was art and then there was A'n'Rt.

What happened just before Now with one major label acted as an example of why The Fifth Season kept their distance.

As a metaphor for the condition of popular culture at the time, Ingenue Enfrazzle and her solo performances with a loop pedal were perfect – minimum musical input and maximum digital involvement combined to deliver a homogeneous, competent product with as little variation and human dynamic as could be imagined and with as little effort as possible.

Ramped up on sales and adoration, Ingenue – with the support of her record label – declared, without any hint of irony, that she had followers and that those followers came to see her at a series of venues that could be described as places of worship.

Using this as the premise to apply for religious status no doubt appealed to Ingenue, a performer so breathlessly self-absorbed and excited about herself that she thought the most important thing in the world was her own reaction to it.

However, in reality, it was an attempt by her label and management to reduce her tax exposure, an inevitable end-result of years of how-do-we-make-more thinking which, with the collapse of religion Now, failed to fly but should perhaps be recognised for its audacity. Or, the band thought, its cynicism. At the very least it showed that karma could play the long game where necessary.

Kick was shrewd enough to know that The Fifth Season was in a subtly different industry – one in which reputation at least partly defined success – and aware enough to realise that he was not and never had been part of its target audience; he simply wasn't *supposed* to get it.

Unlike Zip, who dismissed mainstream music by saying he would listen to it in ten years' time once the relentless grind of modern culture had worn down his expectations enough to make it acceptable, Kick thought there was room for everything in the end.

Whilst Kick tired of the marketing of a person who had been given a persona and that persona then sold as the person, pretty much any song that put a smile on a child's face as they bounced around to it was fine by him.

They were only young because they didn't know any better after all and as long as there was still artistic variety, should they want it, once they grew up then he could sleep well at night.

Sleeping well during the day, Iodine dozed off to the side as Bat and Kick let the smiles slowly fall from their faces. Riot and Zip were so withdrawn from the band that they might have still been there only for the sake of winning a bet but it was Bat that Kick had really wanted to speak to anyway.

Zip and Mangler had once spent every moment between songs at a sound check debating whether or not a caricature is what the mind sees and a portrait is what the eye sees.

Mangler, hands on hips with his 'I'm God's Gift To Women, He Just Didn't Wrap Me Very Well' T-shirt, had, against his better judgement, been unable to resist engaging with Zip, this being – as usual – entirely the wrong time to do so.

Despite the outcome being typically less than conclusive and probably best described as on-going, what Kick did know for sure was that no detail would be missed if something was looked at by Bat.

So, there in the sun, Kick recounted his evening with the Out-Of-Towners and the details of his visit with Myelle. He spoke at greater length about the boy and the promise he had made to Eventually Kelly, something that Bat only now became fully aware of. He spoke of how close he felt to the boy, like he was right next to him, that he would surely turn and see him, just to his right, always just to his right, almost where Bat was now, tantalisingly close.

As Bat considered the words and their context, Kick's gaze tumbled down the grassy slope – over Zip's head he could see Riot and his love waist-deep in the lake, still holding hands, their communication wordless yet comprehensive in the way they looked at each other.

They may have been moving further into the lake – it was hard to tell from this angle and distance – but if they were it was in painstaking increments, the surface of the lake barely troubled by their presence.

'I think you need to go to Maskelyne,' said Bat and, turning to him, Kick would not have known that he would never see Riot again.

'I know,' said Kick, 'although I don't know why.'

Bat picked up another olive, bringing it to his mouth, the subtlest of pauses as it got close (do I *really* want another?) and used the hesitation to suggest that, if U.S. had the boy, then that might be where they have him.

Kick tasted the idea much as Bat did the olive, found it less satisfying.

'That doesn't feel quite right somehow,' he said, his eyebrows coming together in a frown as he considered the possibility, 'but if he is, if they have him…I could…trade.'

His words faded off a little, their significance not lost on either of them.

'I made a promise,' he said by way of qualification and he turned his gaze away again, past Zip, past the now empty lake, off towards the sea.

He heard a howling in his left ear, Mister Five maybe but was that rage or triumph? He turned to Bat and the sound faded to nothing, perhaps only a breeze through the forest trees.

'What do you think Myelle was on to?'

Bat, eyeing another olive as though it offered a battle of wills as well as a salty sourness, asked, 'About Powdermouth?'

Kick nodded, unwittingly taking the olive that Bat had been considering.

Hastily, Bat took another and said, 'You have years invested in Powdermouth Kick; he has never let you down, never let any of us down.'

Kick gave a small nod as he stared off towards the sea again, acknowledging the point that Bat was making and Bat took the opportunity to move the plate of olives slightly out of his reach.

'Besides,' continued Bat, 'even if she was on to something, he's allowed to have secrets.'

Kick reflected on this; Powdermouth, perhaps the most mysterious person he knew, or maybe really didn't know.

Bat gestured with his head towards Zip, who was wrapping up his interview.

'Isn't one of the tattoos on his back "trust"?' he asked and went on, 'I think Myelle was just working on you. I think she was working on what you believe, trying to break your trust or your faith in it. Weaken you. It was a little move but well-designed. Gets at you where you live, you know.'

'She did a good job.'

'She is…exceptional,' said Bat and both men smiled.

Bat expanded a little for his old friend.

'She softened you up plenty Kick. She knows that as an empath you had to close down almost totally the more she ramped up the intensity. She knew that would have been uncomfortable for you – no, *painful* for you – if you had not put up your defences. And then, just at the point that all you had left was a survival instinct and a beating heart, bang, she hits you with something that would make you feel more vulnerable than anything else.'

Kick was glad to have run this past Bat who added, 'With all the resources you needed to assess it accurately withdrawn in self-protection mode,' to stress the point.

'That sounds very calculated,' said Kick but he knew that what Bat said was close to the truth.

'Would you really put that kind of detail past them? All things considered?'

Kick realised that he would not. In fact, it was a simple move for them and he nodded an agreement to Bat's next comment.

'Besides, those like Myelle have an instinct for that kind of work. She could easily have had an agreed strategy and improvised or even gone rogue if she felt your reaction was going a certain way. She also knew you would reflect on it later.'

Zip made his way uphill towards them and Kick recognised the metaphor, wondered how long he would be willing to do so.

Zip stood on the terrace, said, 'I'm glad that's all done,' before picking up the bowl of olives, pouring the remaining ones into his mouth and making his way into the house, adding, 'Now for a whole bunch of nothing else.'

'Karma is a wonderful thing,' said Kick knowingly, biting on a smile.

'Mmmm…' said Bat, finding nothing funny in that whatsoever, although the water glass of sliced cucumber looked pretty good now that he came to think about it. He settled into a crunchy new thoughtfulness, a few minutes later asking, 'What if the boy isn't there?'

Kick had been thinking the same.

'I have no idea. I don't even have an idea what to do when I get there. We both know I need to go though… where else?'

The two men sat and looked at the scene before them, the grassy fairway, the lake, the trees, the sea; each with their own thoughts.

Despite Mister Five randomly finding his ear, Kick felt confident that he could hide his thoughts from them; years of practice had made him almost as silent with The Maze as Dessel but almost was not enough when going into the home of U.S.

'I'll need to hide somehow,' he said.

'Then you will need to find a way to hide me too,' said Iodine, a look of sincere commitment on his face.

Kick and Bat were not sure how long he had been listening or even awake but unlike Entenne, whose approach was an accurate and simple reflection of her contractual obligation, Iodine took his role of protector very seriously indeed and Kick could see no way of talking him out of it.

'Yes,' said Kick, 'we will.'

He missed Honeytongue with a sudden, almost physical pain.

♪

Few stand at the edges of a dense forest, staring in, and experience something that isn't somewhere on the spectrum of fear. It may be trepidation, caution, reluctance, a challenge. Those furnished with high-powered weapons and years of experience might feel anticipation and excitement but take those weapons away and that same experience might well counsel a more considered approach.

The forest is rarely less than intimidating even for those armed with more than simply knowing where the trigger is.

It makes no promises to keep you safe and the forest needs to eat, and this may not encroach upon your awareness until you engage in the action of stepping deeper and deeper into it.

Armed only with instinct, which over centuries, has been blunted from neglect, few would enter willingly, spooked – even unreasonably – by the shadow and veil of its brush and shrub, the stoic dispassion of the trees, their canopies holding uneven darkness tight to the earth.

The tropical forests of the Eastern Lands may lay claim to the greatest content, the greatest dangers, to being the least forgiving but all – including the one framing The Sun Shrine – held their mysteries just out of sight like unspoken cautionary tales.

Whilst few held predators larger than humans, some did and base survival instincts, when appraising the array of textured gloom, reported back that all held at least some and they were surely nearby and waiting.

Here, a creeping sense that you are not alone acts as a stark reminder that you really are.

Regardless, the devil, they say, is in the detail and the detail of the forest is in the holes and burrows that would snap a leg; in the plants and their poisonous embrace, the spiders and their unforgiving bites, the parasite in the tempting water hole, the snake with its palette of squeeze, spit and tooth.

The wrong fruit, a graze calmly incubating the wrong infection and the insects that pay its succulence their total attention, spreading the wound and the wounding, tiny mouthfuls at a time.

Under these circumstances and more, if you are far enough into the forest, or far enough away from another human ear, then the outcome most likely is that you will never leave.

There is something to challenge each of your defences and overwhelm any of your immune responses, disarming your ability to fight, and this is only the first of the energies that the forest will claim as its own.

And once it has this, the forest can wait, its most ruinous weapon being patience.

So, stand staring into the forest and accept that each step you take into its depths is a step deeper into a living creature made up of many others. Accept that the forest has no shame, remorse or regret and that you are food, a fuel to enter the system, perhaps painfully, perhaps only a little at a time.

Because the forest is innocent and the forest needs to feed.

♪

Kick loved the waterfall, its outstanding natural beauty making it a stunning example of its kind. It was a long way from The Sun Shrine, isolated in a small clearing in the trees, the light coming from the break in the canopy spinning rainbows and refracted starbursts through the spray thrown up as the water crashed onto the flat rocks at its base.

It fell as a thin curtain, huge volumes of water reduced to a thrilling but comfortable contact anywhere that you stood in it, vigorous enough to wash away any thoughts and strip things to essential.

Kick never missed the chance to come here and accept the hypnotic chatter of the water and its invigorating stab – he would swim in the deep pool beneath the waterfall, perhaps staring up at the sky through the break in the trees, re-establishing himself in the real world and washing away whatever needed washing away. But for now the waterfall held his attention totally.

He opened his eyes at the sound of Tempra Kay's voice. He thought to cover himself up a little but he wasn't so sure that he had actually heard her. The water distorted his vision and his hearing and just maybe he had merely expected her; maybe he had hoped she would be here.

Maybe nothing.

No. There it was again and he was sure that she was here, calling him. There was something in her tone that told him it was okay to stay under the waterfall, no need to get out or cover up. He accepted this and closed his eyes again, letting the water beat its crisp tattoo on his skin as he listened for her.

In amongst the falling water the question she asked him was, 'Do you feel better now? Now that you have made the decision?'

He realised that he did, the trepidation at the distance that Maskelyne was from his true self reduced to the smallest of concerns when laid against the peace he now felt.

As though she understood, as though she knew, through the water, in the water, all around, her voice said, 'Don't worry, you will be coming home very soon.'

I AM TIME

Chapter Nineteen

The light was mostly gone now, having done what he had been unable to and found a way to escape the confines of the meadow.

All noise and all movement evidencing life of any kind had fallen below minimum, his presence now almost fundamentally at one with the meadow which was, atom-like, mostly space.

Not even the subliminal airy swoop of bats broke the darkness.

The rushing sound of water had lost its urgency and, at some point that was hard to define, had disappeared entirely. With waning effort he tried to think backwards but he had no access to short-term memory, the meadow and the what-next allowing no room for the how and when he got to this moment.

The only identifiable object was the silver birch, wanly reflecting what little light there was and, having no other ideas, he walked towards it, the dimensions of the meadow becoming more definable as he did so.

He stopped half way, reluctant and demoralised.

Suddenly very thirsty.

He sat down, his fingertips brushing against plants

and grasses and he thought about lives spent growing alone, spent growing alongside, spent growing together.

He no longer felt a connection to the environment or anything in it and he accepted the responsibility of being here.

The thirst left him.

He stood, feeling for the first time since finding himself in the meadow that all of his body was awake at the same time and he felt sure that he was getting lighter and taller with each step he took towards the tree.

Chapter Twenty

Peaceful
                Calm

gliding on

                                  gentle air cushioned

    slow rise

                lifting away

  from

                                    fond embrace

        soft light easing in

                                        friends
                          laughing

caress of breeze

                    a cool smooth palm

                        I'll see you soon

fresh

the last rush to awareness
                              where
                                      making

Kick opened his eyes, now fully awake and the eye that wasn't deep in the pillow closed a little to greet the sunlight coming in through the open window.

The breeze that cooled both Kick's face and the arm that wasn't undercover was fresh enough to insist he stay awake – perhaps a little too fresh for the curtains, bashfully falling back into place between its playful gusts as though trying to protect the modesty of the room from its curious probing.

Kick rolled onto his back, the crisp sheets scrunching around him. He wouldn't fall asleep again. As he raised his arms above his head in a victory salute stretch, he realised that he hadn't felt so refreshed, so *even*, since before the tour began.

He had a lot on his mind, sure, but he finally felt restored enough to deal with it; lighter.

He wasn't sure what time it was but he knew he had slept on after the others had risen, their voices travelling like faint fragrance from the terrace on the other side of the house, a quick assessment finding no Riot, which he had expected, but no trace of Powdermouth either which was odd given that his voice was a fresh tendril in the The Sun Shrine's layered sounds.

He could tell that Slopehound, Crunch and Mangler – with his 'Don't Get Mad Don't Get Even Just Get On With It' T-shirt – had mixed feelings this morning and that Iodine was not in a good mood…but nothing from

Powdermouth. He thought again of Myelle's words, allowing them to glance off him, letting trust embrace the mystery as to how Powdermouth could travel with no emotional footprint. Or, for that matter, could arrive unerringly in the right place at exactly the right time.

'Morning all,' said Kick as he made a loose-limbed appearance on the terrace.

The assembled group responded with something that sounded a bit like "heygoodmorn you'rereadybothernoonbeansd" which he chose to take as welcoming, for the most part at least, before sitting down and wondering out loud if there was anything left for breakfast after Bat had hoovered his own requirements into his mouth.

He nodded at Powdermouth who nodded back, contained but expressive responses of old friends delighted to see each other.

'You want to speak with Furious about food hoovering,' said Bat, gesturing towards Zip, clearly still bitter about the previous day's olive-related misdemeanours.

Zip waved a non-committal hand in the air as he stared towards the lake – he either didn't know what Bat was on about, didn't care or wasn't listening. Probably all of them thought Kick, realising that this tour was all but over for Zip.

It wasn't lost on Powdermouth who spoke to Kick for the first time but before he did, he closed his eyes and appeared to listen, turning his head as he did so.

'I've cancelled the last few full-band shows,' he said as though satisfied with the silence.

Kick opened his mouth with questions, perhaps to protest but Powdermouth's raised hands silenced them at source. The crew had gone ahead and more than anything Kick didn't want their efforts to have been wasted and if they had, he didn't want them to go unacknowledged.

'Don't worry,' said Powdermouth, 'they're all okay. The tour has done well, financially they're looked after. They'll still be paid for the last few shows.'

Kick wanted to ask about the audiences – ticket-holders owed a show – but again, Powdermouth was a step ahead.

'Think it through Kick. Without Riot you can't do it anyway,' and this raised a host of other questions in Kick, none of which formed any shape in time to actually get asked.

'I've scaled back the shows. They're more,' Powdermouth looked at the remaining band members before going on, 'acoustic now. I've booked more suitable venues. Ticket holders can use their old ticket or get a refund. Yo-Yo is on to it. Like I said, the tour has done okay. We can absorb it. It's not ideal but we can do a free festival if there's a next time.'

Kick didn't know what to make of the choice of words, especially as chosen by Powdermouth, so named because nothing slipped out of his mouth by accident.

Powdermouth looked at him levelly.

Kick asked, 'Why?' and immediately felt like a five-year-old repeating it after each explanation of a previous 'why?'

'Well,' said Powdermouth, 'I have manipulated the itinerary a little, bent it a little closer so that it's not obvious you're coming.'

'Closer?' asked Kick feeling really very slow to understand.

'I need to get you close to Maskelyne without it looking like you're going to Maskelyne,' said Powdermouth, 'don't you think?'

Thinking of Myelle's provocative words, Kick looked to Bat and then back to Powdermouth – they really had been busy while he slept.

Owning the decision now, yes, he did think that.

Powdermouth turned his eyes to Iodine, who was trying not to scowl, really didn't want to be scowling.

'I'm sorry friend,' said Powdermouth directly to him, 'we will keep you on as long as we can but they will see you coming if we take you to The City,' and then, with both an understanding of the situation and a typical empathy, added, 'If you want to help, do what you can to not actually think about it.'

Kick knew that Iodine understood. Hated it. But understood. And felt better having a way to contribute.

Powdermouth turned back to Kick.

'We'll pick up Giggles Mahoney on the way just in case,' he said.

♪

Zip lasted for two of the remaining gigs before, like the tired final sigh of air leaving a tyre worn too thin, his residual energy source seemed to simply expire. The impression of him slowing to a stop before falling face-first into an insurmountable hill of sand was strong in Kick's eyes and, if that image were real, Mangler would have taken a few more steps before just sitting down, perhaps a little higher up the slope but not much.

Kick had accepted this without resistance. He had learnt over many years that, for Zip, not giving up was a success in itself but there was something especially draining about this tour, despite the recuperative quality of the time spent at The Sun Shrine.

There was little for it, Bat would have to blow the dust off his piano fingers and they would have to play a very limited set reflecting that for the remaining shows.

There were only four left but Kick was frustrated that he was unable to provide the show originally on offer to the audience. This was not The Fifth Season that he had expected at this point; but nor was he particularly surprised.

From the moment Eventually Kelly had hovered into his awareness he had realised that there was more to this story than just the story, the loose ends of which (even down to Riot's subtle evacuation without goodbyes) he would simply have to get back to when the insistent forward momentum let go of him a little.

It was in a small satellite village about a day's travel from Maskelyne that Zip and Mangler finally took their leave. Oddly tropical, dark-leafed trees crowded the small alleyways of what amounted to little more than a traveller's stop of a place; shops, small bars, a refuelling station and trashy overnight stays for those unwilling or wise enough not to arrive at Maskelyne at the limit of their fatigue and far enough away to have a sense of being the first safe stop when leaving.

Nonetheless, so close to Maskelyne invited a renegade element, most of whom formed wordless queues of one at the bars, each feeding money into the one-armed bandit of a beer pump handle, the guaranteed liquid gold pouring out with repetitive precision being the only jackpot they required.

The reduced band and crew pit-stopped here at a functional eatery with dishes in a price range that suggested they wouldn't be poor but nor would they be memorable. Whilst most took time to sit and eat, Zip and Mangler chose something to go and explored the narrow, criss-crossed alleyways in a weary, disinterested meander.

Kick looked around the table at the silent, distant, close group, Powdermouth's reassuring presence a little unlikely at this stage of the tour but more so here, now.

Bat, Crunch and Slopehound focussed on their food, as though assessing the merit of each mouthful before expending any energy on chewing it and Kick realised that this was unsustainable, too much to ask of the individuals and the audiences; the tired end.

'Where's Guilty?' he asked, suddenly anxious that so much was passing him by, slipping through his fingers and evading his fitful attempts at order.

'He's safe,' said Powdermouth, 'Riot took him.'

Kick wasn't sure whether to believe this but believed also that it wasn't a lie. Guilty was safe. This he knew. He didn't need to think any more about that. His old friend had reassured him. He went back to eating. Each mouthful mechanical. He realised that he didn't really have much of an appetite. Looked down at his plate. Full. Despite eating for ten minutes, the dish remained uneaten, as served.

He smiled, almost laughed. Sat back. Scratched his ear.

He looked up to share the oddness of the experience. All of them, plates full. Looking at him. He felt fear.

'Go and find Zip,' said Powdermouth.

♪

'Hi Kick,' said Zip warmly over his shoulder when Kick found him and Mangler in a tattoo parlour, the door closing with a discrete click behind him as he entered, the empty streets now replaced by the almost reverential silence of the parlour, the artist working alone in the shop and without any apparent interaction with Zip.

Zip's shirt was off, his back and its flourish of colours and shapes turned to the artist – what Kick knew to be the final piece was stencilled on, the tattoo artist prepping the colours, vivid in their tiny pots, a blur pattern of careless smears on his latex gloves.

Despite it being somehow familiar, he couldn't quite make sense of the last element but as a whole, the piece was a solid, flexible construct that emphasised the strength of Zip's back and complemented its shape. For no reason he could articulate, it reminded Kick of armour and it dawned on him that, if you are flexible enough, nearly all of your stresses go away.

Mangler – off to the right – stood up from the sofa where he had been browsing a portfolio. He came and stood next to Kick, regarded Zip's back, his hand on Kick's shoulder.

'You have...balance,' he said with an obvious fatigue but Kick didn't know who to and before he could agree, disagree or ask for clarification, Mangler had left the parlour, his eyes lowered.

As if to break the spell Zip spoke to him, looking at Kick's image fondly in the mirror he had turned back to face, as the artist, new gloves on, checked the gun with a short bottled-wasp old-school burst.

I AM THE SKY AND EVERYTHING IN IT

'The only other God is thought,' said Zip with the same weariness as Mangler.

Kick could see the image now and it made a beautiful sense, the complexity of the design distilling to an elegant simplicity. Zip's God, designed by him; decided by him.

Zip smiled at him. A small shake of his head. Kick, uncertain but sure, returned the gesture and the small smile.

'Ready?' asked the artist. And again Kick wasn't sure who was being spoken to and, as is the way in tattoo parlours, if you are not giving or receiving you are mostly in the way so he stepped out to find Mangler.

Out onto a four-way junction, long narrow roads in all directions. No sign of Mangler on any of them. No shops. No doorways. No hiding places.

He turned back to the parlour. Closed. Dark inside. Panic takes over for a brief moment. Makes him bang his head on the glass as he rushes to look in. (Is this how it happens? Losing control and dignity? A little at a time?) The fall of the shadows inside suggests an empty store, having been empty for a long time.

'Kick.'

Powdermouth.

Kick's fingertips stay touching the glass. Or maybe it was the cold, smooth surface of a giant glass marble, impossible to get effective purchase on, impossible to get around, too big and too close to get an accurate perspective on and implacable in its steady forward motion.

He turns to his friend.

'Come on there's work to do,' said Powdermouth cheerily, 'and it simply wouldn't be the same without you.'

It's Powdermouth. So he goes. Zip had shaken his head. Right?

Back of the vehicle. Bat staring out of the window. Crunch the pilot. Slopehound short on words. Iodine will be gone soon.

Four gigs to go.

♪

Two gigs blurred by, the audiences as welcoming as ever but still Kick felt like he was passing tests on both nights.

He found it harder and harder to maintain his concentration; taking a back seat as his autopilot took the controls, he did those shows without experiencing them, the feeling of separation broken only when he missed a cue on the second night.

Bat saved the moment, bringing indulgent smiles from the forgiving crowd by commenting into his mic that, on reflection, he preferred it, 'the other way.'

Kick had smiled, smothered his disorientation, raised his game enough to reply that, yes, no matter how they tried, the new version never did feel quite right and managed to hold his focus through to a second encore, the last lines of the night delivered with his usual commitment but at a greater cost:

> In all that we seek, when should we speak?
> When should we listen?
> So we can get close to making the most
> Of all that we're given?

The reality was that only bit by bit since the tattoo parlour had he regained any of his connection to the sense of well-being he had felt so very recently.

Powdermouth's presence was a large part of that – if he was relaxed, then so should he be.

Bat was with him too, apparently unsurprised and unconcerned by any of these events and Kick took from their lead, these two men he trusted more than any other. He subscribed to their disposition despite being unable to understand why they *were* so composed when so much was so obviously falling apart – especially that Zip and Mangler had simply disappeared, following Riot's earlier example.

He wanted to ask them but each time he meant to do so, something would get said that would distract him, convince him that he could find the answers to all of that later, just sometime later.

Yet, like a regret that visits late at night, it disrupted him enough to keep him from settling.

For now, hey, the gigs needed doing but more than that, much more than that, he needed to find the boy. The grown-ups in his life could all look after themselves and, given where he needed to go, maybe it was for the best that they weren't near him.

And with the five people who were now with him, apart from Iodine who was still a little bent out of shape that he wouldn't be going to Maskelyne, being so serene, why should *he* worry?

Except, hang on, a large touring party has been reduced to six people, absolutely none of whom have said a word for well over an hour. That's not right. No, that's not right.

Kick stared at his hands, nestled redundantly in his lap, while his fellow travellers stared ahead with the impression that they knew far better where they were going than he did.

He looked at Powdermouth, in front of him and to the left. There was never anything to read from Powdermouth but he tried anyway. Why was that? Actually. No, really. He'd never really thought about this before but why *was* that?

He looked at the others, opened himself up wide and whilst there was frustration coming from Iodine, there was nothing else, just that. The others…the others were fading.

Like dreams which upon awaking are destroyed almost by the act of trying to remember them, his companions' emotional presence was little more than trace, dissipated and dissipating.

And yet they were so relaxed. There was almost nothing left of their connection to the world and they were just sitting here like it was nothing? And Powdermouth, he's overseen this? This is acceptable to him? Part of some kind of plan? And why the hell can't he be read anyway? Where's Zip? What the hell happened back there?

'We're here,' said Powdermouth.

'Oh good,' said Kick, 'that's great.'

♪

The satellites of Maskelyne appeared to be much the same, Kick noted. If Crunch had decided to travel a full circle and bring them back to the small village where they had last seen

Zip and Mangler without telling anyone, Kick would not have been surprised, the narrow streets, sparse provisions and tropical foliage making the resemblance unavoidable.

If anything, though, there were fewer people here, the raised pavements that dropped down like mini canyons onto the single lanes were almost entirely unoccupied.

Bat and Iodine eyed the outside tables of a small bar and said that they would wait there while the rest of them followed Powdermouth to a massage parlour, a traditional but spartan establishment, with some of the massage spaces separated from the streets only by transparent floor-to-ceiling drapes.

Giggles Mahoney was so hairy that when Kick saw him that first time receiving such an intense massage his first thought was 'What *is* that woman doing to that gorilla?' – a thought followed by one, only slightly more coherent, that wondered how such a large man could be so clearly losing a fight with such a small woman.

By the time Slopehound and Crunch had wandered off for their own massages and the masseuse had reached the end of her sequences, making those double-handed clacking slaps on the man's back as though concerned that her work would go under appreciated and so giving herself a round of applause just in case, Kick had finally grasped the situation accurately.

In fairness to him, the squeaks and phuts and other sounds of stress emanating from Giggles throughout the process, and continuing now to a lesser extent, suggested a man under duress more than it did a man undergoing a relaxing tactile experience and despite having listened closely to Powdermouth's briefing, it was hard not to be surprised by the scenario.

Rumour had it that many years ago Frank 'Giggles' Mahoney had seen something so funny that he had been unable to stop himself laughing about it ever since. No-one had been with him when it happened so no-one could verify this but one day Giggles was a dry, staid, solid salesman of air conditioning units, the next he was a physically unpredictable presence, struggling to maintain some kind of body order around convulsions and fits of laughter.

At first there was hope. Everyone in his life, including Frank, thought it would pass; then as slowly as viscous liquid dripping, the doomy reality set in.

Each attempt to extract the source of his sudden travails and each attempt on his part to convey what happened raised the image in his head, rendering him entirely unable to do so. The fragments gleaned and released hinted at an event that, incredibly, was *too* funny but no-one knew for sure except Giggles.

For the first few years, he spent most of the time simply trying not to think about it, his sense of future and planning reduced to any destination that might be reached in neutral, his presence to anyone who encountered him reflecting a kind of madness as he wrestled with both his internal world and the external one that fell apart inevitably around him.

He had even welcomed it in at one point, tried to laugh it out. However, letting the genie out of the bottle had only led to a debilitating few days of no sleep or food, with water dabbed on his gums to sustain him as the doctors found their own concentration destroyed by the infectious nature of his laughter when he presented to them and, through weeping eyes, had tried and failed to communicate the urgent need for intravenous nourishment.

The genie went very reluctantly back into the bottle only when the doctors opted for a sedation strategy, the thick haze of which the laughter still managed to pierce and Giggles was managed slowly off the medication, allowing an incremental introduction of coping mechanisms along the way.

The sedative in many ways had left him defenceless but he was at least hydrated and alive. As time went on, despite the occasional grunts and minor convulsions that Kick was witnessing now, he had developed strategies to scramble his own thoughts, strategies that would allow only fleeting glimpses at those images in his head that, even now, after so much destruction, he was unable to resent enough to consider as anything other than the funniest thing he had ever seen.

Giggles stood up after his massage, a big man, slightly out of shape but handy-looking – more bruiserweight than cruiserweight – and turned to the small woman who had just massaged him.

'Thank you-oo-ee. Ar, ar,' he said.

She bowed in response and made her leave.

Giggles turned to Powdermouth and Kick.

'Mahoney,' said Powdermouth by way of greeting.

Giggles hated being called Giggles. Giggles got mad if you called him Giggles and a man in his position giggled more when he got mad, his concentration broken in that way. It was potentially life-threatening for Giggles to lose his concentration.

'Hi Frank,' said Kick.

Relaxed from his massage he had lost a little control.

'Hi ee yup hee yuh yuh hi yuh Kick,' said Giggles and Kick knew exactly why Powdermouth had thought to bring him along.

There was no doubt that U.S. would know by now that Kick was coming to Maskelyne. Kick could shield his thoughts, and Powdermouth never seemed to actually have any that could be read but Bat, Iodine, Crunch and Slopehound were open books to any U.S. superimposers with reading skills – even if Slopehound might well have made for limited reading in many ways and Iodine was working hard not to think about any plans.

Giggles, however, had a brain trained to randomise his own thoughts, a simple yet ferocious ability to scramble them, strong enough to make Kick a little tired himself just from proximity. Despite his own ability to screen things out, the intensity of Giggles's survival technique of permanently changing random thoughts intruded to such an extent that he knew it would also jam any attempts made by U.S. at finding them.

They knew that Kick was coming but with Giggles alongside him with the thought processes of several people together at once, they would never be sure exactly where he was – a slim advantage but Powdermouth was right in thinking that it was one worth having.

Powdermouth and Kick waited while Giggles gathered his things from somewhere deeper within the building, returning with a message from Crunch and Slopehound.

'They said to go on ahead – ah,' he reported and strode purposefully past Kick and Powdermouth towards the bar where Bat and Iodine were waiting. Powdermouth followed him with Kick making up the rear, glancing back every few paces towards the massage parlour and wanting everything to be going just a little bit slower.

As they approached the bar, maybe fifty paces away, Bat turned and saw them. He looked at Kick then at Giggles who stopped and, taking his lead still, Powdermouth and Kick did the same.

Bat looked into Powdermouth's eyes and then at Kick again but now he is smiling tenderly as he stands and motions to Iodine, sitting with his back to Kick, to stand too.

Iodine does but he doesn't turn to look at Kick; instead he tries to pick up his bag as though to leave the bar. A powerful man, Iodine can't seem to lift his small kit bag and he looks first to his palms, almost laughing with confusion, then back to his bag.

Like a drunk man wondering where his drink has gone before realising it has fallen through his fingers and is spilt on the floor amongst shattered glass, his movements are slow, his comprehension even slower as he tries again to lift his bag. Again, he fails.

Now lost, now frightened, now helpless, he looks to Bat who glances at him, puts his hand on his shoulder and then turns his eyes back to Kick.

'It's time to go Kick,' he said softly but the words travel the distance between them effortlessly.

'Bat...' started Kick, disarmed and distracted by Iodine's distress, perhaps not least as a way of avoiding dealing with his own. No Bat. No band. Kick alone. Everything was different.

'...but we have two gigs to go...'

He knew he was pleading; he knew it made no difference.

'Be at peace with not achieving everything you wanted old friend,' said Bat.

And with Giggles phooing and scrawing next to him and such little room left for clear thinking, Kick felt this as a descent into a dire unknown, a blind fall backwards into a hole with no holds to reach for.

He looked at Powdermouth who stared back at him; clearly, he understood this and the steadiness of his regard was so seductive.

He turned back to Bat with Iodine next to him still staring mutely at his hands but before he could say anything he heard:

Kick.

The sound was loud in his head. Giggles shouting? Why would he shout at me?

He wanted to speak with Bat but instead he was overwhelmed by a realisation.

Powdermouth had just spoken directly to him, directly into him. He found himself returning once again to Powdermouth's hypnotic gaze and as their eyes met an immense wave of The Maze careened through him before being safely clipped off.

So much became clear to Kick in the moments that followed, a thousand memories, seemingly unrelated, now tying together to create one giant mesh explaining Powdermouth, his mystery. His benevolence.

Powdermouth broke the eye contact, releasing Kick to do the same.

Bat looking at Kick. He nods, waves and puts one arm

around the shoulders of the glazed Iodine. With his other arm, he picks up the kit bag and hands it to a passing child before steering Iodine away and around a corner.

♪

Kick watches him go as Giggles tenses next to him, the briefest of flexes in contrast to the languid accommodation of Powdermouth's eyes, a seductive place that Kick returned to now.

And in moments, each sliver of information delivered not in words but in understandings, as natural as ideas, Powdermouth told him much of what he needed as they looked at each other.

I'm coming with you.

Haven't I always?

I have my own reasons.

And in the presence of a superimposer whose abilities dwarfed his own, Kick's resistance lost the last of its hold. With his understanding on its way to becoming complete, his fight received its strength.

And Powdermouth went seamlessly back into being entirely unreadable.

Invisible.

Chapter Twenty-One

It was not possible to look down on Maskelyne without a privileged status, its almost circular spread the relief found at the peaks of various extensive natural slopes travellers might stand at the bottom of and be at least a little intimidated by before pressing on. Or choosing not to.

Access from the rear of The City was denied in totality by a semi-circular, implacable cowl of steep, hard-edged, angular cliffs that also served to hide what lay beyond, perhaps the sea. Perhaps nothing.

The most senior of U.S. executives may have laid claim to the indents of luxuriously-featured abodes high in the rock but this was left unknown. In truth, there would be little need since Maskelyne was their domain, their home, theirs, the dark arterial crevices in the jagged features a manifestation of a philosophy, pervasive, total and of course, entirely native.

For some, a nightmare of technology moving faster than evolution, yet, seen through other eyes, Maskelyne, positioned as it was with a sympathetic natural climate and an almost zero percent crime rate, was undeniably a utopian vision, conceived, designed and executed with aggressive efficiency with no detail overlooked.

The public spaces, reassuring, natural and green wherever possible, were designed with order of mood and behaviour in mind. Urban rambling through Maskelyne's public spaces would offer a minimal display of dark corners. Shadows, too, were few with the exception of those cast by the trees, which would have been chosen for the high, airy lightness of their canopies.

Scattered statues of the beings that returned to end The Past, decorated Maskelyne, often with deferential groups standing before them, paying a kind of respect as part of their daily routine.

The cultivated tranquillity of the environs did not preclude Maskelyne from operating at a high-tech level, the green spaces sitting alongside – and often hosting – functions automated for convenience.

Members of its several golf courses would most usually play with a set of golf clubs of traditional design but with an in-built sensor to log and count their shots, not for the purposes of saving participants from having to tot up a series of small numbers but so that the Clubhouse computer might compile a monthly report offering advice, congratulations or, in a mail-out proving computers have a sense of humour too, a query of 'Have you ever wondered whether golf is really for you?' The recipient of such usually ended up waving it around the Clubhouse as a badge of honour before accepting, graciously, that it must surely be their round by way of punishment.

This would be a rare, almost sanctioned, ribaldry with silence (or at most, restrained noise) encouraged. Even vehicles were limited to those that were strictly necessary, most transport being a gliding, unobtrusive network of gently whooshing trains, depositing well-dressed, glowing citizens through automated doors and on to their destinations. These would be offices perhaps, or tranquil shopping centres designed for the glazed activity of diffident shopping that might best be described as retail grazing.

No-one was overweight here, not one of its population over-eating through fear of not knowing where the next meal was coming from, or fear of anything else.

Maskelyne assessed that historical problems of race or culture were often just representations of what people were really afraid of, that being change, so the population was stable and kept so, barring incremental, statistically satisfactory adjustments.

For many, the bland serenity of Maskelyne was no place to live but for many others it was the perfect place to die.

Another day working for or servicing U.S., another day happy doing so; another day in the countless days of an endless future.

Most corners of the grid-system streets hosted hologram posters displaying public-information notices, adverts or maybe even the Golfer of The Month, as determined by the data-collecting clubs.

If the screen sensed the DNA profile of a particular citizen passing by it might remind the individual about an imminent dental appointment or health check and if the subject matter was of a more delicate nature, its sensors could establish whether the said individual was alone or not, relaying location information to all other screens and they would wait until a more opportune moment.

Maskelyne connected with its people and its people accepted its presence in this way, each door in every building opening without resistance if the correct DNA was recognised in the trace moisture of the body requiring entrance and staying resolutely closed if not; keys being rendered all but obsolete, universally celebrated for their vintage kitsch whenever seen.

Orderly, beautiful, safe, a place where even dirty movies might be discreetly wiped clean, Maskelyne was, nonetheless, not without its downsides, even for those citizens enamoured with its municipal competence.

There was an unspoken caution beneath the gilded veneer, an almost imperceptible compression, so subtle as to be only vaguely apparent and only then to tourists, none of whom would quite be able to put into words the something that felt like a benign but conditional containment.

This might manifest in a variety of ways but was always dressed as, and statistically proven to be, for the benefit of all and was consequently met with little resistance.

A citizen might be denied access to a particular building if traces of anything contagious were detected in their medical footprint, most often and especially when the medical footprint of a corporately-important significant other already present would show them to be particularly vulnerable.

Most of those denied access smilingly accepted the situation and reported to the nearest medical centre where their insurance covered a kind of cleansing.

Occasionally a more heavy-handed approach was taken; though still benign, two individuals might step out of the background firmly into someone's foreground and escort them away unchallenged for detoxification or some other such renewal.

The statistical analysis of the individual in question, maybe their biometrics and their performance levels, maybe even their exercise against pharmacy-visit ratios, or other behavioural pattern, had found them to be a possible health threat to the general population and in this example, the evasive heart of the tourists' disquiet could be found.

Most police and policing was understood to be undercover, behavioural standards maintained by this suspicion alone, and the science of statistics, as generated and processed unquestionably by U.S., provided the philosophy of The City's function.

Long ago U.S. had concluded that with the correct application of science and its principles, a society could be constructed and managed to an optimum. The partisan nature of democratic politics, they felt, led to paralysis and a swinging, tilting bias that provided only an obstruction to the healthy exchange of ideas, something that would be considered unacceptable in any other science.

Without irony, U.S. had the leverage to jettison democracy entirely for a population compliant and willing enough to subscribe to the wisdom of the application of statistics.

And unlike most police, who, in continual interaction with crooks, ran the risk of becoming at least a little crooked, those in Maskelyne were impervious to such temptations, committed as they were to the idea of Maskelyne and what it should be. Either that, or they were already crooks, just gainfully employed ones.

What uniformed police there were provided directions for new citizens or visitors and, on very rare occasions, might have made arrests for drunken exuberance. No-one was ever jailed in Maskelyne, they were re-educated by a process that made them the victim of their own crime. If they stole, the equivalent was taken from them so that consequence was fully understood. Or they were banished.

This was an unlikely outcome with all citizens being fully paid-up members of the Maskelyne ideology. They wanted to be there. They succumbed to Maskelyne, this place where science was no longer humble.

Tax rates were low – although all humans in all Lands would complain about them – but giving to charity was actively encouraged, U.S. being (statistically) aware of a society's need to feel good about itself and Maskelyne was no different.

Naturally, the charity was for other regions. Maskelyne was in rude health.

Surviving is not just about what you digest, it is as much to do with what you filter out and Maskelyne had its own system. If you didn't want to be here, if you were not a believer, Maskelyne knew.

Maybe from the seers, the mind readers or the other superimposers in its employ. Or it may simply have been as instinctively aware of threats as a living organism. It was most definitely as cold-eyed in eliminating such a threat as any apex predator – if you didn't want to be there, Maskelyne would make sure that you were not.

Everyone was happy. Everyone was Maskelyne. A jail that you had to be good to get into and for those who liked it – where everyone smiled and didn't wonder how they got here.

The cheap labour force that built it, that delivered its effortless infrastructure precisely and on-time, were never seen beyond the duration of their contracts.

Long enough ago to be almost folklore, the story understood down the generations was that the workers were rewarded with the life-after-death deal, an option they, to a man, took up instantly.

No-one in Maskelyne had ever asked questions testing this, and no-one outside Maskelyne believed it, but Maskelyne knew – as it would have known the exact level of the belief within each of the workers in the project they were working on.

As it now knew about each of its citizens, all of whom had a comprehensive insurance that protected their health – even from the contagious microbes of fellow citizens – and of course, their life after death.

Stepping into any building alerted the mainframe to their presence, the in-situ medics instantly aware of their level of cover and the priority given to any sudden problems they might have.

It was important to each citizen of Maskelyne that they were kept alive to die properly – there was little need for criminal behaviour but suicide prior to your 40th birthday rendered your insurance for life after death invalid.

Of course, those wanting to die young and leave a youthful corpse as a gift to themselves for a future life eternal could pay a significantly higher premium legally but this was prohibitive for most and the majority settled for the cosmetic surgery allowed in the policy after 40 and an assisted suicide on their 50th birthday as a cost-effective solution.

Some opted for the surgery to be post-mortem, many years hence, trusting in the intervening medical advancement to do a better job.

Whilst treatment centres and departure lounges were assimilated effortlessly into the glossy shine of Maskelyne, sitting alongside entertainment, administration and retail buildings, research of the highest level was also a significant element of Maskelyne's conception.

U.S., typically, took a global approach to this. Secure after The Thinning, it consolidated its position, trading again on the fears of an anxious species, and established (deep within its own resource centres) a comprehensive, real-time database of all research being conducted everywhere, by everyone.

When seeking answers, it is often more advisable to speak with someone with experience rather than someone with qualifications, years of practical knowledge and instinct being more informative than time spent in lecture theatres.

Not so with the scope of this endeavour, the panoramic overview allowing U.S. computers to make connections between hundreds of thousands of superficially unrelated projects that would have taken endless man-hours to notice, if they ever did at all.

In this way, the relationship between the significance of alterations in the brain chemicals of breeding doves and, say, the rate of growth of tulips in soils of differing acidity might produce insight and solutions for another entirely separate on-going study being simultaneously scrutinised by U.S.'s all-seeing eye.

This all-encompassing perspective, the understanding of how all things relate to all things and how this might be used was, naturally, available to U.S. and U.S. alone.

Much of its own research was conducted behind closed doors, such as the development of genetically-engineered animals that could only be seen under ultraviolet light, the practical application of which was yet to be determined, but clearly of great potential to a mind like Maskelyne's.

Others were displayed in public, such as The Affinity Ball. In a sedate square, close to the centre, a metal-like ball danced through the air in a reinforced glass case, making jarring, unlikely changes in direction, apparently defying gravity and making light of inertia.

This was not strictly true, although the truth was close. U.S. had developed a material that could absorb such immense forces and had varying sensitivities to the gravitational pull of things in its proximity.

Naturally most sensitive to the pull of the Earth, at the flick of a switch, under the control of a bored, desensitised operator sitting off to the side, the sphere might suddenly feel an affinity with a passing car, a dog, two lovers walking past, a cloud.

Even U.S. couldn't quite defy gravity so they chose instead to manipulate it until such time as they could.

And it was stunning.

But not to the operator off to the side, a fairground worker who had seen this ride many times before.

A small beep caught his attention from the screen poster to his left. A disembodied voice with no accompanying image spoke to him.

'Your pulse and breathing suggest that you may be falling asleep. Kindly stay focussed Harvey.'

♪

Tick   Tick

           Tick   Tick

Chapter Twenty-Two

It was into this, the construct of someone else's philosophy, that they intended to travel; Kick, Powdermouth and Giggles. On foot.

Kick still wasn't sure why he was here or, more accurately, why it was here that he felt he needed to be. In this was a kind of denial and one that he was finding harder to sustain.

Especially since The Maze was increasingly apparent though, unusually, not in a way that it was being thrust at him. It was more like he was simply getting closer to it, its proximity the reason it was harder to keep out – and why their journey across Maskelyne would prove to be mostly unopposed but exhausting.

Yet it wasn't denial that had brought him here, it was trust. He had promised to find the boy and while The Maze was making reasoned thought difficult, he had chosen to trust Powdermouth when it hadn't been.

They had stood at the city limits, the urge to find the boy and the fear of failure becoming increasingly uncomfortable in Kick. Giggles took a few, deep, shivering breaths and Powdermouth, pale and intense, turned to Kick.

He said, 'This is where it gets difficult. Are you ready?'

What Kick thought was, 'Am I ready? Well. Let's see. Apart from the obvious answer of "what for exactly?" it would seem that I am miles from anything I might call home, stripped of all and any support that might be provided by nearly every one of my oldest and closest friends who seemed to just fade away without goodbye or explanation and I am standing on the edges of the last place I would ever want to be, looking for someone I don't know because I made a promise to someone else I don't know, and I have no idea what I am going to do even if I find him.

Beyond that, I can't help feeling that I am involved way, way beyond my brief because if this ever gets to be my idea of normal then my idea of normal is really not very normal at all; I seem to have bitten off more than I can chew but keep chewing all the same and, what's more, I have no idea how this happened because, in the end, I am just a singer for fuck's sake.'

This last thought forced laughter to spill from Kick with such force as to make Giggles eye him and wonder – perhaps just for a moment – if his condition had suddenly become contagious.

'Yes,' was what Kick actually said. Powdermouth seemed to be sure of where he was going after all.

♪

The first impression Kick had of Maskelyne as they stepped cautiously into its glossy ease was that it was organised, beautiful and precise, yet, somehow, coldly unattractive, as though, as with a woman, it needed a little flaw, some idiosyncrasy to make it more than merely perfect.

Being close to Maskelyne brought all kinds of problems, with passers-by tested and checked for sincerity and their reasons for being in the vicinity. In contrast, being in Maskelyne brought no problems at all, the powers-that-be correctly assessing those present as willing, vetted, participants.

Superficially then, there seemed little threatening about it and with Powdermouth leading – apparently listening in some way – they travelled unopposed. He would make sudden decisions to take a left or a right or just hang around for a while and then move off again with no indication as to why.

The screens would occasionally flash up as they went past, flicking off just as quickly, as though confused, as Giggles's scrambling rendered them unsure as to how to respond and so choosing silence in an unlikely display of human discretion.

If other people were around, especially in a group, the screen might, for example, come on to display a disturbingly young female singer, resembling little more than a boy who had had hormone treatment, gyrating luridly in an apparent attempt to wriggle out of what tiny items of clothing that had succeeded in clinging to her as she'd left the house that day.

No doubt, thought Kick as he glanced at this girl, Acutely Cute – impersonating what she thought an adult might do and who often talked candidly about her sexual conquests – she was 'exploring her sexuality', but Kick thought that this kind of growing up did not need to be done in public and proudly displaying what was the worst of male traits didn't really need to be done at all. By either sex.

With little to do but follow Powdermouth, he allowed his thoughts to drift.

It is the prerogative of the young to make mistakes but it is also the duty of the adult to point them out, and Kick wondered where the wisdom was in her life, seeing only the shadows of older men, and the bigger shadows that were their bank balances, regardless of how empowered she considered herself.

Trying to outrun her earlier child-star innocence by taking her clothes off was a lot easier than trying to outrun taking her clothes off once she finally got to be the woman she thought she was now being.

On several occasions he and Bat had knocked this subject around, wondering if these kind of girls had some kind of attention deficit disorder, addressing any perceived deficit of attention by revealing more to get more.

Kick had to also accept that these performers almost certainly didn't care about his concerns.

He tried to shake himself out of the daydreaming, unwilling to lose too much focus on his circumstance, but the sweet of thinking of Bat came with the bitter – he was unable to keep out the memory of his friend and the conversations they often had on this subject.

They had reflected that, generations ago, in The Past, at the beginning of the 20th Century, puberty would begin in humans at around 13. A century later it was beginning at 9. As an expression of the urgent evolutionary desire to succeed and dominate, this development was flawless and it married with technology developing at the same pace.

However, with intellectual and emotional maturity – inhibited by social media and AI – failing to show the same acceleration, the species rapidly expanded its ability to reproduce whilst reducing in itself the overall skill-set required for effective parenting.

Bat had suggested that, like so many empires, it is possible that the species became too big and too successful to sustain itself. The Thinning may or may not have been a natural consequence of this – being satisfied with the status quo has never been in evolution's nature, happy as it is to tear things down and start again without consequence to itself.

Then, as now, Kick looked at Acutely Cute, staring as she was into the camera with the same passive open-mouthed fuck-doll availability as any compliant adult star and wondered if we ever learnt anything.

Whilst she played to a certain type of male and his fantasies – and the timeless economic impetus of this was undeniable – it did little to explain why established female singers continued to do it once successful.

Perhaps it was a display of a more male trait, the desire to beat the competition. Perhaps simply there was always a next generation of horny (increasingly young) pubescent audiences to make money from – fewer and fewer developmental years of uncomplicated unknowing; the sexualisation of youth, ultimately a betrayal of us all.

Bat had wondered why they simply didn't promote someone called Pixie Jailbait and have done, get the experiment over with. A year later, to no-one's great surprise, they did.

And yet, here was Kick, several years even later, having the same idea sold to him and as the frantic rhythmic clatter of Acutely Cute's track added insult to injury by failing to form the simultaneous sequences of sound that even he would reasonably consider music, he realised that he had already paid it far, far too much attention…and it was he that now felt a deficit of some kind.

He recognised that this was a glimpse of a future he was not conditioned for and with this he started to become aware of the noise and his environment once again.

Thinking of Bat had made him a little sad, a little confused and he longed for his friends suddenly, now firmly but reluctantly back in the present.

He wanted to tell Powdermouth that they should just stop, turn around and go back. Where were they headed anyway? Come on, let's just have a look around and go home.

'This way,' said Powdermouth over his shoulder and Kick followed.

♪

It was as they entered a small, leafy square that the tone changed. Groups of people sat on the grass, lunch-break-free and sunning themselves; yet no-one noticed the screens flash up in each corner with an image of Honeytongue, smiling, her beautiful voice calling to Kick and disclosing an address where he could find her in Maskelyne.

It stopped Kick in his tracks.

No-one in the square noticed. Giggles didn't notice. Powdermouth turned to Kick.

'Ignore it,' he said.

They walked on through the square and beyond, Powdermouth picking up the pace a little.

The images of Honeytongue had been screened across Maskelyne simultaneously, knocking everything else off the screens. To the residents it appeared to be a moment of silence, a glitch that Acutely Cute would no doubt have experienced as a momentary deficit in the attention she required.

It was for Kick's eyes only, with Powdermouth's abilities allowing him vicarious insight.

U.S. knew he was here but not exactly where, and not exactly with whom. Despite its gloss, despite its apparent composure, Maskelyne was panicking a little.

♩

And, so they traced their path across Maskelyne, a random zigzag maintaining a general forward motion towards the collar of the rock on the far side, Powdermouth still apparently listening for what Kick was increasingly convinced were directions, maybe also warnings.

He would variously step into a side street, urging Kick and Giggles to make haste in joining him or simply step across and close to Kick, maybe shielding him from prying eyes.

On a couple of occasions, no doubt reluctantly, he would ask Giggles what was so funny anyway or even deliberately call him Giggles, forcing Giggles into working harder at scrambling and, if Kick had looked in the right direction, he would have seen watching eyes change from curious to disinterested, perhaps police, perhaps superimposers thrown off the scent.

Kick felt as though Maskelyne was alive, a dense tapestry of changing images, half-seen in shadow, close but barely tangible. Alive and very alert to his presence. Every screen in sight periodically sparked into life with either the soft touch through Honeytongue or the hard-edged barrage of threats from a villainous-looking Head of Maskelyne Security.

'Hand yourself in sooner rather than later motherfucker and we'll go easy on you and your slut' was a good summary of the general theme.

The influence of superimposers (apart from the periodic raging howl of Mister Five in his left ear) was in sinister manifestations, extra mouths projected on to the cheeks of passers-by imploring him to find Honeytongue, hand himself in, leave Maskelyne, die, live forever.

The tiny moving mouths of stick men were projected onto the teeth of smiling others, crawling and wriggling on the perfect enamels like so many freaky insects carelessly missed by the aesthetically-orientated dentist community of Maskelyne.

But it was a scatter-gun approach, intimidating but intermittent and crude and, as Kick watched Powdermouth visibly paling with the effort of orientation, he was certain he had to trust him.

With a loose sense of reassurance, he was now sure that Powdermouth was not simply listening but being led.

He wasn't the only one listening – or being led; Giggles's abilities, after all, whilst useful, were nothing against the collective might of Maskelyne.

The only time that concern threatened to encroach upon the expression of complete concentration on Powdermouth's face was as they first entered the shadow cast by the rocky slopes. Standing next to a fountain, Powdermouth hugged Kick, pressing his face into his shoulder and aggressively provoking Giggles with what seemed to Kick to be unfair slurs, the urgency in Powdermouth's voice leaving no room for reluctance on this occasion.

Giggles rose to the challenge by in no way reacting, the response deep and internal and Powdermouth closed his eyes, as though accepting there was little more he could do.

At just that moment there were shouts and four nearby men ran off in the direction Kick had come, shouting about how their target had been seen on the other side of Maskelyne.

Powdermouth let out a long breath, let Kick go from his gripping embrace, and said to Giggles simply, 'Sorry.'

This time, the plain-clothed police and their seer had come too close for comfort. The seer went with the plain clothes but was clearly less than convinced.

Deeper into the shadow of the cliffs they went, Maskelyne getting quieter as though only having been alive in the sunlight behind them. In their past.

Powdermouth stopped in front of what appeared to be a storage bay, the lift-up door displaying an indifferent 'Do Not Enter' sign.

He stood there looking for a way in.

The streets around them were grey, lonely. Giggles scanned around, making a twitching turn where he stood, whilst Kick just watched his friend, Powdermouth, worn out.

'Shit!' said Powdermouth, 'In here! Now!'

The three of them ducked into the doorway of the adjacent building as the storage bay door began to lift and six men ran out, splitting into three even groups and sprinting, in as many directions, away and deep into Maskelyne.

'In,' said Powdermouth, grabbing Kick by the arm and with Giggles bringing up the rear they ducked through the door as it closed behind the departing security men.

The scramble over, the first thing that struck them was the silence. And the space.

Kick felt it now, unavoidably aware that they had been led to this place, the front of the storage bay being exactly that, a front. Even Mister Five could not reach him here.

They stood on the edge of a wide grass strip, perfectly-kept and curving around Maskelyne in both directions, following the base of the cliffs, a green moat between the rocks and the city perimeter.

Twenty-five paces wide at most; backstage at Maskelyne.

From a simple wooden chair at the foot of the rocks Frankie Finesse regarded them with the silence of a desert.

As they noticed him and took in their surroundings, Drumbeat stood from a rock he had been sitting on and took a position to the side of Frankie, his movements a little uneasy and stilted; it took Kick a moment to realise he was hurt. His injuries were hidden beneath the carefully-tailored suit that would allow free movement when needed – but they were there nonetheless.

The absence of Tapper was also notable and made more apparent when Drumbeat spat, 'Fuck,' at them and even the aching silence seemed to expect an 'off' from another man's voice to complete the greeting.

Or maybe a 'you' such was the versatility of the erstwhile double act.

Drumbeat winced a little as he moved but no such concerns for Frankie, motionless in the chair, his immaculate right boot resting on the knee of the opposite leg, a soft leather coat hanging like poised liquid around him, the image completed with a silver-topped cane upon which his right hand rested, his arm almost at full stretch.

The two of them blocked what seemed to be a narrow natural archway in the side of the rocks, something Frankie made reference to by hooking a thumb backwards over his shoulder.

'*They* sent everyone off looking for you.'

And then, displaying the lack of trust he was so well known for, he continued, 'Not sure where they are sending everyone but, well, I figured you'd end up here one way or another so thought I'd just…wait.'

'Where's the boy?'

Kick surprised himself at the impatience, the directness, the imperative of the question.

Frankie's eyes widened in faux amusement and for a moment Giggles stopped twitching.

'Calm down,' said Frankie.

'Have you ever known anyone actually calm down when that gets said to them?' responded Kick.

'Now that you come to mention it…' said Frankie, staring upwards in a parody of reflection.

'Where's the boy?' Kick repeated patiently.

'We can't *find* the boy,' Frankie growled, suddenly angry, and as his mouth worked to contain his intemperance, the blood on his teeth showed for the first time, alerting Kick, Powdermouth and Giggles to the advantage they held.

So, it became Kick's turn to toy with Frankie.

'Calm down,' he said, as they ventured a step forward and Drumbeat braced a little.

'No,' said Frankie petulantly, emitting a cough that released a fine red mist, only perceptible as some of it settled on the front of his white dress shirt.

Noticing this, Frankie – his lips tinged with the red of his own blood now – appeared to feel it appropriate to offer his guests an explanation, his left hand waving at the air, as though his situation was little more than an inconvenience.

'An old friend...' he said, smiling a ghoulish and almost embarrassed smile.

The rage on Drumbeat's face as Frankie had spoken, and the story now coming to Kick from him and through Powdermouth, suggested that the fight had been significant, that the old friend had taken Tapper but had been rendered thoroughly deceased. Still, Drumbeat had revenge to exact. On someone.

Frankie wasn't lying. They had not been able to find the boy, the old friend had made sure of that.

'You look like good luck has been treating you bad,' said Powdermouth as they took steady steps across the grass towards Frankie and Drumbeat.

Their pace increased slightly as they realised that Frankie was sitting as still as he was because he was actually too injured to move, his left arm being his only effective limb, his left hand now busy trying and failing to remove the blood speckles he had coughed up onto the beautiful boot resting, perhaps stuck, on his left knee.

Offended by the insincerity of Powdermouth's concern, he scowled and through the pain that harried his concentration, managed to retort, 'Like I need your concern. You are clearly overestimating your role in my life.'

'Fuck,' said Drumbeat, stepping forward to stand alongside Frankie now.

'It's a good job you're charming on other occasions,' said Kick which Giggles reacted to with a skirmish of mixed noises, the distance between the two groups of men closing evenly all the while.

Powdermouth turned to Giggles and said something only they heard and Giggles struggled harder with his emissions, more obviously trying to hold his composure now.

Reassessing the situation, Drumbeat moved his hand towards a small button pinned on his lapel which his thumb now pressed. Back-up was on the way.

'Stay there, cunts,' he said, giving Powdermouth the opening he had been waiting and working for.

'Three words all at once,' he marvelled.

'Yes, but they *were* monosyllabic,' countered Kick, picking up on Powdermouth's intent.

'But there were *three*!' said Powdermouth.

Kick kept the momentum of the exchange going.

'He must feel like being a grown-up is just around the corner.'

Powdermouth turned to Drumbeat and asked in the tone of one speaking to a shy child, 'Have you stopped dazzling...are you sprouting hair?'

There was nothing more than schoolboy-funny about this exchange but Giggles seemed to like it. Giggles wanted to like it. This seemed as good a place as any to Giggles and Powdermouth knew it, turning to him and saying something else that only they heard, smiling as he did so and ending with a more audible, 'Almost old friend. Thank you.'

They were close to within touching distance of each other now and Kick could clearly see the cave-like entrance that Frankie and Drumbeat were so intent on obstructing, knew it was where he needed to go, could feel it.

Frankie knew this, had always known.

'Are you sure Kick?' he asked, obviously fading.

Powdermouth said something else to Giggles. Giggles squirmed. Howled.

'Because...the closer you get to something...the more essential it becomes...and the harder it is...to get away from,' continued Frankie, struggling, looking at Kick.

And a silence fell around them again as the words, uttered with such effort from a dying Frankie, sought resonance and meaning against the blank nonchalance of the hard rock surrounds; a silence broken only by the gnarling of Giggles, whose engine appeared to be revving up to take-off point.

Powdermouth, aware of this and also that Frankie had maybe a dozen breaths left in him, knew exactly what to say.

'That's quite an injury you have there Frankie,' he said calmly, finally, the oddest of matador's raised swords.

'It's okay,' said Frankie, his eyes barely open now, 'I've got insurance.'

The straw that breaks the camel's back is only ever a straw and it was this, the smallest of things, that set Giggles off, years of suppressed glee screeching from him in a glorious release, rendering Drumbeat paralysed and immobile.

The left hook knocked him back into the moment and he engaged as men of his kind always did, both he and Giggles breaking through pain barriers and years of difficult lives, with only one of them now laughing about it.

Kick and Powdermouth took their opportunity, the screaming madness that Giggles was taking to Drumbeat (and would continue to deliver to the reinforcements turning up in moments) would buy them time, but as they moved past Frankie, his last act befitted the street-fighter cunning he had always had beneath the sophistication of his appearance.

His last breath gone, he used his left hand to knock his right foot off his left knee. It swung down as they passed him and knocked the cane across their stride, tripping Powdermouth who took Kick down with him.

As Frankie slumped, they struck the ground and the hard face of the rock on the side of the entrance.

But Frankie had gained little more than their grudging respect – some cuts and bruises accompanied the pain and surprise but nothing more. They scrambled up and entered the cave, leaving Drumbeat to deal with the mounting momentum of Giggles's energy.

It was a kind of madness and it sounded that way to Kick as he and Powdermouth limped along the narrow walls of a passage cut through the rocks.

But Giggles was learning that, if you are ready and you let it in, it doesn't hurt at all.

Kick found himself smiling despite the pain and felt a brief flare of his own relief.

♪

That relief was short-lived. An insistent nausea hung in the air, like so much mist to be inhaled, as they made their way cautiously, painfully along the corridor in the rock, the only light somewhere ahead beyond a series of twists and turns.

It wasn't unbearable for either of them, but it made their progress very difficult, affected their balance, hearing and forward motion.

There was no doubt in Kick's mind that he was coming to the end of his journey in whatever form that might be.

The Maze was very close yet somehow it was contained, controlled and channelled and as they turned a last corner into a circular man-made space with stone-bricked walls, Kick saw why.

He knew instantly – perhaps from Powdermouth who had known all along – that the body-like forms in this pit of a cellar were the beings that had led them in, had distracted and misled superimposers, guards and police, had made them safe, had wanted them to be here.

Chained to the wall and opposite each other, just out of each other's reach.

Kick knew more now.

The Maze actually was being channelled – the form twisted and scorched so that it barely resembled a human anymore, was MessHead, a powerful seer, the most powerful superimposer of all.

Selectively forced down The Maze by U.S., MessHead was kept only just on the edge of its destructive crush, was referred to as The Font by senior U.S. executives and was, unwillingly, the power that U.S. wielded – from a safe distance.

When their all-pervasive digital reach could find no answers, there was MessHead.

The stress of the circumstance rendered MessHead's appearance as that of a human candle; melted, frozen in rigour.

The other figure in the room was less compromised, the lithe elegance of its tall body shape clearly apparent under its caramel skin.

The Haunted Ghost, cynically, deliberately had been placed one step removed, held in a stasis that could access MessHead.

Whereas MessHead cramped to such an extent that speech was impossible, The Haunted Ghost, slumped and immobile, was able to speak, able to interpret and relay the information careening through MessHead to those in whose interests it was to have them.

The only light came from a circular glass window in the ceiling high above them and the sustenance they needed, nutrients, water and – no doubt – a cocktail of sedatives and truth drugs, needed to maintain this grotesque co-operation, were delivered through the IV tubes that led straight into the stone walls, along with leads from several microphones and a speakerphone, incongruous modern intrusions in a primitive captivity scenario.

With horror, Kick realised how long they must have been here – the source of all superimposers that U.S. had fed into society.

He recognised kin and knew they loved each other, and that, despite everything else, there had been centuries of despair watching each other suffer.

That they were just, only just, unable to reach out and touch each other expressed the cruelty of this design.

A single solid wooden door broke the craggy uniformity of the circular stone wall opposite where they had entered – it unnerved Kick a little. Given the scene before him it seemed, frankly, like the least of his concerns but as Powdermouth acted, fighting his own exhaustion, Kick couldn't ignore the feeling.

As though he had always known what to do, Powdermouth went unerringly to a particular brick that was sitting a little proud of the wall, upon which was a key.

'Crouch down,' he said evenly to Kick, indicating that he should replicate the two tortured figures' seated height.

As he lifted the key from the stone, the chamber exploded with sound and light, fireballs of screeching static electricity speeding savage routes above their heads, howls not dissimilar to Mister Five's rang random and projections of gruesome imagery flickered a malevolent intent on each surface.

The security system would not endanger MessHead or The Haunted Ghost so, crouched at this level, Kick and Powdermouth were safe, although, with their energy ebbing away, they were fighting hard to concentrate.

In that moment, Kick knew that Giggles was dead and that he had taken Drumbeat with him. He knew that any surviving reinforcements would not enter this hell. He knew that Powdermouth was here to free MessHead and The Haunted Ghost. He knew that they did not want revenge.

They wanted release, they wanted to see the sky.

He knew, with a smile on his lips, that this would bring down U.S. and that Myelle was somewhere, even now, very pleased with the work that she had done – she had forced him to take a position, to decide if he trusted Powdermouth all the way to the end.

Kick could see how Powdermouth, now methodically releasing MessHead and The Haunted Ghost from their shackles, in his agenda for the tour, might have seen Myelle as a useful tool, with a practical use.

He would have known that she would have burned with ire that whatever power she may have had always had been, and always would be, in the gift of U.S. He would have known that she would consider that as no real power at all. He would have known that, to her, power and her expression of it, would have been in taking down U.S., regardless of the cost to herself.

In pushing Kick to make a decision on Powdermouth, she had facilitated this.

Her gift to him, his own power.

Whilst Powdermouth would have wanted Kick here, as all of his own story and part of a bigger one, Kick felt sure that somewhere Myelle was laughing.

She would survive and thrive and she had said so.

As Kick watched Powdermouth tenderly help The Haunted Ghost towards MessHead, The Maze so close, so much of his energy spent on balming its crush, he wanted to intervene, to tell his old friend not to enable this, that surely this degree of knowledge could be used positively, that they could both see the sky and also recover.

Powdermouth looked up at him, The Haunted Ghost now almost but not quite touching MessHead, and spoke to him again without opening his mouth.

'You are not the first to think that my friend.'

Kick had little time to absorb this but above the shrieking and the fireballs and through The Maze, the imperative remained.

'Where's the boy?' he shouted over the maelstrom, his voice dense with stress.

This time Powdermouth spoke aloud, clear above the noise, his eyes black and endless behind his words.

'Only you can find the boy, Kick.'

And in his next words those secrets of the Universe available to Powdermouth became a little clearer to Kick, The Haunted Ghost so close now to reuniting with MessHead.

'My job is to get you this far,' Powdernouth said. And, noticing the struggle that Kick was having in resisting The Maze, added, 'You have to let it in Kick.'

The Haunted Ghost stretched out a wasted arm towards MessHead, with Powdermouth attentively supporting the ruined frame.

Kick could take no more, the only option being the door, going back the way he came being unthinkable.

And, in making that decision, as his hand reached up and turned the ornate handle, a stillness came over him. The violence of the noise in the contained space was still there but he was beyond its reach.

Before stepping through the door, he turned back to Powdermouth, who was looking back at him with affection, a kindness, with a touch of humour that seemed to say 'How come you get all the peace and quiet?'

Although Kick found himself smiling, he was also concerned for his friend.

'Don't worry about me,' said Powdermouth, 'this is what I do.'

'Of course,' thought Kick and as he stepped through the door, The Haunted Ghost embraced MessHead for the first time in what had seemed like eternity.

Chapter Twenty-Three

The door closed, heavy, behind Kick before he realised his best option might have been to get back through it.

Alarm oiled its way through him as he noticed that the door, which had opened outwards, had no handle, presenting him with no purchase points and as many options. He was stuck here on this crumbling ledge on the far side of Maskelyne, high above dense white clouds that obscured everything beneath him.

His current situation consisted of the thin ledge running around the mountain, its wall on his left a steep prohibition of unforgiving rock preventing any movement upwards. On his right, a deep fall through clouds skimming along on the assertive breeze, into and onto the unknown.

Aware that the ledge petered out behind him, he really was stuck here.

With Dessel.

Blocking the only direction Kick could reasonably take, he stood casually regarding Kick and demonstrating his ongoing ability to hide his presence. In truth, The Maze felt like it had been left in the stone room and, despite a light touch of vertigo – and that odd temptation to jump that so often comes with standing at a perilous height –

Kick was free to drop his blocks almost entirely for the first time in as long as he could remember.

His body reacted to the release of a life's worth of control, throwing him slightly off-balance, his foot clipping the outermost point of the ledge which fragmented, spilling particles of its uncertain edge into the void below.

'So here we are,' said an unmoved Dessel.

Regaining balance of both body and mind, Kick offered a considered response.

'Arsehole,' he said.

Dessel didn't bite, instead puckering his lips in thought before conceding, 'Yes, that comment is probably an accurate representation of the distance between us,' the humour in his eyes at odds with the circumstances.

'Unfortunately,' he added. And Kick believed him.

Buying time to assess this unlikely scenario and with little to lose, Kick pressed his point further, succumbing, all this time later, to his irritation. 'Why would I want to have anything to do with you Dessel? You're little more than a low-rent hood, promoted because of, and for, the thrill you take in murder and intimidation, and your ability to marshal the same in others. You're charmless, dishonest, crude, yet soullessly efficient in the execution of your duties. Plus, you're an unquestioning company man.'

Dessel didn't rise to this either, smiling back at Kick and saying, 'Oh darling, I thought you could see past that.'

They stared at each other, high on a ledge.

Kick exhaled, feeling better but a little self-conscious for having indulged in name-calling; he didn't need to do that again, hadn't realised he had needed to in the first place.

'How did you find me here?' he asked wearily, 'You've got a really bad habit of not leaving me alone.'

The smile retreated from Dessel's face, replaced not with his usual cynical sneer but a conversational matter-of-factness.

'This is where I live Kick,' he said looking around and continuing in riddles, 'You were always going to end up here if I couldn't find a way to stop you first.'

But Kick didn't believe this. Kick suspected that Dessel was lucky to be here, his measured disposition an illusion to cover the fact that he, unlike Kick, was a long way from where he was welcome, that being here took immense effort.

A little baffled by Dessel's words, Kick mocked, 'Is that from one of your favourite songs?' and a flash of the other Dessel spat a response that Kick couldn't quite hear over a rush of wind but it sounded like, 'Or maybe one of your poems?'

The gust dissipated, howling away as though skidding around a corner and off a road. An elevated road with a view, perhaps.

(Flames)

The two men continued to regard each other.

'You know, Powdermouth isn't the only one who listens,' Dessel paused, allowing that one to sink in.

'Ever noticed how everyone who has anything to do with him tends to disappear?' Dessel added mischievously, this time moving on almost immediately, deliberately giving Kick no time to consider the comment.

His tone nettled.

'I guess Frankie sitting right outside where you needed to be was a last-minute signpost that could have been avoided. He could've sat anywhere but, no, right where you needed to go.'

Dessel's voice betrayed more than a touch of irritation but he caught himself and, almost apologetically, continued more reasonably.

'In fairness to him, Powdermouth *was* being led in and Frankie's judgement would have been compromised, what with him being in the process of dying and all but, well…' and here Dessel appeared to struggle to find the right words.

'He was…bless him, he was an effete thug.' And satisfied with the context he had found, he expanded, 'An effete thug at the top of his game, no doubt, but barely scraping the bottom of mine.'

Kick wasn't sure if this was Dessel's ego speaking, his insecurities, or even whether he was making some kind of last-minute job application and, in the absence of certainty, said nothing.

For a moment Kick thought that Mister Five had returned to his ear with renewed vigour but realised that it was another gust of wind instead, peeling past them and out of reach around the cliff side.

'It's getting interesting up here,' said Dessel.

Kick remained silent, measuring the increasing flurries in the lift and drop of Dessel's hair.

He recognised the familiar, contained, threat in Dessel's tone.

'Soon I won't be able to save you from what I'm going to do to you,' said Dessel before adding, 'I might just bring your death to life…slowly.'

Kick assessed the situation. There was no obvious route back to anything or anyone he knew, he was stranded and exhausted high above he didn't know what, on a crumbling ledge, with the wind building, and he was in the company of the most dangerous individual he knew, who would be fully prepared to fulfil his promises of violence regardless of the somewhat pantomime nature of his threats.

'Join us Kick,' said Dessel, just as aware of Kick's limited options, and, after glancing over the side of the ledge to the cloud-covered uncertainty below, continued almost compassionately, 'Make this the biggest decision of your life…not the last.'

Kick's eyes had followed Dessel's gaze over the ledge (still that odd temptation to jump) but it was the only thing of Dessel's he was prepared to follow.

'Dessel do you really think that if your threats worked on me that we would have ended up in this situation? Seriously?'

Dessel lowered his eyes. 'That's far too good a point to make to me when I'm trying to threaten you,' he said, his tone of weary acceptance acknowledging that, finally, this approach had run its course.

Now, two men stood merely talking.

'Who…what do you represent Dessel?'

Dessel, reluctant to the end to interact reasonably, didn't answer straight away and appeared to be chewing his tongue behind his closed mouth as he considered his options. Having decided he was also out of them, he engaged with Kick and engaged fully.

'I represent The Future, Kick,' and, nodding over the side of the precipice, added, 'The alternative to *that*.'

Kick responded in kind to this change in manner.

'Why are you so sure? Every time I do something I wonder, is it the right thing to do, could I do better, what could I have done differently? You…you're certain.'

'Yes Kick, I am. Look what we are doing Now. Just think what we could do in The Future. I believe in what U.S. can do.'

Dessel's voice was rising as he spoke, the wind now tugging the men's clothes, Kick feeling the need to hold the side of the cliff.

'I believe Kick. It's why, despite what you think, I am not trying to fool you into some kind of compromised position. With you on board…'

Dessel's voice trailed off as he struggled to frame the case he was presenting. He approached it from a different angle.

'Most animals evolve by adapting to their habitat but we…we adapt our environment to *us*. *We* are evolution now Kick. It is our luxury, our destiny, our…'

The wind took away the last of Dessel's words but it looked like he had said '…our responsibility.'

He then surprised Kick, his eyes widening in cartoon wonder, as he asked, 'I mean, if evolution was so clever, how come I *hate* the sound of a baby crying?'

'I'm sure your boys will eventually find a way to create one that's noise-free,' commented Kick cynically.

'Now that,' countered Dessel instantly, '*that* is exactly the kind of thinking that makes you so valuable to us!'

Kick couldn't help smiling with Dessel, despite the peril in his circumstances.

Holding onto the cliff face with one hand, Dessel pointed over the side with the other and, in a break in the wind, Kick heard, 'We don't need to do…this anymore.'

The two men stood, maybe ten paces apart, both in a hugging struggle against the wind.

Dessel, now almost shouting to be heard, 'Think about it Kick. We already out-manoeuvred The Thinning. We *can* solve everything. Just think, if we are all together on this, what we could achieve. The Future is ours Kick. Believe it. Join us.'

And with this, in the face of the buffeting wind, Dessel let go of the cliff-side, the wind tearing at his nondescript suit, pulling and clawing at him as he began to take slow steps towards Kick, his palms raised at shoulder height as though in surrender.

Kick knew Dessel was sincere, he knew that Dessel wanted the best for him, he knew it was not Dessel's intention to harm him. Had never been. None of which made Dessel's increasingly close proximity any less menacing and instinctively he took a step backwards, inevitably stumbling on the inconsistent terrain.

Dessel stopped. 'Kick. Okay. I've stopped. Look. Don't move.'

There was genuine concern in Dessel's eyes.

'The only thing you want to do quickly now is stop and think. Nothing else.'

And at that point, the wind stepped up its campaign, almost throwing the unsecured form of Dessel completely off balance before he managed to steady himself.

His eyes widened again as he looked over to Kick.

'Close one, eh?' he shouted and as the wind screamed to disturbance, followed with, 'What do you believe Kick? And are you really prepared to die for it today?'

With his legs bending and giving to resist the grabbing wind, he looked straight at Kick and shouted, 'I am.'

Kick, still crouched and holding on to the cliff-side, had the instant thought 'Yeah but you don't die do you?'

He straightened, looked flatly into Dessel's eyes and deeper into the darkness of Dessel's being, realising that, more accurately, Dessel was eternal.

For the first time in weeks, he decided to take control, realised that he could.

He said clearly, 'Where's the boy Dessel?'

The change in Dessel was instant, a fury that at this stage, in this position with no options, Kick was still focused on finding the boy.

The anger was not only at Kick, not only a threshing rage of frustration that he could not get his way.

'We can't *find* the boy!' he spat.

In those words, Kick found hope.

In the next thing he said, Kick found release.

'One of us, one of *us* kept him from us,' Dessel screeched. 'Some fucking twisted attempt at redemption for past sins. Gave his fucking pitiful life to save the boy's.'

Kick looked down. He watched with no great surprise as the bones in his shins snapped – and it hurt. A crushing pain in his pelvis followed without pause – and it hurt, but Kick understood.

Zip's arresting answer to the man in The Religious Zone came back to him, as his own – he could decide when his God was complete.

Peacefully, with Dessel's blazing eyes above his thin-lipped fury widening as realisation dawned in them, Kick fell over the ledge.

♪

Kick's fall jarred to a stop and his thoughts banged and rattled in response so that it took a moment for them to settle from, hang on, surely that drop was further than that, to realising that Dessel had covered the distance between them and was now flat on his stomach, clinging to Kick's arm with decreasing purchase and increasing alarm.

Instinct took over and, with nothing beneath his feet, Kick clutched at Dessel's wrist, instantly taking a sharp intake of breath, the cold-air shock to his lungs less than a footnote to the bursting images in his head flowing from the direct contact with Dessel.

Kick could see everything now and as acceptance pervaded every sense, he raised his gaze to see nothing but panic in Dessel's eyes.

'Hold on Kick, I've got you,' said Dessel, his voice choking with emotion and exertion.

Dessel, in this place where his powers meant nothing, was trying to reassure himself that this was true, despite not really believing it.

But Kick could see clearly what Dessel *did* believe. He believed in what he represented and in the steps he took to represent it.

He believed that U.S. had the answers, that everything could be fixed, that death was little more than a pause, a temporary setback.

He believed. But he didn't know.

He didn't know that his bosses had not given him the full information, that he, too, was just a believer.

He didn't know what Kick now knew.

Kick smiled at all of those on this tour who had spoken of the effect of time on things, that which we currently call evolution, and the irony that this included Dessel.

That Dessel would ultimately be denied by the elegance of the implacable process that he claimed to own, that each and all of us are born into our era, to live and die in the time we are designed for, to be someone else's history, part of the sequence, hopefully leaving something better behind.

That no-one is ever in charge, although some may feel they get to hold the reins for a while.

Dessel would never know that evolution only ever comes from the bottom up; life's profound expression of dissatisfaction with circumstance forcing a tireless, avaricious reach for improvement.

It was the youth thinking that the old have got it wrong and, though they may themselves be misguided, the motion forwards and upwards was undeniably right – it was nature's consensus and inevitable in its conception and execution.

Evolution was endless questions and the humble knew this and, whilst Dessel had found his answers, Kick realised that he had really only reached the point where he had no more questions of his own.

He knew that Dessel could also see into him in this moment – but he knew that the depth of his vision would have a limited scope, despite his immense powers.

Dessel would see everything but would be unable to assimilate it, unaware of, and unable to, make any essential connection between the internal and the external world.

Dessel would know the score but the story of the game would always be beyond him – though he could see far into Kick, he would never comprehend the details that made him who he was.

He could see the tattoos on his back but would never understand the sequence in which they arrived, the context, the reasoning behind each, who Kick was before and who he became afterwards. The good the bad and the everything that happened, as unique to Kick as his DNA; the things that Kick could not remember but had never needed to.

The details stored as experience and the experiences that made up the details of who he was.

Dessel's perception fell short of seeing his own flawed assumption that he could offer anything that would allow for all of this. In Kick. In all.

A fiery engine at the core, tensions and pulls, pain and moments of beauty.

Coming to a stop.

Kick saw the realisation in Dessel's eyes just before he broke the gaze, the serenity on his own face reflecting how he now felt. As his ribcage collapsed, a smile played on his lips – it hurt a little less now.

He thought of stepping out onstage, the headiness of the noise, the rush, the thrill and always the surprise of the heat. The light that intensified everything but often blinded as it did.

He thought of those who threw themselves around in the moment and of those who stood off to the side, observing as a way of participating, of those who came close and those that watched from a distance, those engaged and those a little distracted.

He thought of giving his best and not always achieving it – and of those who would forgive him this because his intentions were good.

He thought of the silence at the end when the show was over and he hoped only that it was because the energy of the event had been taken away to live beyond the moment in the memories and the lives of those who had witnessed it.

The wind had dropped, the silence made more so in contrast, so that, as Kick closed his eyes and Dessel said, 'Kick...' it carried clearly between the two men.

Everything he wanted was in his past and all that was left was his future, whatever that was, and being an empath had been no great cost.

Dessel didn't matter anymore.

With the last of the bones that would break shattering in his neck and his head falling onto his broken chest, Kick let go.

Chapter Twenty-Four

The lightness of falling continued a confused narrative. In tiny increments he became aware that the surface he was on was not moving, but that he was; a comprehension reluctant to integrate with his conviction that he had landed.

It raised his curiosity enough to make him open his eyes – he struggled a fractured effort to think backwards through the yesterdays in search of a coherent narrative as to how he got here.

He smiled up at the boy whose arms were beneath his body, his thoughts still sprinkled in a benign disarray. He didn't chase them, he quite enjoyed letting them spill away and up into the sky.

He knew he should be hurting, but as the boy eased his body into the water and it took his weight, bathing him in a cooling comfort, there were almost no other sensations of any kind – maybe the touch of the boy's hands under his back, taking what weight the water could not, his whole now less subject to gravity, less bound to earth.

The boy looked down, the frank simplicity of his regard belying the responsibility he now carried for both of them as effortlessly as he moved, waist-deep and certain, through the water.

He looked into the boy's eyes, which appeared to be so close as to be his own.

'I promised her I would find you,' he said, breaking a silence he hadn't been aware of.

For a moment the boy looked puzzled, his facial expression taking a few moments to resume a fond compassion.

'She hasn't been seen for a long time,' said the boy, softly. Carefully.

The touch of the water became his world again as he looked back at the sky, relinquishing control once again to the boy.

His thoughts slowed, simplified, stilled. Made small by what he saw.

A vastness of everything he had seen and all that he could accommodate.

Everything he had encountered and all he could imagine.

The boy was unafraid. Possibly he was lucky that way. Maybe he had been raised well. Perhaps by all of us; the presence of any God weighted correctly in his mind.

As he looked again at the boy and then the fading sky, he could say that he had kept his word, that he was who he claimed to be.

He raised his head a little, enough to see a surface ribbed by the waves they caused as they moved.

Ahead of them, as though gliding, he glimpsed a silver tree breaking the endless surface, a lazy branch shaping an informal arch. He lowered his head back into the soothing embrace of the water and noticed that it was now chest-deep on the boy.

'I think we're going under,' he said.

'I think we are,' the boy replied and a few seconds later added, 'I know the way.'

He became aware that the boy was leading them towards the tree.

'What's through there?' he asked.

The boy looked at him, again his eyes so close as to be sharing the same view.

'Anything you want.'

Acknowledgements

Many people have put their time and their skills into the work that you see here and I am deeply grateful to them.

Huge thanks to Lisa Sargent-Small and Pascal Cariss for their input, advice, sound-board abilities and patience throughout the entire process. I asked a lot, you gave it and you're still talking to me.

Alexander Dommett thank you for your comments and the well-timed confidence boost you provided that this whole thing had been worth doing.

Daryl Gibbard at Jolt Creative – thanks for the fantastic graphic design work for Deaf Fret, used in this book.

Maz – you know why I am thanking you. One day soon the world will see your brilliant work.

Thank you to Miles Skarin at Crystal Spotlight for such an extraordinary book cover design.

Rob Skarin at Crystal Spotlight – thanks for the beautiful website you have created for this book at www.theoriginalheart.com

Special thanks to Jessica Woodward at Troubador for guiding me so gracefully through this process. I hope my appreciation shows in all of our exchanges.

Thanks also to Chloe May, Andrea Johnson, Jonathan White and everyone else at Troubador involved in the production of this book.